Praise for 43 Light Street

NOWHERE MAN
"...a to-die-for hero, chilling suspense and an unforgettable love story."†

"...one of the most heart-wrenching, moving works of romantic suspense in years."*

FATHER AND CHILD
"...great, one-sitting romantic suspense that will keep readers on the edge of the seats from start to finish."*

FOR YOUR EYES ONLY
"Few write suspense like Rebecca York."‡

FACE TO FACE
"Harlequin's first lady of suspense...a marvelous storyteller, Ms. York cleverly develops an intricate plotted romance to challenge our imaginations and warm our hearts."†

PRINCE OF TIME
"Get ready for the time of your life.... Breathtaking excitement and exotic romance...in the most thrilling 43 Light Street adventure yet!"†

TILL DEATH US DO PART
"Readers will delight in every page."‡

TANGLED VOWS
"A bravura performance by one of the best writers ever of quality romantic suspense."†

*Harriet Klausner, Amazon.com
†Melinda Helfer, *Romantic Times*
‡Debbie Richardson, *Romantic Times*

Dear Reader,

We all have favorite themes in the romance novels we read. One of mine is the good woman who isn't married but who becomes pregnant—and then must cope on her own with the emotional turmoil and problems of unwed motherhood. Will she tell the man she loves that she's carrying his child? If she does, how will he react? Do they have a chance of happiness together now that he unexpectedly has to face the responsibilities of fatherhood?

These are some of the issues I deal with in *Shattered Lullaby,* the story of Jessie Douglas and Miguel Valero. And, of course, because it's the kind of book I love to write, all these personal problems play out against a background of intrigue and danger, since Miguel is on the run from a man who will go to any lengths to kill him—and anyone who gets close to him. Miguel thinks his fugitive status limits his choices, but he doesn't realize that in Jessie Douglas he's found a woman strong enough to cope with his deadly dilemma.

Since I've been writing on my own as Rebecca York, I've been able to explore many of the themes that fuel my own fantasies. In the Light Street Book I'm writing now, *Midnight Caller,* I'm telling the story of Meg Faulkner, who thinks she's working to overthrow a man beneath contempt, a man with terrible secrets that must be exposed. But once she gets close to Glenn Bridgman, she doesn't know whose side she's on anymore. Think of it as a kind of "Beauty and the Beast story," although Glenn Bridgman's anguish comes from his tortured past, not his considerable physical presence.

I hope you enjoy *Shattered Lullaby* and the many more 43 Light Street Books I'm planning.

All my best,

Ruth

Ruth Glick, writing as Rebecca York

Rebecca York
SHATTERED LULLABY

Ruth Glick writing as Rebecca York

HARLEQUIN®

TORONTO • NEW YORK • LONDON
AMSTERDAM • PARIS • SYDNEY • HAMBURG
STOCKHOLM • ATHENS • TOKYO • MILAN • MADRID
PRAGUE • WARSAW • BUDAPEST • AUCKLAND

ISBN 0-373-22500-8

SHATTERED LULLABY

Printed in U.S.A.

Directory

4 3 L I G H T S T R E E T

	Room
ADVENTURES IN TRAVEL	204
ABIGAIL FRANKLIN, Ph.D. KATHRYN KELLEY, Ph.D. 　Clinical Psychology	509
BIRTH DATA, INC.	322
INNER HARBOR PRODUCTIONS	404
THE LIGHT STREET FOUNDATION	322
KATHRYN MARTIN-McQUADE, M.D. 　Branch Office, Medizone Labs	515
O'MALLEY & LANCER 　Detective Agency	518
LAURA ROSWELL, LL.B. 　Attorney at Law	311
SABRINA'S FANCY	Lobby
STRUCTURAL DESIGN GROUP	407
NOEL ZACHARIAS 　Paralegal Service	311
L. ROSSINI 　Superintendent	Lower Level

CAST OF CHARACTERS

Miguel Valero (aka Miguel Diego)—He was running for his life and ran straight into the arms of a woman he couldn't forget.

Jessie Douglas—She fell in love with a man who was afraid to let her into his life.

Luis—When he wasn't packing a gun, he was just a normal kid.

Erin Stone—She was willing to go out on a limb to help Jessie.

Katie Martin-McQuade—Would Dr. McQuade treat a patient without revealing his identity?

Carlos Jurado—Only one man—Miguel Valero— stood between him and a new life.

Georgie Coda—Jessie Douglas made a fool of him, and he vowed to get even.

Officer Waverly—Why was he making trouble for Miguel?

Ramon Martinez—He had the power to make life hell for Miguel—if he could find him.

Eduardo Sombra—He was a paid killer, so Miguel and Jessie were just another assignment.

Jim Alvarez—He took the moral high ground— when it suited his purposes.

Andres Cuento—Could a dead man come back to life?

Previous titles by REBECCA YORK
43 Light Street books:

Life Line
Shattered Vows
Whispers in the Night
Only Skin Deep
Trial by Fire
Hopscotch
Cradle and All
What Child Is This?
Midnight Kiss
Tangled Vows
Till Death Us Do Part
Prince of Time
Face to Face
For Your Eyes Only
Father and Child
Nowhere Man
Shattered Lullaby

Peregrine Connection books:

Talons of the Falcon
Flight of the Raven
In Search of the Dove

Don't miss the next 43 Light Street:
A Special Duet
August 1999

Chapter One

Lock the office door.

That was the most important rule when working late at night. With a sick feeling in the pit of her stomach, Jessie Douglas realized she'd forgotten to throw the bolt.

Sitting up straighter, she ran a nervous hand through her blond hair. She'd been focused on the pile of reports on her desk, each one representing a family on the edge of desperation—like Mrs. Sierra, who needed help paying for day care because her husband had disappeared and left her with two young children.

Jessie had been writing a request for stopgap funding for the family, when a sound like stealthy footsteps penetrated her concentration.

Was there really someone out there in the darkness beyond the circle of light cast by her desk lamp? Swinging her chair away from the computer screen, she peered into the black well of the waiting room, praying that her weary mind was only playing tricks; praying that all she heard was the pounding of her own pulse in her ears.

Maybe the door actually *was* locked, she told herself hopefully. Or the building superintendent, Lou Rossini, might have let himself into the office and was trying hard to be quiet now that he realized she was working late. *Sure. And maybe elephants can fly.*

Several agonizing seconds ticked by as she wiped her suddenly damp hands against her slacks and waited for confirmation of one of a woman's worst fears. Under the new tile flooring, an old oak board squeaked, the sound pricking the skin at the back of her neck. Someone was out there, all right—someone sneaking across the floor, stalking toward her office, step by careful step.

Her eyes darted around the little room until they focused on the telephone just six inches from her hand. She could call 911.

No good. She'd be scooped up long before help could arrive.

She was on her own. Her gaze darted around her office, and fixed on the green metal Statue of Liberty that a grateful client had given her last year. It was pretty tall, and heavy for a paperweight. Maybe if she hid it below the desk, she could use it as a weapon.

But it was too late for even that minimal protection. Before she could grab the statue, a figure stepped purposefully out of the darkness of the waiting room into the partially lit doorway.

Too bad she hadn't turned on the overhead light, Jessica thought as she squinted at the shadowed shape, trying to guess his intentions, trying to make the image there square with the menacing picture her mind had conjured up.

His body blocked her escape route as he stood dead center in the doorway, with his mouth set in a grim line and his eyes narrowed under their straight black brows. The picture was spoiled by his diminutive height—and by the way he held his scrawny arms with unbearable stiffness. The overall effect was an image of Latin machismo, she thought with sudden insight. He wanted her to see how tough he was.

They stared at each other across six feet of charged space, each gathering strength for the confrontation. Yet despite his grim expression and stealthy approach, she felt relief kindle within her breast.

Good grief, it wasn't a robber or a rapist; it was a boy from the recreation center in the barrio, where the Light

Street Foundation was running sports and other programs for kids who might otherwise be home alone after school, or on the streets. If she remembered correctly, he was ten years old. And his name was Luis. She also remembered they'd had a couple of friendly conversations. Had he marked her as an easy robbery victim?

"Luis?"

He nodded tightly as he dragged in several lungfuls of air.

"You're pretty far from home," she said, keeping her tone conversational.

He answered with another nod. He must have gone to a lot of trouble to sneak up on her; now he looked overwhelmed that they were actually face-to-face.

"What are you doing here at this time of night?"

He took another breath, than let loose a flow of Spanish so rapid, she could barely follow him.

"Slow down." Pushing back her chair, she came around the desk.

"It is an emergency, *señorita,*" he said, switching to heavily accented English as he stared up at her with huge, dark eyes that seemed to dominate his thin face. "You must come with me."

"Where?"

He gestured impatiently. "A house. In the neighborhood," he answered, making an effort to enunciate carefully.

She thought about the dark streets of the inner city, where unspeakable crimes seemed to happen every day. "What kind of emergency?" she asked. "Something with your mother or your sister?"

"No." His weight shifted from one sneaker-clad foot to the other. "But we have to hurry."

"Luis…I can't just go down to the barrio at this time of night. Please, tell me what's wrong."

"You must come!"

"We can call the police if you need help."

She realized her mistake as his expression turned into one

of panic. With lightning speed, his small, grubby hand darted under the open flap of his jacket. When the hand emerged it was holding a shiny little pistol. It might be small, but Jessie was pretty sure it was no toy. And the business end was pointed somewhere in the region of her belly button.

"Luis, be careful with that." She was surprised that her voice could sound so steady as she faced a deadly weapon.

"We have to go," he insisted, a small, scared boy trying to act the part of a tough guy as his voice rose, "or else!"

Knowing his fear made him more dangerous, she replied, "I can't go anywhere if you shoot me."

For another few moments he held on to the hard look in his eyes and the revolver clutched in his small hand. Then his face crumpled and the gun lowered.

Careful. Don't startle him, she warned herself as she took one cautious step closer and then another.

"Put the gun down," she said.

His gaze fell to the weapon as if he were surprised that he was holding it in his hand.

"Put it on the desk."

A strangled sound rattled in his chest. With a thunk he set the revolver down carefully.

The knot of tension inside her released.

"Good. *Gracias.*"

"It's not loaded," he said in a barely audible voice that carried as much chagrin as apology.

She came down on her knees so that her face was a little below his level. When she held out her arms, he hesitated for an instant, then closed the distance between them in a rush and clung to her. She felt his shoulders begin to shake as she smoothed her hands across his back, murmuring words to comfort both of them.

He hid his face against her shoulder, and she knew he must be fighting for control. When he lifted his head, his eyes were large and bright, shimmering with tears that he'd struggled to hold back. "I'm sorry," he whispered.

"I hope so."

"Are you going to call the police?" His voice rose as it reached the end of the sentence.

She should. Instead, she made the kind of decision that her job with Baltimore's underprivileged frequently forced upon her. "Probably not."

He let out the breath he'd been holding. "My stepfather told me I'd better not get in trouble."

"Then why did you come here with a gun?"

"*He* needs your help. I was afraid you wouldn't come."

"Who? Your stepfather?" This man must be very important for Luis to risk so much by coming here and threatening her with a gun.

He shook his head impatiently. "No. Not him. It's Dr. Miguel. He's going to die." The last part came out as a sort of croak.

Jessie's heart lurched. Miguel was a common enough name, yet she knew of only one who was called "Doctor"—even though he wasn't licensed to practice medicine in the U.S., as far as she knew. A sudden image leaped into her mind—an image of a man with fierce dark eyes, lean features, and a mouth held tightly closed when he looked at her. She shook her head, silently denying that it was him.

"You know him," the youngster insisted, his fingers digging into her arms. "He used to come to the center sometimes in the afternoons. He played basketball with us. Now he just sees if anyone is sick. When Senora Morano had the problem with her heart, he told the family what to do. He saved her life!"

She felt a coldness pass over her skin. Dr. Miguel might mend hearts, but he had broken hers—two months ago. And the wound was as fresh as the day she received it.

It had all started when he'd stopped by to talk to her about Ernesto Alcanzo, a boy who needed glasses. They'd begun with a chat about eye care. Two hours later they were still comparing notes on the community, Baltimore, and Don Quixote's relevance to modern life, of all things.

She'd asked Miguel if he wanted to grab a quick dinner,

and the evening that followed would stay etched in her memory until the end of time. They'd sat for hours in a small café off Thames Street, sharing a pitcher of sangria as the conversation grew more intimate—at least on her part. She'd told him about her failed marriage and her decision to go back to school and become a social worker. As she'd talked, she'd felt that she was sharing her hopes for the future with a man who was going to become very important in her life— and very quickly, judging by the man-woman awareness between them that had charged each look, each sip of sangria, each little gesture. The anticipation had built all evening, and she'd known he was going to kiss her when he walked her back to her car through the darkened streets. Instead, he'd only given her arm a quick squeeze and stepped away.

The disappointment had been sharp. It was only the beginning of her disillusionment. Later she realized that she had done most of the talking, and knew little more about Dr. Miguel personally than when he'd knocked on her office door—not even his last name. She'd assumed they'd remedy that situation, but she'd been wrong. The next day, he'd spared her only a curt nod, then turned away after their business discussion. Since that time, he'd been as remote to her as a ship sailing through Arctic waters. And she knew that he regretted their hours together.

She told herself she understood. Doubtless he was in the country illegally. Doubtless he was hiding from the INS. And he was afraid the agents who trawled the neighborhood for fugitives would ask her questions about him.

Bitterly, she'd labeled him a coward, though she wasn't sure whether she was referring to him or to herself. He hadn't spoken to her since that memorable night. Still, more than once, she'd caught him watching her with an intensity that brought goose bumps to her skin. Against her will, she'd caught herself watching *him*, too, when she thought he wasn't looking. But she hadn't seen him for several weeks.

The boy's voice broke into her tangled memories. ''He helps a lot of people who don't have the money to go to the doctor. Like my mother. Now he's burning with fever. He needs *you.*''

Her breath caught in her throat. ''He asked for *me?*''

Luis spread his hands. Again he spoke too quickly in Spanish for her to follow. Maybe this time it was on purpose. He ended with, ''I think he will die if you don't come quick.''

''He won't want *my* help,'' she said, almost to herself.

''There is no one else.''

''But I'm not a doctor,'' she insisted.

''You studied emergency medicine.''

''How do you know?''

''I heard you tell Rosita's mother, when she came to pick her up from the sickroom. The nurse wasn't there that day, and you were doing her job.''

''Yes, but—''

''That's fine. He knows what to do. You just have to get him the right medicine.''

Right. Sure. Against her better judgment, she let the boy's urgent voice persuade her. Probably she was making her biggest mistake of the evening, worse than leaving the door unlocked, she thought as she opened the bottom left-hand drawer of her desk and retrieved her purse. Yet the pinched look on Luis's face told her that there was no time to waste.

''You are coming?'' he asked in a relieved voice.

''Yes,'' she answered, silently promising herself that if things were as bad as Luis said, she was going to call an ambulance. Miguel might not like the decision, but in her judgment, it was better to be deported than dead.

After turning off her computer, she spotted the gun still sitting on the edge of her desk. With a shrug she slipped it into her purse.

THE MIDDAY SUN WAS HOT, burning his skin, burning through his body and into the center of his brain with a relentless heat that sapped his strength and made every step he took a new agony.

Madre de Dios. He needed a drink. Cold water to wet his cracked lips and cool his mouth. He would stand in an icy shower, let the water sluice over his body, and open his mouth to the blessed wetness. He shivered in anticipation, yet part of his mind knew there was no water in this place; only the heat and the sound of insects buzzing in his ears.

He'd run from the killers into the back country, where a man could lose himself—if he kept moving, if he kept his wits. Because *they* were back there, tramping through the underbrush, the men with the automatic weapons, following him. They would catch up, and they would gun him down the way they had murdered the others—Margarita, Anna, Tony, Paco. And it was his fault.

A smothered sound of protest and sorrow bubbled in his throat. He wanted to scream, but he kept the agony locked inside. If he screamed, the sound would bring them to him.

He had to get away. And not just for himself. He had to bring the killers to justice. To do that, he had to stay alive....

His body shuddered, then his eyes opened. For a moment he had no idea where he was as he stared at the dark, bare room where he lay on a narrow, lumpy bed. Then a moment of clarity came to his fevered mind. He wasn't in the jungle. He was in his basement apartment in Baltimore. Sick as hell.

The pounding headache, the heat burning up his body, and the terrible thirst came from fever.

Agua. He needed water. And he needed to remember to speak English, he cautioned himself. This was the United States, where even the poorest house had a kitchen sink with hot and cold running water.

He just had to turn on the tap. It was only twelve feet away, on the other side of the small room. But when he tried to push himself up, his arms shook and he fell back on the thin mattress. The best he could do was kick at the covers, push them away from his hot skin. The effort made his heart pound. With a groan of frustration, he lay back, and the thought flitted into his head that he was going to die in this miserable basement room in a city far from home where nobody knew his real name.

LUIS STUCK CLOSE TO Jessie as she led the way to the elevator and then out the back door to the garage across the alley, where she'd parked one of the vans that belonged to the Light Street Foundation.

Pulling out of the garage, she headed down Light Street and turned onto Pratt, taking a familiar route. For the past eighteen months she'd been dividing her time between the Light Street office and their outreach center in Baltimore's growing Hispanic community. Erin Stone, the foundation director, had wanted someone fluent in Spanish. Jessie had thought she was fluent enough, but she hadn't been prepared for the countless idioms and dialects she was now expected to understand. But she was doing her best. And Erin seemed happy with her work.

"Where are we going?" she asked as they turned onto Princess Street.

Luis reeled off an address above Fells Point, in the neighborhood where many Mexican and Central American immigrants—both legal and illegal—lived.

Jessie's hands tightened on the wheel as she drove under burned-out lights that turned the streets into dark canyons looming on either side of them. She passed more than one boarded-up building, and several times she saw figures slip hastily into the shadows as the van's headlights knifed through the dark.

Casting a glance at the boy hunched in his seat beside her, she casually asked, "Do you know Miguel's last name?"

"Diego."

"How did you find out he was sick?" she asked.

The boy hesitated.

"If I'm going to help, you have to give me information," she said softly. "You have to trust me."

He knit his fingers together in his lap, the pressure build-

ing until the skin was white. Then he said in a choked voice,
"He was sitting on the sidewalk around the corner from his
house, leaning against a building. I thought he was...
drunk...or stoned." He gave her a sideways look that made
her throat tighten.

She nodded, wishing she didn't live in a world where
children tossed off such observations.

"I was going to walk past him, pretend I didn't see his
shame. Then he said my name. When I stopped, he pushed
himself up. He had to stand with his back against the wall,
and he asked me to help him get home."

"And you knew he was sick?"

"When I touched him, I could feel his skin was as hot as
a radiator," the boy said.

"Did he say what was wrong with him?"

"I...I don't know for sure. But it's bad," Luis answered
in a low, evasive tone.

"It sounds like Miguel should be in the hospital."

"No!"

"He's illegal?" she asked, trying to make the question
sound as casual as possible.

"He's hiding out from bad men who want to kill him!
That's why he doesn't go to the center now."

"How do you know?"

"I heard it on the street."

"Yes, but—"

"Everyone knows," he insisted vehemently in Spanish.

Everyone but her. After eighteen months of community
social work, she was still an outsider—trusted only so far
by people who were afraid of getting chewed up and spat
out by the system. Since nobody in the barrio had revealed
Miguel Diego's secret to her, she was left with only the
bittersweet memory of their one vivid encounter, and the
image of his face—of high cheekbones, masculine angles,
expressive eyes, and lips that had softened into sensual lines
when he'd talked to her.

Don't be a fool, she scolded. To remind herself of reality, she deliberately changed his features back to those of the hard-edged man who had kept her at a distance for the past two months. That was the way he wanted it, she told herself. It had been *his* choice. Yet the features wavered, and she had the sudden conviction that he was a man at war with himself, a man who couldn't afford the luxury of comfortable choices.

Beside her, Luis sat up straighter as he carefully eyed a line of narrow row-houses. "It's the third one. Right there."

Jessie peered at the dwelling, seeing window frames with peeling paint and front steps listing dangerously to one side. Slowing down, she tried to make out any signs of life behind the grimy front window. All she could see were darkened rooms. "Are you sure this is the right place?"

"*Sí.* Dr. Miguel's apartment is in the back. Downstairs. Through there." He pointed to a dark, narrow passageway between two buildings.

"Great."

She didn't like the looks of the house, or the street. For one frantic moment she wondered if this was all an elaborate scheme. Had some adult persuaded Luis to lure her down here tonight? For what?

As she pulled into a parking space several yards down the block, she shook off the suspicion. The gun told her the boy had acted out of desperation. Their conversation had persuaded her he was trying to help a man he liked and respected.

"Cross the yard and go down the steps," the boy called over his shoulder as he jumped from the van and lunged into the passageway between the buildings, the blackness swallowing him whole.

"Wait." Scrambling to keep up, she followed him into the unlit tunnel, then had to stop abruptly when she realized she couldn't see well enough to keep from bashing into a wall.

Finally, she emerged into a small courtyard enclosed on three sides by a sagging wooden fence.

"Luis?" she called.

He didn't answer.

Then a metal trash can clattered to the ground somewhere nearby, and she almost jumped out of her skin as the ringing noise reverberated along her nerve endings.

Rats, she told herself, when the can continued to rattle as if being rocked by spectral hands. Or maybe a stray cat scavenging for dinner.

"Luis?" she called once more with a mixture of exasperation and fear.

Nobody answered.

After long seconds of silence, she was forced to concede that her young escort had vanished into the darkness.

Chapter Two

On a surge of panic, Jessie flattened her back against the wall as her gaze darted around the enclosure. The only other exit seemed to be a set of concrete steps to her right, descending into a well of blackness.

Luis had brought her to this place—and now he had vanished. The smart thing would be to cut her losses and make a hasty retreat—maybe call 911 and let them take care of the medical emergency, if there was one.

Yet she felt torn between prudence and concern. Again in her mind, she saw Miguel's face. This time, the mixture of diffidence and vulnerability in his eyes had a kind of transcendental effect on her, as if the feelings he evoked were more important than anything else.

Almost as if her feet had made a decision without consulting her brain, she moved away from the wall. When she reached the stairwell, she took a step downward. The worn concrete surface was uneven, causing her to lose her footing in the blackness. She thrust out a hand to catch herself against the rough brick wall.

The misstep knocked her out of her trance. No outside force was compelling her to stay in this place. She had a choice. She could turn around and leave if she wanted. Instead, she went forward.

Only by feel did she know when she'd reached the bottom of the stairs. Then she turned a corner and found herself facing a beat-up metal door with a tiny, high window that glowed dimly with interior light.

Was this run-down place really where Dr. Miguel lived?

With a little sigh, she knocked. When there was no answer, she tried the knob. It turned, and she boldly pushed open the door and stepped into the small room beyond.

A host of impressions assaulted her as she stood on the threshold of discovery. The air was damp and musty. The only light came from a small lamp on an old wooden table that shared a far wall with an iron bed. The lone occupant of the room was a man with a broad chest and narrow hips who lay stretched out on the bed. One arm was slung over his eyes, hiding his face. He was saved from total nudity by a pair of white cotton briefs that stood out like a beacon against the dark tones of his skin.

There was no way of knowing who he was. God, this could be any of a thousand men—and angel of mercy Jessie Douglas had blundered into his bedroom uninvited.

Hesitating in the doorway, she took in more details. It was obvious he had kicked away the covers, which hung over the bottom of the mattress and pooled on the gray tile floor, revealing his well-muscled body in all its particulars. When she realized which "particular" she was staring at, she felt heat rise in her cheeks.

She should be worrying about his health, not observing the way the cotton briefs molded to his impressive masculinity. Her gaze was pulled abruptly upward as his hair-roughened chest suddenly rose and fell in a series of shuddering breaths.

"Miguel?" she called in a hoarse voice, hardly aware that she had taken several quick steps forward. She wasn't sure whether he heard her call his name, but his arm moved, revealing his face for the first time.

It was him—although the sharp contrast between his previous appearance and his present state shocked her. A fine sheen of perspiration covered his brow. Dark smudges almost like bruises marred the skin under his closed eyes. Black stubble covered his sunken cheeks. And although he seemed to be asleep, the tautness of his features told her he was in pain.

"Miguel," she called again, her own features contorting as she watched his face.

His eyes were closed, and he moaned in frustration as he tried and failed to push himself into a sitting position.

The sound tore at her. She'd been frightened of coming here; frightened of a man she hardly knew, if she were honest with herself. Yet tonight, she knew she was seeing him at his most defenseless, and the realization caused a tide of protective instinct to swell inside her. He needed her help, although she was pretty sure—judging from his past behavior with her—that he wouldn't want to accept that help.

Still, she had made her own decision. Turning, she closed the door, shutting them in the room together. Then she knelt beside the bed and with a hand that wasn't quite steady, she softly touched his cheek.

For several heartbeats he lay without responding, and she was vividly aware of his stillness, except for the rise and fall of his broad chest and the rapid pounding of his heart. His skin was damp and hot to the touch. Luis was right about one thing, at least. He was very sick. But with what?

"Miguel? Miguel Diego?" she said, staring into his face. His lashes were incredibly long and dark—squandered on a man, really. In sleep they heightened his appearance of vulnerability.

She said his name again, and he stirred, as if he'd just realized she was speaking to him. The dark lashes fluttered open, and his expressive eyes found her in the dim room. The last time she'd seen him, they'd been clear and bright and lit with the fierce inner light that spoke of pride and determination. Now they were dull and glazed over by his illness.

"Anna. Oh, God. I thought they killed you," he said in Spanish, his hand coming up to grip her arm, pulling himself toward her.

The raspy sound of his voice was a shock—but not as much as the words. Who was Anna? Had somebody really killed her? Or was he speaking from the depths of a nightmare? All at once she remembered what Luis had told her: Bad men were after him.

"I'm not Anna," she said, answering in English to help him orient himself in time and space.

He blinked, pulled himself toward her, and she saw him making an effort to focus on her face, to anchor himself to present reality. His features contorted with what looked like crushing disappointment. "I thought..." Even as he spoke, he fell back against the pillow as if defeated.

She brushed aside her own disappointment. What had she expected, exactly? That everything would change because she had undertaken this rescue mission?

"I... It's Jessie. Jessie Douglas. From the rec center," she whispered, her breath catching. When he didn't reply, she added, "You remember me?"

"We had dinner. I wanted—" He stopped abruptly, and she saw the color in his cheeks deepen.

His gaze shifted away from her, and he tipped his head downward, taking in his state of undress. "You should not see me like this," he said in a thick voice as his hand began to search blindly for the sheet that had slipped below his grasp.

Modesty was the least of their worries, she thought. Yet she helped him tug the covering over his muscular body, up to chest level. When her hand landed on top of his, she kept it there, her fingers feeling cool against his burning skin. "Everything's okay," she said softly, conscious of the lie, conscious of the need to ask him some important questions—like about Anna.

Turning his head a fraction, he studied her. "What are *you* doing here?" he asked in a barely audible voice.

"Luis brought me," she replied, then felt compelled to add, "He insisted."

"He should not have bothered you."

"He was very worried."

"I will be fine."

Right, and the moon is made of Cheddar cheese, she thought as she watched him lick his cracked lips.

"Do you want me to get you a drink of water?" she asked, half expecting him to refuse even that small service. But his need was too great.

"Sí."

She stood, glad that there was something she could do for him, glad to break the intensity of the contact. Turning, she surveyed the little room. It was sparsely furnished with the iron bed, a chest, an old Formica table, two chairs, and several sturdy wooden boxes stacked against one wall. A tiny kitchen unit was strung out along the adjoining wall. Crossing to it, she opened a battered metal cabinet and took out one of the jelly jars she found on the shelf. As she filled it with water from the sink, she noted that his dwelling might be old and shabby, but everything was orderly and clean. The only thing out of place was the clothing he'd discarded in a heap near the end of the bed.

Returning to his side, she knelt once more. Although his eyes were closed, he must have been listening to her move about the room. As soon as he sensed her presence, his dark lashes flickered open and he extended a shaky hand toward the jar.

"Let me help you."

"I can do it."

Biting back a denial, she handed over the glass, watching the contents spill down the sides as he tried to hold it steady. Neither of them spoke. After a small pool of water had splashed onto his chest, she lifted the vessel from his grasp again and set it on the rickety nightstand.

"Sometimes it's a sign of strength to accept help," she said mildly.

He made a low sound in his throat as he tried and failed to sit up.

She had never dealt with anyone as proud, stubborn and arrogant—to name a few choice traits. Figuring she didn't have anything left to lose, she sat on the bed and wrapped her free arm around his shoulder. When he didn't reject her overture, she lifted him, cradling his body against her chest so that she could bring the glass to his lips. He leaned heavily against her as he drank, swallowing quickly, greedily, as if he'd been caught out in the hot desert sun. She hadn't considered that giving someone a drink of water could be such an intimate act, but holding him like this while he drank was very intimate.

"Have you had enough?" she asked softly, when he'd downed half the liquid.

"More, please."

She allowed him to drink his fill as she cradled him in her arms. When he was finished, he sank back heavily against her and sighed, the effort to simply quench his thirst having been almost too much for him.

She let him rest for a moment, then eased away, leaving him propped against the wall.

"Gracias," he finally said.

"You're welcome."

When he turned his head and looked at her, she asked, "Do you know what's wrong with you?"

"Malaria," he answered in a hoarse whisper.

"In Baltimore?"

"A relapse. I got it in San Marcos. In the hill country."

She knew that could happen. One of her clients had had a boyfriend from El Salvador with the same problem. The man had gone into a coma and died.

"You should be in the hospital," she said quickly as she inspected the dark streaks marring the skin under his eyes. He looked almost as if a couple of goons had pummeled his face with their fists.

He regarded her steadily. "Impossible."

"Why not?"

"I do not have…the energy to explain," he replied with profound weariness. It wasn't just from his illness, she thought. This man was worn-out from some heavy burden he had been carrying around for a long time.

Or was she reading too much into his ragged voice and

haggard expression? All she could tell for certain was that the brief conversation was rapidly sapping his strength.

"If you can get me mefloquine I will be okay." He paused for breath. "Or maybe pyrmethamine," he added, reeling off the names of the medicines with a physician's precision.

And where was she supposed to get either of those drugs without a prescription? Maybe from her friend Dr. Katie Martin McQuade, who was married to medical researcher Mac McQuade. They owned Medizone Labs, which specialized in developing the medical potential of plants from around the world. "I may be able to get you what you need."

"Without disclosing the name of the patient?" he asked, apparently following her train of thought. Avoiding her gaze, he stared into the darkness beyond the circle of light from the lamp.

"Yes."

"You would do that for me?"

She nodded, shifting on the bed so that she was facing him.

"Why?" he asked.

"My job is helping people," she said evasively, knowing he was more likely to accept her offer if she kept the transaction impersonal.

She sensed he was making a decision about whether or not to trust her. Sick as he was, he held on to the balance of power in this encounter. As she waited for his approval, time stretched like wire pulled taut. She wanted to say all sorts of things that would push him in the right direction, but she knew that nothing she could say would matter to him. He would keep his own counsel.

"Come back in the morning," he said after several tense, silent moments.

"I don't think that's smart," she answered quickly.

"You can't stay. It is…dangerous."

The word hung in the air between them like the sound of a bomb ticking.

"Luis said that you were on the run—" She hesitated for a fraction of a second. "From the INS?"

His gaze held steady. "Worse than the INS."

"Who?"

His Adam's apple bobbed. "The less you know about me, the better. For your own sake."

She wanted to push him for explanations, make him give her more information. At the same time, she felt a little bud of hope unfurl inside her. The night they'd gotten close, he'd made her think the two of them could eventually mean something to each other. The next day, he'd ruthlessly turned away from her. Was he finally giving her a valid reason? Had he been afraid that her getting close to him would put her in danger?

It was all she could do not to grab him by the shoulders and shake the truth out of him. But she could see every word he uttered was stealing more of his strength. Even so, his eyes locked with hers in silent defiance. God, this man was something else. Too sick to get out of bed, yet fighting like a raging bull every step of the way.

"But you'll let me get you the medicine?" she asked, pushing for clarification.

He ignored the challenge. "From whom?"

"Katie and Mac."

"Who are they?" he asked, the hard edge of suspicion back in his voice—along with a little tremor as he tried and failed to keep his teeth from chattering.

"They're good friends." If she'd had more time for pleasantries, she would have explained that they were part of the group that someone had dubbed the Light Street Irregulars—friends who rallied around when one of their own was in trouble. They were there if you needed them and didn't press for inconvenient explanations when it was better to leave the details vague.

"You trust them?" he asked, cutting to the bottom line with the precision of a surgeon.

"Implicitly," she answered, as she scooped up the covers and draped them around his shoulders. He was starting to have chills. Not good. Before he could come up with any more objections, she said, "I'll be back as soon as I can."

HEARING THE SOFT CLICK of the door behind her, Miguel sighed and leaned his head heavily against the wall, conserving his strength.

Now that she was gone, there was no longer a reason to keep his body from shaking, so he let the tremors take him. God, he hated Jessie Douglas seeing him like this, weak as a newborn baby and almost as helpless. He was certain she knew how he felt, too. Hiding his emotions had simply been too much effort.

His eyes squeezed closed and his face contorted as he struggled to blot out the images of her in this wretched place—and the feel of her body as she held him while he drank a glass of water.

Desperately, his mind scrambled for a refuge. He succeeded only in calling forth another vivid scene—the first time he'd seen her. He had been talking to one of the boys in the big room with the Ping-Pong tables when he'd been distracted by a flash of movement from the corner of his eye. Lifting his head, he'd turned and seen what looked like an angelic image in a Renaissance painting. He'd told himself she couldn't be real. But when he'd blinked to clear his vision, she was still there, blond and lovely and serene—in the midst of grubby chaos.

As soon as he could breathe again, he'd started weaving his way across the crowded room so he could get her into a conversation that would lead to the two of them ending up alone together in some quiet, comfortable place.

He'd stopped himself before he'd reached her and spent the rest of the afternoon fighting the impulse to learn more about her.

He'd kept on fighting the compulsion for weeks. Finally, he'd come to her with a story about a boy who needed glasses. The story was true enough, as far as it went. He had delivered his message and ordered himself to leave. Instead, they'd started talking, and he'd found himself dropping his guard for the first time since the fiasco in Mexico.

Perhaps he'd been hoping she wouldn't be as charming as she looked or that he could find something about her to dislike. But she'd been everything he'd imagined and more. They had liked each other at once; had found so much to talk about, even though he was careful not to reveal his background. While they had shared a meal, he had drawn her out, fallen deeper under her spell.

His mind had flashed him images of dark, hot fire igniting between them as he kissed her good-night. Somehow, though, while he'd walked her to her car, he'd ordered himself back to his senses. The next day he had found the strength to coldly cut off any chance of a relationship with her. Still, the craving for her had grown like an addictive drug spreading a seductive warmth through his system. Long after he should have gone underground, he had found himself drifting over to the recreation center so he could at least feast his eyes on her. And to his secret gratification, he'd seen her watching him with the same intense interest he felt toward her. He even knew she'd asked some questions about him.

All she'd found out was the standard story. He was Miguel Diego, a man who didn't want to talk much about his background and who supported himself by wielding a mop and a broom at night. He hadn't told her or anybody else that he was really Dr. Miguel Valero, fugitive from the law, in danger of being sent back to San Marcos to face murder charges.

His hands clenched convulsively at the corners of the blanket she had draped over his shoulders. He was so worn down that the idea of simply closing his eyes and going to sleep forever had a seductive appeal. But he hadn't sunk to quite that cowardly level. He had to stay alive. As long as he drew breath, there was still a chance he could get the men who had turned his clinic into a slaughterhouse and made it look as if he were the one who was responsible.

He'd read about it in the papers as he'd traveled north,

hiding like an escaped criminal. The story was that the greedy Dr. Valero had gotten into a drug deal and then turned up short on cash. So the cartel had come gunning for him. Only he'd been out of the clinic when they'd stormed inside. Unable to find him, the gunmen had taken out their vengeance on innocent people.

It sounded plausible in a country like San Marcos where the allure of making a fortune in the drug trade was all too tempting. If he died now, no one would ever hear the real story. He'd simply be another statistic. Along with Anna and Margarita, Tony and Paco, and the rest of his staff. And the patients—five innocent women who had been at the wrong place at the wrong time; women whose haunted eyes he saw in his nightmares. One of them had been a charity case from a village near the coast. The great plastic surgeon Miguel Valero was going to fix the ugly birthmark that covered half her face. Instead, she'd been executed in a hail of machine-gun bullets.

Soon there could be another woman on his conscience— sweet, innocent Jessie Douglas, who had shown up in his miserable basement room and wanted to help him.

It was wrong to let her get this close to him. If she was an angel of light bathed in reflected radiance from heaven, then he was the angel of death, slipping out of the shadows of darkness. He could bring her harm if she was caught anywhere near him. Yet he only needed her for a little while, he rationalized. Then he could leave Baltimore, go on to the next city. And Jessie would be safe.

As SHE REACHED THE sidewalk, Jessie stopped for a moment, wondering where to find a phone so she could call Katie. Then she saw a flicker of movement near a flight of steps to her left. Someone was watching her from the shadows.

Goose bumps rose on the skin of her arms as she quickened her pace. She'd be safe in the van, she told herself, unwilling to give in to panic. But it was already too late for escape.

"There she is. I told you," a voice hissed from behind her, and she realized there was more than one watcher.

A hand grabbed her arm, pulling her to a stop. "What's your hurry, sweet face?"

From the darkness, a group of shadows swarmed, then circled around her, imprisoning her with a wall of bodies as surely as if they had enclosed her with iron bars.

She saw young men—teenagers—their faces bright with the excitement of the hunt. They were all dressed in baggy pants and orange shirts or jackets with black stripes. Gang colors. The colors of Los Tigres, to be exact. Although she'd heard nasty rumors about the gang's exploits, she'd never seen them up close and personal like this.

They must have spotted the van, seen her park and get out. Then they'd hung around, waiting for her to come back. At least she should be grateful that they hadn't barged into Miguel's apartment and caught both of them.

She tried toughing it out. "Let me go," she said in a tight voice. "I don't have time for this. I have work to do."

Several of the group laughed. "Work. Yeah."

"There's only one kind of work a woman does at night," another voice observed. It belonged to a guy who shouldered his way forward, the crowd parting deferentially for him as he approached. He was taller than the rest, meaner looking, with rank orange hair and a safety pin piercing the skin over one eyebrow.

"No," was all she could manage.

"Then what are you doing down here at this time of night, blondie?" he asked. "Slumming?"

"You give it to her straight, Georgie," one of his cohorts approved.

The rest of them snickered at the brilliant witticism, and Jessie fought not to cringe as their leader took a menacing step toward her.

Chapter Three

The guy called Georgie formed his lips into a smile that made her insides curdle.

Her eyes darted to the windows of the houses across the street. A few still showed yellow lights behind closed blinds. People were awake, but even if she screamed bloody murder, probably no one would want to get involved.

The creep's eyes swept up and down her body, lingering on her breasts as his tongue flicked out to lick his lips. "We're going to have some fun," he said in a voice that made her skin crawl.

She tried not to let him see her fear, for all the good that would do her.

Behind him some of the others murmured their approval—and she caught a note of gathering excitement.

"You'll like spending some time with us, *caramelo*," the spokesman continued, playing to his audience, calling her "caramel"—in this case, a mocking Spanish endearment. "We have a nice safe place where we can all take turns getting to know you real well."

"No," she said, fighting to control the terror in her voice, fighting to pretend that she wasn't so scared she could barely keep her knees from buckling.

Georgie's lips quirked into a parody of a smile, his expression telling her that she wasn't fooling anyone. "You don't have much choice," he told her. "You're pretty stupid to come down here all by yourself in the dark, so I figure you're getting what you deserve.''

She stood facing him, her knees locked, her skin clammy. "What's in that expensive purse of yours?" he asked.

Her gaze dropped to the pocketbook slung over her shoulder, and the answer to the question leaped into her brain. *Not just a wallet and keys,* she thought as her hand reached into the partially unzipped opening.

Swallowing to moisten her dry throat, again she tried to sound tough. "I'm not as stupid as you think." As she spoke, she pulled out the shiny little revolver Luis had brought to her office. He'd said it wasn't loaded. Maybe he'd been lying, she told herself. Or maybe it didn't matter—if she acted like she was going to scatter this flock of turkeys.

A collective gasp issued from the flock, and her confidence leaped. Obviously, they hadn't expected any kind of defense on her part.

Georgie's eyes fastened on the gun.

"Back off, or I'll spatter your guts all over the sidewalk," she hissed, hardly recognizing her own voice. With deliberate care, she leveled the weapon at his midsection.

Several gang members backed away. Those on the fringes of the group began to fade into the shadows.

When Georgie didn't move, she spoke again, "Get the hell out of here."

For endless heartbeats, he stood his ground, his eyes filling with hatred. Too late, she wished she hadn't stooped to using such ugly language.

"I'll get you for this," he snarled.

"I wouldn't count on it."

He gave her one more deadly look, then spun on his heel and sauntered down the block, probably trying to create the illusion that the decision to disengage had been his.

A violent tremor shook Jessie as she stared down at the gun—the gun that probably wasn't even loaded, she reminded herself. To keep herself from whimpering, she crammed her fist against her mouth and backed toward the van. When she felt the cold metal touch her hips, she whirled and shoved the key into the lock. Opening the door, she sprang inside, jammed her hand on the automatic lock, and started the engine with a grinding noise that seared her nerve endings. After laying the weapon on the seat beside her, she yanked at the wheel with both hands. Somehow she managed not to mow down the car in front of her as the van leaped out of the parking space like a bronco from the chute. She sped down the silent block, ran a stop sign, and didn't slow down to below the speed limit until she was several blocks from Miguel's.

Pulling around the corner, she nosed behind a stop sign and quietly began to cry. They had intended to rape her. There was no doubt about that. But would they have let her out of their clutches alive?

Several minutes passed before she felt enough in control to drive again. Fumbling in her purse, she brought out a tissue and blew her nose. Lord, now what? Since she'd left the office with Luis, she'd been taking this one step at a time. She'd planned to call Katie, go back to Miguel's with medication, and then check on him in the morning—if it was reasonable to leave him alone. Los Tigres had changed those plans. It was no longer safe for her to pop in and out of Miguel's apartment. If she was going to help him, she'd have to take him someplace else as quickly as possible.

The decision didn't sit easily with her. She hated being pushed into a course of action without considering the consequences. But the alternative was abandoning Miguel or turning the job over to someone else. Since she didn't know whom to trust with that kind of responsibility, she turned the van around and headed in the direction from which she'd come.

But no way was she going to park on the street again, she thought as she made a wide circle around the scene of the near disaster. Instead, she found the alley paralleling Miguel's street and drove cautiously up the cracked pavement, squeezing past several trash cans as she looked for the third house on the left. All the yards were hidden behind high wooden fences with gates. The third gate was open a couple of inches, and she realized that must have been where Luis had slipped out. She just hadn't been able to see it from where she'd been standing in the yard. As she turned off the headlights, her breath grew shallow. Driving back here was one thing. Getting out of the van again was quite another.

For several minutes, she sat with her hands clamped to the steering wheel, her eyes probing the darkness. Finally she pulled forward so that her door was as close as possible to the gate, and cut the engine. Then she picked up the gun, made a rapid exit from the van, and slipped into the backyard.

She entered the apartment to find Miguel was sitting slumped against the wall. His head jerked toward the door as she stepped inside.

"You... We have to get out of here," she said.

He focused on her face, his eyes glinting. Probably she looked like she'd been crying, she realized suddenly, sorry that she hadn't thought to check her appearance in the mirror.

"What happened?" he growled, pushing himself up straighter.

Before she could think of what to say, his gaze zeroed in on the revolver still clutched in her hand. "Tell me," he commanded sharply, "have they found me?"

She didn't know who "they" were. Probably not Los Tigres. "No," she answered, then concluded from his tense expression that a one-syllable answer wouldn't suffice. "Some members of a gang saw me park the van. They were waiting when I came out."

His eyes narrowed as he studied her. "I told you to get out of here. You should have taken my advice."

"Yes. We'd better go," she agreed.

"Where did you get the gun?"

"From Luis."

His gaze bored into hers. "He gave it to you for protection?"

"Not exactly."

Apparently she didn't have to draw Miguel a picture of the encounter. "That boy! He is going to be sorry when I catch up with him," he growled, although she could see that the long exchange was sapping his strength.

Jessie slipped the weapon back into her purse and gave him a few minutes to rest while she collected some toilet articles from the bathroom and stuck them inside a travel bag she found there. The bag went into a pillowcase, along with some extra clothing and the wallet lying on the floor beside the bed.

When she'd finished packing, she knelt beside Miguel, a T-shirt in her hand. He was dozing lightly. His eyes snapped open when she gently touched his arm.

"Let's get you dressed," she said briskly. Nurse Douglas. Only she was afraid she lacked some of the critical training. She might need some coaching from Dr. Diego.

"I can do it!" He managed to get the shirt over his head, then sagged against the wall, breathing hard. She helped with the sleeves, wanting to tell him that he didn't have to prove anything to her. She was certain he wouldn't welcome any discussion of the subject.

Getting his pants on was going to be harder, she decided as she knelt on the floor in front of him. But she'd always loved a challenge. Without comment, she bunched up the legs, slipped his feet through the bottoms, and worked the fabric upward. As she tugged the pants over his hips, she kept her eyes averted and her hands carefully away from the front of him. So it was several seconds before she realized that the elasticized waistband had gotten caught on the most prominent part of his lower anatomy.

He made a strangled sound and reached to free the pants. She reached at the same time, and their hands collided squarely over the stumbling block.

"Sorry," she murmured, sure her face had turned the color of tomato soup.

"I will do it," he said roughly.

She pulled her hand away and let him complete the task while she picked up his shoes and socks and sat back down on the floor in front of him. There was no danger of his seeing her face now. This should be the easy part, she told herself. Yet there was something very intimate about handling a man's feet, she discovered. His were narrow and well shaped, with bluntly cut toenails and high arches. When her fingers moved against the sensitive flesh, his body twitched. It was a relief to finally announce, "All done."

He answered with a grunt that might have been construed as thanks.

"You'll have to walk to the van," she told him as she got to her feet.

He closed his eyes, leaning back against the wall as if he were gathering strength for a trial by fire.

"Ready?" she asked.

"I suppose you have been told before that you are stubborn," he answered without opening his eyes.

She shrugged. Apparently they had that trait in common. This time she had won—because he was simply too sick to fight her.

He leaned forward, his fingers gripping her arm. "Promise you won't take me to the hospital."

"I—" How could she agree to something like that? What if his life depended on hospitalization?

"Promise!" He lifted his head, and his gaze burned into her.

"All right. I promise," she agreed, feeling trapped. Yet she understood that giving her word was the only way she could get him to cooperate. Because she couldn't take too much of his scrutiny, she bent and slung an arm around his shoulder.

They were both silent as she grabbed the pillowcase and her purse before helping him to his feet. When they started across the small apartment, she realized it was going to be a longer trip than she'd anticipated—if he made it at all.

TWO THOUSAND MILES SOUTH of Baltimore, in the country of San Marcos, a man with lean cheeks and hard eyes touched a finger to his face, then turned his head from one side to the other as he inspected his reflection in the mirror. The tiny scars just in front of his ears were healed now— like the scars at the sides of his nose, and below his eyes. They had been made with surgical precision by a master craftsman. And they were all but invisible.

The larger wounds that marred the back of his neck were still a little red, but they were hidden by hair that reached his collar. Delicately, he fingered one of the slashes. Every week, it was less noticeable to his touch. Soon, even these scars would be undetectable to all but the most intimate of explorations, and he could put the next phase of his plan into action.

He smiled, pleased with his appearance. Pleased with Miguel Valero's work. The doctor had fashioned a wonderful face. And now he was the only one left who could prove that Carlos Jurado was not dead; that Carlos Jurado had turned himself into another man.

As he thought of the last barrier to complete success, the satisfaction he felt evaporated like spit on a blazing sidewalk. His hand balled into a fist that he almost smashed against the mirror. But prudence stopped him.

He gave a bark of laughter. There was no need to get angry, no need to push his blood pressure up. He had men looking for Valero. Competent men. They had almost caught up with him once in Mexico, even though he had changed his name and gotten false papers. A woman had betrayed him. And someone would betray him again—if the price was right.

As JESSIE GUIDED MIGUEL into the darkness of the stairwell, every instinct urged her to hurry. But she had to let him set the pace as they hobbled slowly up the steps. When they finally made it to the yard, he stood still, breathing heavily, and she wondered if he could go on. But he was made of strong stuff. In a few moments, he began to move again slowly but doggedly.

"*Perdón,*" he murmured as he stumbled on a patch of loose paving. Jessie struggled to stay on her own feet as his weight came down on her shoulder.

"It's all right," she said, hoping she had kept the fear out of her voice. This was the worst part—being in the dark, exposed and defenseless. It felt like hours before they reached the van, and all the while she kept imagining menacing shapes coming at them from the shadows.

As Miguel leaned against the vehicle, she opened the side door.

"You can lie down in back."

He sucked in a breath and blew it out. "I can sit in the front seat."

She might have taken the time to argue, if she hadn't heard the sound of feet coming toward them along the pavement. In a panic, she pushed Miguel into the back seat, scrambled in behind him, and slammed the door. Seconds later she was in the driver's seat, shoving the key into the ignition. The moment the engine came to life, she bulleted down the alleyway, almost taking out a cluster of trash cans on her left.

When she reached the street, she spared a glance in the rearview mirror. Two boys were running toward the van— two boys wearing gang colors.

With a frantic moan, she pulled out into the street and made a tire-screeching getaway worthy of a Hollywood stuntman.

Not until she'd traveled several miles did she glance behind her again. Miguel was propped in the corner, his knuckles white where he clutched the shoulder strap for support.

"Are you all right?" she asked.

"More or less. What happened?"

"I saw them. Two of the boys from the gang—Los Tigres."

"They are bad. And now they're your enemies, I think."

She wasn't sure how to answer as she sped into the night.

"Another stone weighing down my conscience," he muttered.

"It isn't your fault."

"Of course it is," he snapped.

They rode in silence for several minutes before he asked, "Where are we going?"

"My house."

"No."

"At the moment, you don't have much choice." Maybe it wasn't such a great idea, but she couldn't think of anything better.

Their eyes met in the rearview mirror as she left the harbor area and headed up I-95 toward Catonsville. She broke the contact first, because she had to watch the road. But she felt his gaze like a laser drilling into the back of her head.

By the time she reached the red brick rancher she'd bought when she came to Baltimore, he was asleep, lying on his side with his feet jammed against the end of the seat.

He didn't stir when she pulled up beside the kitchen door and cut the engine. Quietly she climbed into the back and eased down onto the floor, looking at his flushed face in the dim glow from the overhead light. He'd worsened visibly in the time it had taken her to get him out of his apartment and drive home. She suddenly realized how much responsibility she'd taken on by bringing him here.

Gently, she pressed the back of her hand to his hot cheek, stroking the stubble of his heavy beard. He hadn't shaved in several days. How long had he been sick?

The dark lashes fluttered open, his eyes registering confusion—then alarm—until they focused on her and held like a compass fixed on magnetic north.

As she saw his expression soften, she felt a dangerous

warmth well up inside her and knew she was getting too close to a man who could hurt her badly.

"Let's go inside. You'll feel better in bed," she managed, the last part coming out in a little croak.

He pushed himself up and his eyes locked with hers for a moment. She was the first to look away. Awkwardly she helped him slide off the seat and exit the van. It was slow going into the house—even slower than before.

"What do you need before you sleep?" she asked.

"Bathroom…water…aspirin," he gasped.

She led him the few steps to the bathroom, wondering if it was safe to leave him alone. Knowing he wouldn't allow her help, she waited in the hall until she heard the sound of water running. She found him leaning on the sink, supporting himself on his elbows, splashing cold water onto his face. He followed by scooping some into his mouth from the faucet.

"Miguel?"

"I am fine!" he retorted, his words slurred. When she touched the side of his neck, his skin felt as if it were on fire. Maybe the aspirin would help. Opening the medicine cabinet, she shook two tablets out of the bottle.

"Here."

He stared at the medication, then shook his head stiffly. "Did Carlos Jurado buy you, the way he bought Juanita?"

"Who?"

"Carlos—" He stopped abruptly, his expression confused.

"That's the man you're hiding from?" she asked quickly, pressing for information.

He nodded.

"Is he a cop?"

"I wish." The observation was followed by a gritty laugh.

"Why is he after you?"

"I know his name, and I know his secret!"

"Which is?"

His eyes narrowed. "If you want to stay alive, do not ask me questions! He killed everyone at the clinic. Everyone except me."

"When?"

"October."

Six months ago. A long time to live like a fugitive. Was it really true, or was Miguel in the grip of some paranoid delusion brought on by his illness?

At the rec center, she'd taken care of a child with a high fever—a little boy who had started hallucinating. He'd thought monsters were under the sickroom bed, and there had been no way to calm him. Yet Miguel's case was different. She had no doubt that *something* real—something *terrible*—had happened to him.

He blinked, as if trying to figure out where he was and what she was doing there. So much for the moment of connection they'd shared in the van; or perhaps it had only been her imagination.

"It's okay," she said softly. "I'm Jessie Douglas. You're at my house. You're safe here. Remember?"

He gave a little nod, but she didn't know whether he believed her. She'd brought him home because it had seemed like the best alternative. Now she realized just how dangerous a situation she'd set up. What if he decided she was the enemy? Restraining a hysterical little boy was one thing. Defending herself against a large, aggressive man was quite another.

"You'll feel better if you take the aspirin," she said carefully, wishing she could get him into a tub of cool water. That might help lower his fever, but she doubted he'd let her take off his clothes and bathe him—even if she thought she was up to it.

To her relief, he finally accepted the aspirin, then allowed her to steer him into the only room in the house with a bed— her bedroom. Flopping onto the spread, he lay with his eyes closed, breathing heavily. Jessie straightened his legs and removed his shoes and socks. She was tugging on the waist-band of his sweatpants when his eyes came open. The look he gave her made her jerk her hand away. A little smile played around his mouth as his gaze slid over her, starting with her mouth, caressing her breasts, ending below her waist. She felt every nuance as if he'd actually touched her.

"Don't," she said in a weak voice.

"I wanted to take you to bed the first time I met you," he said thickly, his hand capturing hers. "And now, here you are, undressing me."

"I—"

"You wanted it, too. I saw the way you looked at me."

"Don't say that," she protested, fighting the fluttery sensation in her stomach.

"Why not? It's true." His speech was slurred slightly, his brain apparently incapable of censoring his words or his actions. "You have the face of an angel. And a very sexy body. That night we had dinner, I could hardly keep my hands off you."

His thumb stroked her palm seductively, sending prickles of sensation across her skin and up her arm.

"Do I?" she asked, her own voice unsteady.

"Yes." His eyes drifted closed, and his breathing became more quiet. Just like that, he had fallen asleep.

Shaking herself, she pulled from his grasp. Forget about his pants, she told herself as she began to tug the covers out of the way.

The movement jerked him awake again, and a deeply puzzled expression flitted across his face. "I thought…" He was silent for several moments, regarding her gravely. Then he said, "You fuss too much, Anna. You must learn to relax."

An unexpected stab of disappointment pierced through her. Was he talking to her or to someone else?

Setting her jaw, she fought for perspective. Her reactions were absurd. He might be lying in her bed, but she had no right to be jealous. If he had told the truth earlier, Anna had died violently. At the clinic he had talked about?

He lay very still, and she realized he'd slipped back into sleep. He kept doing that—then waking up, confused. He was getting worse, and she wondered if she could handle this by herself.

Leaving her purse and the pillowcase full of clothing beside him, she went into the spare room she used as an office and flipped through her Rolodex. It was late for calls, she realized, as she found Katie's number. But she didn't have many options. It was either call her friends or call an ambulance and break the promise Miguel had wrung from her.

After several moments' hesitation, she dialed the number. Katie answered on the second ring.

"I know it's late," Jessie apologized quickly. "I hope I didn't wake you."

"No. As a matter of fact, Mac's on a research trip and I was sitting here watching a dumb movie. What can I do for you?"

Jessie dragged in a quick breath and let it out in a rush. She'd been hoping Mac would volunteer to come along.

"Jessie?"

"There's a medical emergency. Something confidential," she added, wanting to make things clear from the outset. "I have a guy here who's pretty sick." She cleared her throat. "But he insists that he won't go to the hospital."

"Why not?"

"He's a fugitive from somewhere in Latin America."

"Is he in trouble with the law?"

Was he? Making a decision to take Miguel at his word—at least for now—Jessie answered, "No."

"Tell me what's wrong."

Quickly she gave Katie a brief summary of the facts she knew.

"There are several distinct malaria strains," her friend said in response. "We can't be absolutely sure what medication he needs until we do a blood test. But I'll stop by the lab and pick up the best treatment alternative. I can get to your house in about an hour."

"I appreciate it," Jessie told her with sincerity, wondering if she'd done the right thing. After hanging up the phone, she hurried back to the bedroom to see how Miguel was doing. She'd only been gone a few minutes, but she found the contents of her purse and the pillowcase strewn across the bed. Miguel's sweatpants were lying in a twisted heap on the floor, and he was sitting with his back propped against the pillows, his head bent, and his arms partially hidden by the edge of the sheet.

"Are you all right?" she asked anxiously.

His head jerked up. Eyes glazed, forehead beaded with perspiration, he stared at her. Or was he seeing someone else?

"Miguel?"

His arms came free of the covering. Clasped in both hands was the shiny little revolver she'd taken away from Luis—the same weapon that she'd used to fend off Georgie. Too bad she'd been too scared and too busy to check whether or not it was loaded.

"You are back," he growled, speaking in Spanish, moving the pistol so that it was pointed where it would do the most damage. "I always knew you would be back to finish the killing.'' He seemed to be looking right through her as his face contorted in anger.

"I'm not your enemy. I'm Jessie," she gasped. "Jessie Douglas. I brought you to my house, remember?"

"Lying scum!" he growled, still in Spanish. "Carlos Jurado sent you to kill my staff. Kill my patients. But you are not going to get me."

The gun wavered, and she wondered how long a man in his condition could hold it steady. Maybe he wouldn't be able to shoot straight. Maybe there weren't any bullets. But she couldn't trust her life to either eventuality.

"Please," she tried, taking a step closer. "Put the gun down."

"You must be crazy!" he spat. The weapon listed to the side, but she could see he was working hard to hold it on her.

"Miguel, it's Jessie. Jessie Douglas," she cried out again, her voice rising in desperation as she saw his finger tighten on the trigger.

Chapter Four

Jessie braced for the impact of a bullet. It never came.

Despite her numerous deadly mistakes this evening, she was living a charmed life. Springing across the room, she threw herself against Miguel, the impact of her forward motion knocking him backward into the pillows.

She heard the breath hiss from his lungs as he took the force of the collision squarely in the chest, but the pistol stayed in his hand.

"Miguel, it's Jessie," she repeated urgently. "You're safe. Nobody's going to hurt you."

Paying no attention to her words, he kept fighting her with his remaining strength.

"I brought you home," she panted. "You're at my house. Please, trust me!"

It seemed she was wasting her breath.

"No." He made a mighty effort to push her off him, then struggled to get the revolver into position for another shot. What if there really was a bullet in one of the chambers? she thought frantically as she tried to wrest the gun from his grasp.

Under ordinary circumstances she would have been no match for a well-muscled man, but she felt his strength flagging fast. Her fingers on his, she pried the pistol from his hand and lay across his chest, panting.

When he stopped moving, she eased away so that she

could look into his face. His expression had changed dramatically, and for the first time since she'd returned to the bedroom, she was sure he recognized her.

"Everything's okay," she whispered, her hand pressing over his, trying with her touch to bridge any gap between them.

"Oh, God," he gasped. "I thought—" He was silent for long seconds, then said in a shaky voice, "Jessie, I had a gun in my hand. Did I just try to shoot you?"

She nodded. His teeth clenched as he sank back against the pillows.

"It's all right. You didn't know what you were doing." Without thinking, she wrapped the fingers of her free hand around his, carried them to her lips.

"That is no excuse! You cannot keep a loco in your house," he choked out, trying to yank his hand away.

She kept hold of him, determined to maintain the contact. "I think it's called 'delirium' when it's caused by a high fever, Dr. Diego," she said quietly.

His face contorted, but she continued quickly, "You need medicine and someone to take care of you until you're feeling better."

"What if I…threaten you again? What happens then?"

"We'll deal with it. Lie still."

"I'm getting worse. Delusional."

"My friend Katie is coming over to bring you medication. You'll start feeling better soon."

"You called her? When?"

"While you were getting the gun out of my pocketbook."

Miguel made a guttural sound.

After checking to see that the revolver was really empty, she set it on the floor, then moved to the head of the bed and cradled him against herself, stroking back the damp hair from his forehead, murmuring low, soothing words. She could feel his warm breath penetrating the thin fabric of her blouse, heating her skin. She tried to stay detached, but when she thought she detected the touch of his lips brushing her shoulder, she felt her heart melt.

"Why are you doing this?" he murmured.

He had asked the question before. Last time her answer hadn't been entirely honest. This time she whispered, "I want to," then, "Everything's going to be all right. Trust me on that."

"It has been a long time since I trusted anybody," he replied in a barely audible voice, as if the admission were welling up from some hidden place inside him.

"I know."

"How?"

"It's pretty obvious. I think it's turned into a bad habit."

He gave a short, mirthless laugh. "Changing my habits kept me alive."

She thought about the things he'd inadvertently revealed earlier and wanted to ask about Carlos Jurado. Who was he and what had happened between him and Miguel? But she knew this wasn't the right time—not when he'd finally settled down a little.

Several silent moments passed till she felt the tension ebb from his rigid shoulders, felt him calming in her arms, felt her own heartbeat returning to a normal rate. There was something elemental about holding him close like this that was an antidote to all the uncertainty that had come before.

Exhausted, she curled against him, rested her cheek on the top of his head. Her eyelids were impossibly heavy, and she let them drift closed.

"HIDE!" MIGUEL'S VOICE was low and urgent as his hands pushed at her shoulders. "Get away from me. Hide!"

She lifted her head, blinked as she tried to remember what they were doing together in her bed. The chiming of the doorbell penetrated her consciousness, then the sound of loud knocking.

Miguel's eyes were dark and fierce, his cheeks flushed as

he turned and began searching frantically on the surface of the bed. "Where is the gun?"

"You don't need the gun. It's my friend Katie at the door. She's coming to bring you medicine. Remember, I called her?" she asked, her gaze locked on his. "We're safe here. You don't need the gun," she repeated. "I'll be right back." Standing, she used her foot to slowly push the weapon farther under the edge of the bed.

Then she hurried to the front door. Peering cautiously through the peephole, she was relieved to see a distorted image of her friend.

"Sorry I took so long," Katie apologized. "I don't usually need to put my hand on medication, and I had some problems finding it. So I called Mac, and I've got some great news. There's not much malaria research going on in the U.S., but it turns out Medizone is working on a medication that's designed to be effective against all strains of the disease, and with reduced side effects. The drug's still in the testing stages, but Mac says it's better than anything on the market."

Jessie nodded, then put a hand on her friend's arm. "Before you meet Miguel, you'd better know he's, uh, having a little trouble remembering where he is, and that I'm one of the good guys."

"A high fever will do that."

"I know," Jessie said as she led the way to her bedroom.

Miguel was sitting up, his head turned toward the door, but she could see it was taking considerable effort to maintain the position.

After Jessie introduced them, Katie stepped closer. "I'd like to examine you, if that's all right. And get you started on a course of treatment as soon as possible."

He nodded.

Jessie stood uncertainly in the doorway.

Katie looked from the patient to her. "Why don't you have a cup of coffee or something while I'm checking him out."

"Yes. Right." Miguel wouldn't want her as a spectator. She'd just have to trust that he wouldn't try to murder the doctor.

Making a quick exit, she headed for the kitchen and automatically filled the kettle. But when the water boiled, she turned it off again, knowing she was too jittery to drink anything. Pacing back and forth, she kept watching the clock. After twenty minutes, she tiptoed down the hall and found Katie had pulled a chair close to the side of the bed. She and Miguel were talking peacefully in low voices.

Katie looked up. "I've taken a blood sample to find out what malaria strain we're dealing with, and I've given him an injection that will take effect very quickly. But he needs to continue with a course of treatment over the next few days." She picked up a bottle of tablets from the bedside table. "He should have one of these every six hours until the bottle's empty."

Jessie nodded.

"He'll feel a lot better very quickly," Katie continued, "but the effects don't last unless the course of medication is completed. I've explained to him that he's going to have intermittent good and bad periods, but he should stay in bed for the next three or four days. His fever may spike again and alternate with chills."

Jessie nodded. "He's already had those."

"It's important not to overdo when he's feeling better. You can be the bad guy and enforce the bed rest."

"Thanks."

Katie turned back to Miguel. "Do you have any more questions?"

He shook his head.

"I'll be back in a minute," Jessie said, as she and Katie stepped into the hall. "How is he?" she asked tensely when she judged they were out of earshot.

"It's a good thing you called me tonight," Katie replied. "He's in pretty bad shape."

"But he'll get better?"

"I can't give you a guarantee, but I think so."

Jessie let out a little breath.

"He's worried about you," Katie added. "About your being found with him."

"Something happened to him back in San Marcos. He won't tell me much," Jessie hedged.

"Well, he's trying to protect you. If he hadn't been so sick, he never would have let you bring him here."

"I know."

They walked down the hall to the front door.

"Phone me tomorrow morning and let me know how he's doing," Katie said. "Here's my private number at Medizone." Reaching into her purse, she took out a card and handed it to Jessie.

"Thanks. And I really appreciate your coming over so late."

"That's what friends are for," Katie answered, giving Jessie a quick clasp on the arm. Then she drew back and searched Jessie's face. "Is there anything else you want to tell me?"

Jessie hesitated. "I don't know much."

"But you trust him?"

"Yes."

"Call if you need anything."

"I will," Jessie promised, anxious for her friend to leave.

"One more thing. He may not remember the conversation he had with me. You'll have to make sure he follows doctor's orders."

"Understood."

Miguel was sleeping fitfully when Jessie returned to the bedroom. She stood with her arms crossed, looking down at him before flopping into the chair Katie had pulled next to the bed. For a while, simply sitting with her eyes closed was a profound luxury. Soon she realized it wasn't enough, particularly since she didn't know what she would be facing in the morning.

She needed to sleep, and she needed to stay in this room.

And the only way she was going to do both was to occupy part of the bed.

After a quick trip to the bathroom, she donned a T-shirt and sweatpants, then set out the medicine and a glass of water on the nightstand. Finally, she climbed under the covers and lay on the far edge of the bed. Right before she fell asleep she had a fleeting worry that she was doing something improper.

MIGUEL MOANED AS THE nightmare assaulted him again. It always started the same way, when he entered the clinic waiting room and saw the pool of blood flowing from behind the reception desk.

Rushing around the desk, he found Margarita on the floor, bullets riddling the front of her plump body. He didn't have to search for a pulse in her neck to know she was dead. But he did that anyway, stooping to touch her smooth skin—skin that was still warm.

Good God, he had been gone less than an hour—to the airport to pick up some medical supplies that he'd been waiting for.

He bolted toward the back of the building, praying that the others were all right. But it was already too late. He found Tony in the hall. Then Anna in the lab. And Paco in the lunchroom. They were all shot, all dead. And so were the patients.

All except the VIP patient who had come to the clinic three days ago. He was missing.

Miguel was staring at the empty bed when he heard stealthy footsteps coming down the path that led from his private residence.

"His car is back," a harsh male voice hissed.

"Get him. One of you go in the front. The other take the back." The speaker was his well-heeled patient.

For several heartbeats, Miguel stood in the middle of the room, paralyzed. When he heard the front door open, he knew he had only seconds to react. Climbing onto one of the beds, he dived through the window into a flowering jasmine bush. He picked himself up and ran, skirting the guest cottages where rich patients came to vacation while they were recuperating.

His luck ran out when he rounded a corner of his own luxury villa and almost slammed into a man directly ahead of him—a man holding a machine gun, his back to the path, his eyes trained on the thick trees that marked the edge of the lawn.

The assassin must have heard a noise behind him, because he started to raise the weapon and turn. There was only one option as the weapon came into firing position. Miguel leaped forward, under the muzzle, his head butting hard against the man's chest, knocking him to the ground, pummeling him with his fists even as they went down. A burst of automatic fire shot into the air.

No! The noise would bring the others.

Wresting the gun away with strength fueled by fury and fear, Miguel slammed the stock into the man's face. Blood spurted, punctuated by a scream of agony. Miguel leaped up and sprinted for the woods, breathing hard, clutching the gun against his chest.

JESSIE AWOKE TO THE sound of ragged breathing. In the light from the hall, she looked around her room, then remembered why she was sleeping on the wrong side of the bed. Miguel was on the side near the door, his body shaking the mattress as he muttered something about guns and bodies.

Chills racked him, and at the same time his arm lashed out, catching her in the ribs. Gasping, she wrapped her arms around him, using her grip and the weight of her body to keep his still.

Her breasts flattened uncomfortably against the hard wall of his chest, and her hips wedged intimately against his so that she could feel every male contour as he struggled with her.

"Don't. It's okay," she gasped out several times while

she tried to defend herself from his flailing arms without hurting him. Gently she told him again and again that he was with her, that he was safe.

Finally his eyelids fluttered open, and he stared at her, surprise registering on his face.

"Where am I?" he grated, his teeth beginning to chatter.

"With me. With Jessie. You have malaria. I brought you to my house. And Dr. McQuade gave you some medicine."

He listened, taking it all in. "Jessie," he repeated, some of the anxiety seeping out of his voice. Yet his body was still shaking.

"I'm cold."

She pulled a blanket around him. "You need to take more medicine."

She got the pills from the bedside table and handed him a tablet and a glass of water. This time, even though his hands were trembling, he managed to drink by himself. When he was finished, she folded him close against her.

"It's all right," she murmured, stroking him gently, feeling his tremors lessen. Finally, he relaxed against her, his arms moving up to clasp her.

FROM THE FIRST TIME HE had seen her, he had wanted to hold her. He had wanted to lie in bed with her, although this was not exactly what he'd pictured, he thought with a harsh inward laugh. He'd cast himself in the role of a lover who could turn her beautiful green eyes into shimmering pools of passion. He'd imagined drawing little gasps of gratification from her lips as his hands and mouth caressed her, learning what gave her pleasure; then he had imagined himself inside her, moving with urgent hunger above her, driving her higher and higher into a world where only the two of them existed.

But simply making love with her wouldn't be enough. In the dark hours of the night, when he felt more alone than any other man on earth, he'd dared to dream of a safe haven in her arms, an end to his wanderings. Now that he was in her bed, he was caught by the power of that ultimate fantasy. The safety of her embrace felt more true and more real than anything else since he'd been on the run.

"Everything's all right," she murmured.

"Yes." *At least for now. For this moment. In this bed.*

Too weak to resist his need for her, he let his trembling hands glide over her narrow shoulders, along her slender arms, feeling her skin tingle under his fingertips. One hand moved to her silky hair, shifting the strands between his fingers like spun gold.

She made a little sound in her throat, but she didn't pull away. He touched his lips to the tender place where her hair met her cheek. There was no way he could make love to her now. But even in his weakness, he wanted her—more than he had ever wanted any other woman. Or had it become impossible to separate sexual desire from the need for comfort?

They held each other in the darkness, his face against her shoulder, her hand cupping the back of his head, and after a while his shivering subsided. He was warm again, warm from the inside out.

"Better?" she asked, her lips close to his ear.

"Yes. I think Dr. McQuade's medicine is starting to work."

"She said you'd feel better quickly. But you have to stay in bed for a few days—and keep taking the medicine."

"Um," he answered, noncommittally. It didn't matter what the doctor had said. He must leave as soon as he had the strength.

Perhaps Jessie knew what he was thinking, because she drew back so that she could study his face. He was glad that the sliver of light coming from the hall hid his expression. Not a muscle in his body or his face twitched as he held himself very still.

"You have to take care of yourself."

"Of course," he agreed, but he couldn't let her start asking questions about his motives—or his fears—so he made a quick change of subject—one that he knew would throw her off balance. "Is this your bed?" he asked.

He watched her swallow before answering. "Yes."

"Dr. McQuade will think we are lovers," he heard himself say.

She drew in a quick breath, and he knew he'd succeeded in distracting her.

"Lucky for you I'm harmless at the moment." Well, relatively harmless, he thought, as his hand moved to the front of her and cupped the fullness of her breast. Somewhere in his mind he was astonished—and horrified—that he was taking such liberties with her. It was as if the combination of being sick and waking up in her arms had made him drunk, and he was no longer in control of his actions.

"What are you doing?" she asked in a strangled voice.

"Something I've wanted to do for a long time," he admitted, holding his breath, waiting for her to pull away. Instead she closed her eyes and lowered her forehead to his shoulder. Her breast quivered in his hand like a soft, frightened bird. Gently, his fingers stroked her, feeling her nipple harden at his touch, hearing her breath quicken.

"You shouldn't do that," she whispered in a voice so low he could barely hear.

"Yes," he agreed huskily, turning his head to nibble along her cheek, amazed to find that his body could respond more fully than he'd expected. *"Querida,"* he murmured, his free hand sliding downward to cup her softly rounded bottom and pull her closer.

"What did you say about being harmless?" she asked in a low, inquiring voice.

"You must have magic powers."

"I hope so," she replied, sounding half teasing, half serious.

With a little sigh of regret, he forced his hand away from her. "In the morning, you should remember this as a dream."

"It's not a dream. It's real. If you want it to be real."

"It cannot be," he answered with a kind of desperation.

"So this is like the night we had dinner," she challenged. "We got close, then you acted like I didn't exist."

The pain of rejection in her voice made his insides clench, yet he went on relentlessly. "No, this is different. Tonight I've been using my illness as an excuse to touch you."

If he thought he could force her to drop the subject, he was wrong.

"You want to touch, but you don't want to get close," she accused.

He longed to tell her she was mistaken. He wanted every sweet, tender gift she was willing to bestow on him, but he had vowed to hide the depth of his need.

Instead, he fell back on male bravado. "We are very close," he murmured, moving his hips against hers.

But she'd caught on to what he was doing. "Stop trying to change the subject. You know I don't mean physically. I mean close in the sense of sharing our feelings."

He said nothing.

In the darkness, he heard her swallow. "Miguel, being pushy with men isn't my style. I'm saying things to you that it's hard for me to admit."

"I know that."

"Then don't back away from me this time," she pleaded. "You and I could…could mean something important to each other. I think we both know it."

He dragged in a breath and let it out, cursing himself for giving in to temptation. "I shouldn't have started anything," he said with a weary sigh.

"Why did you?"

I need you—more than I have ever needed anyone in my life. But the words stayed locked in his mind. Instead he made a dismissive little noise. "This discussion is using up my energy." Easing away from her, he flopped onto his back, feeling as if he were the one who had been abandoned.

In the darkness, he felt her hurt radiating toward him. Then her fingers dug into his shoulder. "Be honest with me.

What are you afraid of, exactly? That I'll end up like your lover, Anna?''

He turned back toward her. ''What do you think you know about Anna?''

''Enough.''

He made a sharp sound in his throat. ''Not as much as you imagine.''

''All right, what do you want to tell me about her?'' Jessie challenged.

It didn't matter. He should let her think what she wanted. Instead he answered the question. ''She was my sister. Not my lover.''

''Oh. I'm sorry.''

''She died because of me,'' he added hoarsely. ''After my father died I thought I was helping her live a better life. Instead I got her killed.''

''How?''

Desperation sharpened his tone. ''Jessie, do not ask me about the things that have happened to me. Do not get involved.''

''I *am* involved. Isn't that obvious?''

This time he didn't allow himself to answer, hoping against hope that she would let it alone.

Instead she asked, ''Why don't you tell me about Carlos Jurado?''

His whole body stiffened. Was this all some sadistic trick? Was she like Juanita, the one who had tried to trade his life for money? Gripping her by the shoulders, he shook her.

''Miguel, you're hurting me,'' she gasped.

''Where did you hear that name?'' he demanded.

''From you. You said it.''

''I couldn't have.''

''You did!''

His mind scrambled, came up with dim memories, and he cursed richly in Spanish as he eased his grip on her shoulders.

''I'm sorry.'' He snorted. ''And apparently paranoid.''

"Who is he?" she persisted.

"What did I say about him?"

"Nothing I could make sense of," she replied evenly.

Maybe. Tonight, all he could do was hope she spoke the truth. Before she thought of any more questions, he turned his back on her and stared at the faint light coming in around the edges of the window shade, thinking that he should never have let her bring him here. But he was too exhausted to do anything about it.

JESSIE LAY STIFFLY beside Miguel, listening to the harsh sound of his breathing. It had been a long time since she had spent the night with a man. And despite their fleeting intimacies in the darkness, it was pretty clear he'd be happier if she found somewhere else to sleep.

She had thought—

Well, it really didn't matter. The bottom line was that nothing had changed. He still didn't trust her enough to tell her why he was on the run—although he'd certainly given away more than he'd intended.

It would cut the tension considerably if she'd simply decamp to the couch, yet she was too stubborn to flee her own bed. So she lay there in the dark, trying to relax as she replayed the events of the evening. Sometime near morning, she actually fell asleep.

She awoke with a start to find the bed empty. Glancing at the clock on the bedside table, she was astonished to see that it was almost lunchtime.

She should have been at work hours ago. Luckily, nobody had called to check on her. Probably Erin thought she was at the rec center, and the center thought she was downtown at the office.

When she didn't hear any noise in the house, she swung her legs over the side of the bed and hurried down the hall, hoping Miguel was in the bathroom, but it was dark and empty. And he wasn't lying on the couch in the den, either.

He was gone! And she should be happy to be rid of him.

He wasn't worth the agony. But she didn't really believe it. Seized by a feeling of dread, she pulled on a pair of shoes and pounded down the hall to the front of the house.

"Miguel?"

The living room and kitchen were just as empty. Then she saw that the back door was ajar. Slipping outside, she saw her houseguest standing by the van. Dressed in the rumpled sweatpants and T-shirt he'd worn last night, he was inserting the key in the lock—the key that she was pretty sure had been in her pocketbook the last time she'd looked.

"What the hell do you think you're doing?" Her voice rang out as she charged out the door and straight toward him.

His body went rigid. Instead of answering he hunched over the lock, and she felt her anger surge. She'd brought him home, moved heaven and earth to get him the right medication, and done everything she could for him. Now this was the thanks she got. Clamping her hands on his shoulders, she tried to shove him away from the vehicle.

He turned, and she saw his face was beaded with perspiration. *Lord, he shouldn't even be on his feet—let alone drive.*

"Let me go."

"Are you crazy?" she gasped, as she struggled to turn him away from the van. "You're a physician. You know damn well you're too sick to get behind the wheel."

He gave her a long, tense look. "I will manage," he replied between gritted teeth, as he tried to free himself from her grasp.

"Don't do this!"

"I have to. I cannot stay here with you." He redoubled his efforts to escape. In desperation, she drew back her hand to shove at him. It was then that she heard the squeal of tires behind her.

She and Miguel both froze. Slowly she turned to see who was pulling up at the house. To her horror she saw a police cruiser planted squarely across the entrance to her driveway.

Chapter Five

With a feeling of unreality, Jessie watched a uniformed officer climb out and move purposefully up the driveway.

Of all the damn bad luck, she muttered under her breath.

"What's going on here?" the cop demanded in a sharp voice.

"Let me handle this," she hissed to Miguel, hoping he was smart enough to keep his mouth shut.

Without waiting for a reply, she raised her chin and faced the patrolman, noting that the name tag on his shirt read Waverly.

"What's going on?" he repeated in a louder voice, as if he thought they were both hard of hearing.

"Nothing," she answered.

"Your neighbor saw this guy was getting ready to steal your van. Now it looks like you're out here trying to stop him," Waverly observed.

"No!" she retorted in a strained voice. Unfortunately, the cop was no dummy. He had just delivered a pretty good analysis of the scene.

Behind her, she felt Miguel's whole body tense. He would bolt, she thought. And then he'd be arrested.

She cleared her throat, wondering what she was going to say. What came out was, "My boyfriend and I overslept. We were just having a little argument about who gets the transportation this—uh—this afternoon."

"Oh?" Waverly raised questioning eyebrows.

"It's no big deal," Jessie added, moving back so that her arm slipped around Miguel's waist. "Just a little misunderstanding, wasn't it, honey?" she asked, running her fingers up and down his ribs.

Miguel's arm came around her in what she hoped looked like an affectionate embrace.

The cop's eyes moved from her to Miguel, and she wished her houseguest had stopped to shave or comb his hair or change out of the clothing he'd slept in.

"You feeling okay?" Waverly asked.

"We were up late last night," Jessie replied. "That's why we're getting a late start, you know."

"Is that the way it is, buddy, or do you let your girlfriend do all the talking?"

She watched Miguel draw himself up, make an attempt to relax the muscles in his jaw and shoulders. "We were partying pretty late," he answered carefully, yet he wasn't totally able to wipe the soft Latin accent from his speech.

Waverly continued to scrutinize him. "You don't look so good," he said.

Miguel shrugged.

The cop's next words cranked up her tension another couple of notches as his gaze stayed fixed on Miguel. "Step away from the van. Why don't we go into the house while I find out what's happening here?"

Jessie shook her head. No way was she inviting this guy into her house. "We're fine. Really."

He gave her a long look, then focused again on Miguel.

"What's your name?"

"Miguel Diego."

"Let's see your identification."

Jessie held her breath, wondering what Miguel was going to do now. Did he even know she'd stuffed his wallet into the pillowcase last night? Did he have a driver's license?

To her relief, he reached into the pocket of his sweatpants and pulled out the wallet. Calmly he extracted a plastic card similar to her own and handed it to Waverly, who examined it more carefully than he would have done hers.

"How long have you been a resident of Baltimore, Mr. Diego?" he asked.

"Two years," Miguel answered, and Jessie felt her heart lurch. She knew that wasn't true.

"And your country of origin?"

"I am an American citizen," Miguel said, his voice firm.

"Oh?" The syllable held a note of surprise—and challenge.

"My mother was an American. I lived with my father in San Marcos for several years, but I was educated in the States."

"I see," Waverly answered as if he doubted the account. "And what's your line of work?"

"At present, janitorial," Miguel said tersely, sounding as if he'd rather admit that he ate worms for breakfast.

"For whom?"

"I am between jobs."

"What's your address?"

Miguel reeled off an address—not the one she'd visited the night before, she noted.

"How did you two meet?" Waverly asked, keeping the questions coming hard and fast.

"She works at a recreation center in my neighborhood."

"Your girlfriend supporting you?"

"I have money saved," Miguel retorted.

"So why did you need the van this morning?"

"I was going to check in at an employment agency."

"Which one?"

"United Employment."

"You stay here often?" Waverly asked, keeping up the rapid-fire interrogation that he'd established.

"No."

"Why did you need the van?" he asked again.

"I told you, I'm looking for a job!"

Hearing the note of exasperation in Miguel's voice, Jessie

interrupted, ''I think you've established that everything's okay here,'' she told the officer.

He gave her a long look. ''You're sure?''

''Yes.''

After several seconds of silence, Waverly reached into his pocket and brought out a card, which he handed to Jessie. ''Here's my number. If you need any help, call me.''

''I will,'' she said, clenching the card in her palm.

As the officer made his way down the driveway, Jessie gave Miguel a cautioning look. ''Are you okay?'' she whispered.

''Yes,'' he replied, but the edge in his voice was like a knife that had just been sharpened.

''Let's go in.''

He followed her inside. The moment the door was closed, she hurried down the hall to the living room and looked out the window.

Waverly was sitting in his cruiser. Jessie's fingers dug into the edge of the business card as she waited for the patrol car to pull away from the curb. Instead of starting the engine, the officer sat pondering the house.

Hearing footsteps behind her, Jessie turned and almost bumped into Miguel. His expression was grim as he stared through the window at the cop. ''Why is he sitting there?''

''He thinks you might try to get back at me for all those questions,'' she said, then took a breath and added, ''I think we've got to convince him everything is just fine.''

''How?''

Jessie turned toward Miguel. ''Act like you're happy he's leaving us alone, and that you've changed your mind about going anywhere.''

He looked as if he wasn't sure how to accomplish that objective.

''You could kiss me,'' she suggested, trying to sound casual, yet hearing the thickness in her voice. Lifting her face, she looked up at him gravely. ''It won't work unless you make it look like it's your idea,'' she whispered. ''If *I* kiss *you,* he'll think I'm only trying to placate you. You have to pretend you'd rather make love than fight,'' she added in a rush.

He stood without moving, without bending, and her heart stopped. Then a sigh swept over her as she watched his expression melt. Need flared in his eyes as he gazed down into her upturned face. Inch by inch, as if savoring each small movement for its own sake, he bent toward her, his arms coming up to pull her close. She caught the scent of mint toothpaste as his mouth hovered millimeters from hers. Then, with infinite gentleness, his lips settled and began to move over hers.

She'd been daring him to kiss her, daring herself to risk rejection again. The contact of his mouth with hers was like the completion of an electric circuit, starting a flow of current between them. Swamped by her response, she heard a small sound escape from her throat.

He answered with a growl deep in his chest, as he gathered her closer. Moving his lips against hers, he opened her mouth for a more complete invasion.

One of his large hands slid down to anchor her hips against his, the other slipped under her T-shirt so that his fingers could splay across her back. Instantly, her skin heated under his touch—not just her skin, but her whole body.

She forgot that they were standing in front of a window in full view of her neighbors; forgot that the intimacy had started as improvisational theater for Officer Waverly. She forgot about everything except the taste of Miguel's mouth as it moved urgently over hers, the feel of his hands on her, and the pressure of his hips against hers.

The kiss deepened, lengthened, consumed her. Consumed thought and reason. She was dimly aware that he had pulled her away from the window, into the shadows of the hallway where they had all the privacy they needed. He leaned back against the wall, taking her with him and widening his stance so that he could bring her body more intimately against his. He moved his hands downward, cupped her bottom,

rocked her against the rigid flesh concealed by his sweatpants, and she made a little sobbing sound as she held on to
him to keep her knees from giving way.

She hadn't planned anything like this when she'd issued
her challenge. One moment she'd been standing on solid
ground, the next, she was spinning out of control.

She would give him anything he wanted, because she
wanted the same thing—to get closer to him, and closer still,
until there were no barriers left. All she could do was cling
to him and let him take her wherever he wanted to go.

His deft hands rolled up her T-shirt, unsnapped her bra,
then angled her body so that he could bring his hot mouth
to her breast.

"Oh!" She cried out as his tongue circled her rigid nipple.
When he began to draw on her, the exclamation turned into
a sob of pleasure.

Still, somewhere in her fogged mind she registered that
his hands were shaking and his breathing had become ragged. Not from passion, she realized, as she forced herself to
come back to earth. Last night when she'd brought him
home, he'd been so sick he could hardly walk. Perhaps Dr.
McQuade's medicine had worked a miracle, but he was still
in no shape for this kind of activity, and she was crazy to
have let things go this far.

"We shouldn't be doing this," she whispered, dragging
her heated flesh away from his.

Miguel looked dazed, then swayed on his feet when she
moved a few inches away. Lowering her head to hide the
abashed expression on her face, she reached to refasten the
catch of her bra, then pulled down her shirt. When she
looked up again, he had flattened a hand against the wall to
steady himself.

"You should be in bed."

"Yes."

"I mean..." Her voice trailed off as she silently acknowledged that she was the one at fault. She had goaded him

into kissing her—and kissing had quickly gotten out of control.

"You should be resting," she managed.

He looked away from her, and she knew he hated being reminded why she had brought him home.

"Come on." She took his arm and steered him down the hall. Really, what had she been thinking?

When he stood staring at the bed, she tugged on his arm so that he was forced to fight her or sit down. He sat, staring with unfocused eyes at the opposite wall as he kicked off his shoes. They thunked onto the floor.

When he didn't lie down on his own, she took him by the shoulders and eased him onto his back against the pillows. He lay with his eyes closed, breathing heavily, and she started to slip from the room.

"I should take some more of Dr. McQuade's medicine," he said in a low voice.

Her eyes shot to the nightstand, where the bottle had been.

"In my pocket," he answered the unspoken question.

She pulled out his wallet and set it on the bedside table, reminding herself that they had things to discuss. But any discussion would have to wait until he was in better shape. Instead she found the bottle of pills that Katie had given him, shook one into her hand and got water. Miguel took the glass from her and swallowed the medicine.

Then he lay back heavily and closed his eyes again. A few minutes later, he was asleep.

She glanced quickly at her watch, knowing she should make an appearance at work. Yet that would mean leaving him alone in the house. Now she knew that would spell disaster. As soon as he thought he could stagger to the kitchen door, he'd duck out on her.

After tiptoeing out of the room, she picked up the phone in the den and called the staff's private line. The answering machine picked up, and she thanked Providence that everyone had gone to lunch. Quickly, she left a short message saying that she was at home taking care of a sick friend and

wouldn't be in that day. Tomorrow was Saturday, so she
wouldn't have to make up any excuses for the weekend.

MIGUEL LAY IN BED with his eyes closed, breathing slowly
and evenly so that Jessie would think he was sleeping. He
heard her quietly slip from the room, heard her making a
phone call and talking in a voice so low that he couldn't tell
what she was saying. For a moment, he had to fight a surge
of panic. After that scene with the van and the policeman,
she could be calling the authorities, summoning help. Yet
he was still able to recognize paranoia when it swept over
him. She had gone to a lot of trouble to get rid of Officer
Waverly. And afterwards…

His tongue touched his lips, searching for the taste of her
and finding the proof that he hadn't been hallucinating.

He felt his mouth curve into a little smile as he relived
the kiss. Not just his lips on hers—the whole thing. Her body
moving against his, the wonderful taste of her breast.

Jessie had stopped him, but he knew things couldn't have
gone much further—not when a strong wind would blow
him over. Yet she'd wanted him. He knew that as well as
he knew his own reactions. And if things were different…

He allowed himself to contemplate a kinder, gentler world
where he was not a hunted man, and where he could make
choices based on his own needs. In that world, he would
make slow, perfect love to Jessie Douglas. Too sick to resist
the comfort of the fantasy, he lay with eyes closed, imagining that luxury.

He hung on to the delicious daydream as sleep crept over
him. For a while Jessie guarded his slumber. But eventually
the nightmares came. The clinic again. And then another
one—from the time when he was on the run.

He was in Cancún, Mexico, where he'd traveled by bus
from Playa del Carmen. He was staying at a small tourist
hotel where people from many cultures mixed. The vacation
spot was a good place to get the identification papers he'd
need when he crossed into the U.S.

There had been a woman named Juanita who owned a local restaurant where he got into the habit of eating dinner—because he liked the food, and because he was lonely.

In his dream, he was back there again—a man starved for human contact, consumed by the need to prove to himself that he wasn't doomed to an existence in the shadows.

"You eat alone every night," she said as she stood beside his table.

"I like my own company," he answered, hating the way the lie felt in his mouth.

"Where are you from?"

He gave the answer that he'd rehearsed. He was from Costa Rica, and he was a lawyer who was tired of the rat race. He'd taken a few months off and was traveling north, stopping where the spirit moved him. He was enjoying the snorkeling here, he told her.

He thought the performance was convincing. He didn't know he'd picked the wrong audience.

That night she pulled out a chair at his table and sat with him, joined him for a cup of strong, dark coffee after his meal. Soon they were eating together in the back of the restaurant where they could talk in low intimate voices.

She told him she'd been poor as a young woman, but she'd married a man who was much older than she. When her husband had died, she'd moved away and used the money from his insurance to buy the restaurant.

Now she was financially secure—and selective about her lovers. But it seemed that she was taken with the man who was calling himself Diego Marcos. Drawing him into the shadows of the arbor behind her house, she kissed him, inviting intimacies that he was hardly able to resist. The next night they moved from the arbor to her bed. After that, he was there every night.

Perhaps he should have thought more about her background—and her motives. But he was attracted to her, and she made him feel comfortable—too comfortable.

One night after they'd made love, she gently began asking him questions.

"Where are you really from? Why are you on the run? What can I do to help?"

Her soft voice, the touch of her hands, and the warmth of her bed made him let down his guard. Slowly, giving away more and more, he answered her questions. Forgetting caution, he ended up telling her too much about his background.

Not until later did he realize that men had been looking for him in cities like Cancún—and putting out the word that they would pay a fat fee to anyone who turned him in. Juanita had heard about the offer and wanted the money.

So she'd kept him near her while the net closed around him. They were eating dinner at her house one evening, when he heard a noise in the front hall. The evasive look in her eye told him something bad was happening. He bolted from the table seconds before two men with guns burst into the dining room.

As he fled into the night, he heard the shots and heard her scream—and knew that she had taken the bullet intended for him.

He abandoned his clothing and few possessions at his hotel, then hitched a ride on a hay wagon, thankful that most of his funds were in the money belt he was wearing. And as he rode out of town, he vowed never to give in to soft words and seduction again.

Chapter Six

Voices woke him—women's voices, low and quiet, penetrating the vulnerability of sleep. They dovetailed with the dream, and he was halfway out of bed when he saw that the speakers were Jessie and her friend, the doctor. They were standing just inside the door to the bedroom, their faces registering shock as they saw his frantic reaction to their presence.

"It's all right." Jessie moved rapidly toward him, put a reassuring hand on his shoulder, though her expression was still worried.

Dr. McQuade hung back.

He stopped himself in midflight and eased back against the pillows.

"Were you dreaming again?" Jessie asked.

He answered with a tight nod, then asked, "How long was I asleep?"

"Almost two days."

He shook his head in disbelief. "What day is it?"

"Sunday morning."

He must have been in worse shape than he'd imagined.

"Well, I woke you up to take your medicine. And you got up to go to the bathroom. But you went right back to sleep."

He had vague memories of her coming to him—very

vague memories. Had she slept in the bed with him again? He thought not.

"Your body knew you needed rest," she said softly. "Even if you were too stubborn to admit it."

That was Dr. McQuade's cue to come briskly forward, her medical bag in her hand. "How are you doing?" she asked as she pulled the chair up to the side of the bed.

He took a quick inventory. His fever was down. His headache was gone—along with the terrible thirst. And he felt as if he could get out of bed without falling on his face.

"Much better," he answered. "Your medicine is very effective."

"I think you have the constitution of a bull elephant."

He laughed. "Maybe."

"Jessie told me you were up and around the morning after you arrived," the doctor added conversationally.

His nod of agreement was cautious. Had Jessie reported that he'd been planning to leave? Or that he'd been going to steal the van? Neither woman's expression gave anything away.

"I want you to take it easy for at least another couple of days," Dr. McQuade said with a note of mild reproach.

He didn't answer, unwilling to commit himself to anything.

The doctor opened her bag and pulled out a stethoscope. As she warmed the business end in her hand, he eyed Jessie. She stayed where she was in the doorway, watching as Dr. McQuade deftly rolled up his shirt and listened to his chest.

"Well?" he asked when she had finished.

"Heart and lungs sound normal."

She prodded his abdomen, looked down his throat, checked his ears, pronounced him in surprisingly good shape.

He nodded in gratitude, knowing that if it hadn't been for her and Jessie, he might have died.

Jessie walked the doctor to the door. When she came back, she had a tray with food.

"Are you hungry?"

Chicken soup. The rich aroma made his stomach growl.

"I see the answer is yes." She tried for a little grin, and he knew she was feeling uncertain about how to act.

He was just as uncertain. He was lying in her bed. For one night, at least, she had shared that bed with him. Then they'd kissed, and his last pretenses had disintegrated. Now he needed to convince both of them that it had been a temporary aberration.

Twisting away from her, he plumped up the pillows. When he leaned back again, she set the tray on his lap. He wanted to thank her for everything she'd done, but he knew the words would come out wrong. If he sounded too impersonal, she would be hurt. If he said the things he longed to say, she would think he was going to share his burden with her—and that was impossible.

She had brought a mug of soup for herself, and she sat in an overstuffed chair across the room, sipping it while he ate.

"You're a good cook," he complimented her, enjoying the food and the simple fact of being with her, storing up memories for when he would be alone again.

"Thanks. I love being creative in the kitchen," she answered self-consciously.

He longed to talk about things that were important. Instead, he asked about the weather and the news he'd missed.

When he finished the meal, he ran his hand over the stubble on his jaw. "I must look like Robinson Crusoe. Can I borrow a razor?"

"Yes."

"And your shower."

"If you're quick. Then you need to rest again."

He gave a little nod.

When she took the tray away and set it on the dresser, he walked down the hall, through the living room and into the kitchen, testing his strength. For a man who had been at death's door, he was doing amazingly well, he decided, as he opened the refrigerator and took out a carton of milk. He downed a glass and was still hungry, but he knew it would be imprudent to eat too much.

Domestic sounds from the bedroom drew him back. Jessie was changing the sheets. Leaning against the doorframe, he watched her work, taking pleasure from simply observing the grace and efficiency of her movements. Infinitesimally his body swayed toward hers until he caught himself, his feet scuffling slightly as he shifted his position.

She stopped, looked up at him, then quickly turned to slip a pillow into its case, avoiding further eye contact. It looked like he'd let her know where they stood. He should be pleased. Instead he felt his throat tighten.

Grabbing a change of clothes, he headed for the bathroom and started to lock the door behind him, then thought better of it. What if he suddenly passed out, he wondered as he studied his gaunt face in the glass. Honesty made him admit that he looked a lot worse than Robinson Crusoe. More like a refugee from hell. But a hot shower and a shave would go a long way toward restoration.

Stepping under the hot spray was delicious. Once he had taken such simple pleasures for granted. Now he deeply appreciated every luxury of modern life. If he was ever allowed to settle down again he would—

Ruthlessly, he cut off the thought, lifting his face and concentrating on how good the pounding water felt. Then he grabbed the bar of soap. It was already wet. Jessie had been in here not long ago. As he began to lather his body, he couldn't stop himself from thinking about her doing the same thing with the same bar of soap, and he felt himself getting hard.

It was definitely time to leave, he told himself with a low curse.

CARLOS JURADO SAT BACK in the leather chair, alternately staring with narrowed eyes at the phone on his broad mahogany desk and at the antique clock that hung on the wall between the windows. Impatiently, he drummed his stubby fingers on the polished surface of the desk. When the phone failed to ring, he reached into the middle drawer and pulled out a thick manila folder. Once the cover had been crisp, though now it was bent and smudged from frequent handling.

Eyes narrowed, he thumbed through the pages of the exhaustive report, hitting highlights that he had perused many times. Really, he no longer needed to read the words. He had long ago memorized the report, absorbed the clues that would lead him to Miguel Valero. The man had traveled north. He was in the U.S.—near his old hometown. He had to be.

Jurado was on the fifth page when the phone rang. Snatching it up, he snapped, "You are late."

"Sorry, *señor.*"

"What do you have for me?" he demanded.

There was a slight hesitation on the other end of the line, telegraphing bad news. "Valero is not in Washington, D.C."

"Are you sure?"

"Yes. I have been waiting for a report from the detectives I hired. They have checked out everyone from his past who might have given him shelter. No one has been in contact with him."

Jurado's fingers dug into the edge of the manila folder. He'd been playing a hunch—more than a hunch. And he'd thought he was right. Now he reiterated his reasoning. "But his mother is from the suburb of Bethesda," he growled. "She went back there after the divorce. His father was with the San Marcos embassy for over five years. Valero has strong ties to the city. He knows many people there."

"Yes. I checked the relatives on his mother's side. I even checked old friends of her family, people who might have known him before he went back to San Marcos. Nobody has heard from him since before—" The speaker cleared his throat and ended the sentence differently. "Since last winter."

Jurado held back the curse that hovered at the edges of his lips. His operative in Washington knew too much. He needed to be replaced with someone more manageable.

"I can cast the net wider," the man on the other end of the line said quickly. "I can investigate in a larger circle around the city."

Jurado hesitated. Really, the bastard could be anywhere in the States. Yet, when he read between the lines, the report told him that Dr. Valero was on the East Coast—probably near the city where he was born. "All right," he growled. "Widen the search."

"It's going to be expensive," the voice on the other end of the line warned.

"I don't care about the expense. I want him dead." *And you, too,* Jurado added silently.

JESSIE STACKED THE DISHES in the dishwasher, then wiped her hands on the sides of her jeans.

Two days ago a barrier between herself and Miguel had shattered. They'd kissed, and she'd discovered how much he needed her. And not just physically, although passion had flared between them like lighter fluid on hot coals.

It was more than that. She knew it, and he knew it too, damn him. But nothing had been the same since he'd awakened this morning. She could feel him detaching himself the way he had before; could feel him getting ready to leave. And there was nothing she could do about it. The realization brought a mixture of anger, sadness, frustration—and determination.

Two months ago, she'd been hurt, and finally she'd begun to doubt her own perceptions. This time, she understood him better. She knew what game he was playing. And she wasn't going to let him win it. This time, she wanted to hold on to what they were creating together and build on it.

Yet all she'd done was be a good little girl. She'd brought the man a bowl of chicken soup and changed his sheets— then let him take control of the conversation.

He'd gotten them chatting about the weather, for heaven's sake. And she'd let him get away with it.

Viciously she swiped at the kitchen counters with a sponge, then furiously dried them with a paper towel. With a grimace, she tossed the paper towel in the trash and turned toward the back of the house where Miguel was lurking. Really, what did she have to lose by confronting him? He couldn't make things worse than they already were.

Purposefully, she marched down the hall to the bedroom, then stopped short, her heart lurching inside her chest when she saw that the bed was empty.

Panic swept over her. He was gone! Damn him. She had been waiting for it to happen, and now her worst fears were confirmed.

Then she caught the scent of soap and steam coming from the bathroom. He was taking his sweet time in there. He should be back in bed. Damn the man. Didn't he have any sense?

What a question. She knew he didn't!

All the anxiety of the past few days gathered into a knot inside her chest—then burst with the force of a grenade. Rushing headlong to the end of the hall, she pounded on the bathroom door.

"Miguel!"

"In a minute."

"Now!" She threw open the door with a ferocity that shocked her.

"What the hell do you think you're doing?" she shouted, then stopped short as her eyes focused on the man.

"I'm shaving," he said, calmly half turning his head as he spoke. He was standing naked, his back to her, his dark hair tousled from a towel drying and his face partially covered with lather as he raised his hand to scrape dark stubble from his left cheek.

"You're supposed to be back in bed."

"I am almost finished." He dipped the razor in the water-filled sink before starting on the other side of his face. "Are you planning to stand there watching?'' he asked, a quizzical note in his voice.

She didn't answer, didn't move as the razor took away the lather and the dark stubble from his face. He looked better. Healthier.

The air inside the little room was thick with steam from the shower. It held her fast, enveloped her in a palpable intimacy as if the world had shrunk in size, trapping the two of them in an enchanted mist.

He finished shaving, then bent to rinse his face, drawing her gaze to the olive skin of his waist and lean hips. Straightening, he sought her eyes in the mirror. For an endless time, neither of them moved or spoke while the steamy air around them thickened with tension.

''I think there is an American saying about 'getting out while the getting is good.' You should take that advice,'' he said, the warning in his voice abrading her nerve endings.

Was it only a warning? Or did she hear a note of challenge, too?

She moistened her suddenly dry lips with her tongue, noticing him watch the tiny movement. Unconsciously she rolled her shoulder to ease some of the tension knotting her muscles. When she saw his gaze drop to the front of her T-shirt, she realized the action had thrust her breasts toward him.

All at once, she remembered the wet heat of his mouth on her. Judging by the look on his face, she knew he was remembering, too. An arrow of hot sensation shot through her body, lodging at her center.

He was right; she shouldn't have invaded his privacy. Certainly she should turn and leave. Yet her brain wasn't telling her feet to back away.

She dared a glance into his eyes and saw a fierce, aching hunger that stole the breath from her lungs.

''I am going to turn around in a few seconds,'' he cautioned. ''And if you are not out of here when I do, then we'll both be in trouble.''

She had been warned, but she stood her ground, swallowing hard as he slowly turned to face her. She had known from the look in his eyes what she would see. Still, she wasn't quite prepared for the wave of masculine potency emanating from him. His eyes seemed to burn with an inner fire, and his body was gloriously, fully aroused. Yet he made no move to close the distance between them. As she watched his fingers clench and unclench, she knew that he would not reach for her unless she made the first move.

Quickly, before she could tell herself she was doing the wrong thing, she found the hem of her T-shirt, pulled it over her head, and tossed it onto the floor. With shaking fingers she unhooked the clasp of her bra and sent it to join the shirt. Then, in one smooth motion, she slid her jeans and panties down her legs and kicked them away so that she was as naked as he.

He stared at her, unmoving, and for a terrible moment she thought that she had made a mistake. God, what was she thinking?

Then she saw the fire in his eyes flare. "I knew you would be beautiful," he said in Spanish, ending with a low sound of need as he closed the distance between them and swept her into his embrace.

The shock of his naked body against hers was almost too much to bear. A low sob welled in her throat, as her hands caressed his back, his shoulders, slid down to his narrow waist and over his firm buttocks. His hands moved over her in the same frantic rhythm. Then the two of them were rocking together, clinging, finding each other's mouths in a kiss that was more desperate than erotic—more savage than civilized.

He kissed her with a driving need that made her heart stop, then start again, beating in frantic time to the blood pounding through her veins.

When his mouth lifted, his breathing was ragged, and the skin of his face was stretched taut. "Tell me to stop," he growled. "I can still stop if I hear you say no."

Wordlessly, she shook her head, then lifted her hand to stroke the harsh planes of his cheeks.

For heartbeats they stared into each other's eyes. Then his hand moved between them, cupping her breast, his fingers stroking back and forth across the hardened tip. There were no coherent words to express what was happening between them, only the low sounds and breathy exclamations of two people caught in a spiral of hunger for each other.

She forgot where they were. Forgot any sense of caution. Forgot everything but the taste of him, the feel of his hands and mouth on her hot flesh, the joy of being with him like this.

"Please, I need you," she gasped. "Please."

She heard him draw in a shaky breath. Lifting his head, he looked around as if he were coming out of a dream. "Not here. Not like this."

She was too dazed to understand what he was saying.

"Come to bed, my angel," he whispered, taking her hand and tugging her toward the door. He led her down the hall to the bedroom, to the newly made bed, and held the covers aside so that she could slip between the sheets. Then he joined her, folding her close and dropping tiny kisses over her face and neck and shoulders before returning to her mouth for a long, lingering kiss as his hands stroked her breasts.

When he looked at her, his eyes were dark and smoldering. When she tried to speak, he pressed his thumb gently against her lips. "I have dreamed of all the ways I wanted to touch you and kiss you," he said in a thick voice, then lowered his head to one distended nipple.

Her breath hitched as he began to draw on her, while his hand sought the other peak, mirroring the action.

She couldn't speak; she could only lie against the pillows, her hand caressing the back of his head as he sent a wave of heat shimmering though her.

When his mouth returned to hers, it was infinitely gentle and tender as he alternated kisses with passionate Spanish endearments while his hands moved down her body, stroking and caressing their way to the center of her desire. The surge of sensation as he touched her there was so intense that a low whimper welled in her throat.

"Yes," he whispered. "Let me hear your pleasure. Let me know how much you like my touch."

She did as he asked, because she had no choice. He was a man who knew how to please a woman, how to draw out each measure of gratification almost beyond endurance. Sensation built on top of sensation until she was clinging to him, calling his name, begging him to fill the empty ache inside her.

Then, finally, he levered his body over hers, and she guided him into her. He made a hoarse sound deep in his chest, telling her that he felt what she did—the stunning intensity of joining.

"Miguel," she whispered.

"My angel," he answered, his eyes burning into hers.

Her hand moved, gliding over the planes of his face and his lips as if touch could help her remember this moment—a moment more vivid than any other in her life. Then he began to move, and she was lost to anything but the power of this man—in her, over her, surrounding her.

He set the rhythm, taking her with him on a journey that she knew was too intense to last for long. The tempo quickened, lifting her to a higher place where the air burned in her lungs. She clung to him, feeling tears gather in her eyes as she approached a summit of fulfillment beyond any previous imaginings.

She felt her whole body contract, then break apart in a shattering climax that seemed to send her hurtling through the universe. She heard his shout of satisfaction as he followed her, pursued her, claimed her as his own, then brought her back to earth with him.

The glow slowly faded from her body as her breathing returned to almost normal. Shifting his weight off her, he gathered her close, skimming his lips over her hair, her damp face, her mouth.

She wanted to tell him how wonderful it had been for her, but she was afraid that she would burst into tears, so she simply held on to him, her lips moving against his neck and shoulder.

When the cool air on her damp skin made her shiver, he reached to pull the covers over them and settled beside her.

As the silence stretched, she understood that neither of them was sure what to say. Everything had changed. And yet, at the same time, nothing had changed.

JESSIE LAY BESIDE Miguel, dozing off and on, glad to keep him close to her.

Some time later, she knew he was awake again.

"How are you?" she asked.

His hand found hers. "Good. But—"

She didn't let him finish, cutting him off with a quick shake of her head. "Don't tell me you've put me in danger by making love to me. And don't tell me you're going to leave as soon as you feel strong enough to walk around the house a couple of times," she ordered in a strained voice.

"I *have* put you in danger," he growled. "I should have left before I gave in to my baser instincts."

"Is that how it was for you—base?"

His face contorted as she threw the word back at him. "No. It was…" He cleared his throat, then continued more strongly, "It was the best thing that has happened in my life in a long, long time."

"It was that way for me, too."

His hands tightened on her. "That changes nothing."

"Yes, it does! Nothing's going to happen to me because we finally showed each other how we feel."

His expression didn't alter. "Something already happened. A police officer saw me trying to steal your van. What if he comes back to see if I try any more tricks?"

"You were borrowing the van!" she exclaimed, ignoring his question.

"Yes, I was going to call and tell you where to pick it up. But Officer Waverly would not believe it. To him, I'm just another guy from the barrio who shouldn't be sleeping with a nice woman like you."

Her fingers opened and closed over his. "Don't. We know that's not true."

When he didn't reply, she laid her head against his shoulder. She wanted to be close to him. Getting into an argument about Officer Waverly and the van wasn't what she had in mind. After a few moments, she sat up and managed a little smile. "What we both need is some dinner."

The relieved look he gave her made her chest tighten. Sliding out of bed, she reached for the robe on the back of the closet door. In the kitchen she opened the refrigerator and inspected the casseroles she'd stowed there like a squirrel storing nuts for a cold spell, working off her anxiety while Miguel slept.

Deciding on the beef stew with red wine, she set the Dutch oven on the burner and toasted some of the soda bread she'd taken from the freezer. She was stirring the pot when she heard a noise behind her. Turning, she saw Miguel standing in the doorway, wearing a pair of jeans.

His eyes lit up as he inhaled the aroma coming from the bubbling liquid. "That smells wonderful. What is it?"

"Just beef stew," she answered, ladling some into two bowls.

"You made it?" He reached eagerly for a bowl and took a spoonful while he was still standing at the counter. "This is the best thing I've eaten in years."

"You're hungry!"

"And I know good food when I taste it," he replied, carrying the bowl to the table and spooning up several more bites. "You are a wonderful cook. Did your mother teach you?"

She laughed as she sat down across from him. "Mom

didn't come into the kitchen much except to confer with the cook. I started teaching myself after I got married,'' she answered.

"Yes. You said you were married. For two years.''

So he remembered that detail! She took a deep breath. "I told you I was divorced and that I'd gotten a degree in social work before coming to Baltimore. I didn't tell you about my family. I guess I come from what most people would call a privileged background. I lived in Grosse Point, the high-rent suburb of Detroit. I went to private schools. Dartmouth University. I majored in Spanish just because I enjoyed it. I knew I wouldn't need to support myself—especially after I met Jack.''

She gave Miguel a quick look, then continued in a rush. "He was everything my parents wanted for me. Everything I was taught I wanted—a solid upper-crust citizen who jumped right into the fast lane at his father's bank. Things started falling apart after about a year, when I realized that I was utterly bored by my new life.

"But my husband didn't want me to work. He wanted me to stay home and decorate the house, take tennis lessons at the country club and dazzle his business friends with my beauty and charm. I tried to be the wife he wanted, but I felt as if my life didn't mean anything. I felt trapped, and I didn't know what to do about it.''

"You could have had children.''

"That's what my mother said. That's what *she* did. It's not that I didn't want a family. But maybe I sensed that Jack was the wrong father for my children. Or maybe I was afraid that I'd end up reliving my mother's frustrations.''

She saw Miguel watching her intently and found herself clutching the mug of tea in her hands. She didn't usually talk much about what had led to her divorce. Now she wanted him to understand.

"We started having arguments. We had one just before he left for a business trip to St. Louis. I wanted to patch things up, so I decided to surprise him by flying out there and meeting him at his hotel. I walked in on him—'' she gulped ''—in bed with another woman.''

Miguel made a low exclamation.

''It's okay. It made me understand that I was trying to hang on to a marriage that wasn't worth saving.''

''It must have hurt,'' he said, reaching across the table to press his fingers over hers.

''It did, but it set me free to think about what I really wanted out of life. I went for counseling. And career counseling, too. I have a trust fund from my grandmother, so I could afford to go back to school and get my master's degree. Then I found this great job with the Light Street Foundation. I mostly live on my salary, although I do cheat a little. Like I used my trust-fund money for a down payment on this house.''

He gave her fingers a squeeze, then withdrew his hand. ''It sounds as if you turned your life around.''

''I think I made the right choices for myself. I'm happy with my job and how I live. Happier than I ever was growing up. Or in my marriage. I like being able to make a difference in people's lives.''

''Good,'' he said, but his expression was indrawn.

''What are you thinking?''

''Now I know how you got mixed up with me. You have strong instincts to help people.''

''Yes,'' she agreed. ''But, in your case, it was a lot more than that. You know as well as I do that there was something simmering between us from the first moment we saw each other.''

''Yes.''

She appreciated the honesty, but she didn't like the look on his face. Suddenly defensive, she blurted out, ''Maybe you think I do this all the time. Actually, my marriage made me pretty cautious about men.''

''*Querida,* you don't have to explain anything to me.''

Too wound up for prudence, she plunged ahead. ''Maybe

it will boost your Latin ego to know that I haven't been with anyone else since my divorce.''

Her vision blurred as she jumped up from the table and began rinsing out her bowl. He came up behind her, turned her, and gathered her into his arms.

"My angel," he said in a broken voice. "My angel." Pulling her close, he rocked her against him, his hand stroking over her hair and across her back. Softly, he spoke endearments in Spanish, then moved his lips against her cheek. "I've been alone too long. It seems I've forgotten how to communicate."

"What do you want to communicate?" she whispered, knowing that if she spoke more loudly, her voice would crack.

"I want you to know that I cherish this time with you. I want you to know that making love with you was…everything I imagined it would be and more."

"Oh, yes." She nodded her agreement, moving her cheek against his.

"But I am not a free man—not in the way you think of freedom. No matter how much I want to stay with you, I can't do it."

She lifted her face to his. "Miguel, everybody has choices. Let me help you."

"You have. I was very sick. I think you saved my life."

"I don't want to just patch you up and send you back into battle—whatever that battle is. Let me help you get out of trouble."

"It's not simple. A powerful man—a ruthless man—wants me out of the way."

"Why?"

"I know his face," he said with a harsh growl.

"Carlos Jurado."

He cursed aloud in Spanish. "I should never have spoken that name. I told you to forget it."

"I—"

He gripped her shoulders. "What else did I say when I was delirious?"

She swallowed, wanting to minimize his anxiety. Yet she knew she couldn't expect him to be open with her unless she set the precedent. "Well...the part about your sister Anna getting killed. And I know you've been on the run since the fall."

He nodded tightly.

"And you didn't do anything criminal in San Marcos." He hadn't exactly said that, she thought as she held her breath.

"No. I did not." His gaze was steady, his words firm, and she knew for certain that he was telling the truth.

"I have friends who can help you."

"I doubt it."

"At least tell me you'll think about it."

He sighed. "Okay."

"Was Luis right? Are you in the country illegally?" she asked. "Or did you tell Officer Waverly the truth?"

"Yes and no."

"What does that mean?"

He gave her a fierce look. "Jessie, I will not go into long explanations."

She clasped his upper arms, wanting to demand more information—and wanting to push for assurances that he'd let her help him get out of trouble. She sensed, though, that if she leaned any harder, he'd leave.

"You need to rest," she whispered. "We both do."

"Yes," he agreed, his face relaxing.

"Promise me I won't wake up and find you've run out on me."

He hesitated, then nodded tightly.

She felt some of the tension ease out of her chest.

Instead of heading for the bedroom, he started clearing the table.

"You don't have to do that," she objected.

He shrugged. "I wanted to."

She gave a little nod, glad that he was feeling better, yet sensing that he was hiding behind the domestic activity.

"Is there anything I can do for *you?*" she asked quietly as he turned away from the sink.

"Yes." She saw his nostrils flare. "You have been sleeping in T-shirts and sweatpants. I want to see you in a nightgown."

"Miguel. We shouldn't. I mean, you're supposed to be taking it easy...."

"I know. I promise to be good. But I want the pleasure of seeing you in something sexy."

Unable to deny him anything, she gave a little nod. Then, turning, she went down the hall, opened a dresser drawer, and pulled out an ecru silk gown with spaghetti straps that she'd bought on impulse when she'd been shopping for underwear. Quickly she changed in the bathroom, then brushed her hair and put on a little makeup.

When she returned to the bedroom, he had straightened the covers. The look in his eyes when he turned and saw her stole the breath from her lungs. "You are so beautiful."

"Am I?"

"Oh, yes."

When he held out his arms, she came into them, cleaved to him as he embraced her. She wanted this, and not just for tonight—but for the rest of their lives.

He wanted the same thing. She was certain by the way he held her, moved his lips against her cheek, her neck. But she knew he wouldn't admit it yet. They would have to take things one step at a time. So she settled into his arms and closed her eyes, telling herself that all she needed was enough time.

When she awoke, it was still dark. But she was alone in bed. She lay rigid under the covers, listening to the stealthy sound of someone moving about the room. Miguel? What was he doing in the dark?

Then the mattress shifted and he slipped into the warmth

of the bedcovers, his body chilled from his early-morning excursion.

She lay quietly, trying to keep her breathing steady, trying to make him think that she didn't know he'd been sneaking around. Then one of his hands settled on the bodice of her gown to caress her breasts through the thin fabric, and she couldn't hold back a little sound in her throat.

"You are awake," he said in a thick voice.

"Um." His hand was cold, and she shivered.

"I should let you sleep. But I can't keep my hands off you."

"I'm glad you can't." In a quick motion, she pulled the gown over her head and turned back to him, her mouth finding his in the darkness while her body rocked against him. In the sleep-warmed bed they kissed and caressed each other, building to a slow, delicious coupling that left her limp and sated.

Snuggling close, she dozed again in the circle of his arms.

When she awoke a second time, it was to the sound of pounding on the front door.

Miguel was out of bed before she realized what was happening. In the dim light, she saw him reaching into the pillowcase for his spare clothing and pull on a pair of jeans. Then he pulled a black T-shirt over his head.

The pounding grew louder, more insistent. "Ms. Douglas?" a man's voice called. "Ms. Douglas, open the door."

Chapter Seven

"Go!" Miguel ordered. "Go to the door. But make them wait until I can get out of here."

In the early-morning light, she saw him pull on his tennis shoes and tie them with deft movements as the knocking sounded again.

"I'm not dressed!" she called, trying to keep her voice steady. Her gown had disappeared. Crossing to the dresser, she pulled on a pair of panties before grabbing her robe and shoving her arms through the sleeves with jerky movements.

As she fumbled to tie the belt, she saw Miguel looking at her with an expression that made her heart melt. She should go to the door, she knew. Instead, she crossed the few feet of space between them and pulled him close. He hugged her to him, and she closed her eyes. For a timeless moment she convinced herself that if they simply stood locked in a tight embrace, the world would leave them alone. Maybe he thought the same thing, because he held her with a fierceness that squeezed the breath from her lungs.

"Jessie," he breathed, his lips moving over her face, across her forehead, into her hair.

But nothing and no one could shut out reality. The knocking came again—louder, sharper.

Miguel turned her loose, and she hurried down the hall in her bare feet. "Who is it?" she called.

"INS."

"Who? Say it again."

"The Immigration and Naturalization Service. Open the door, ma'am."

"I—" She pulled her robe tightly closed, wishing she'd put on her gown again after making love.

"Ms. Douglas, we have a search warrant. Quit stalling, or we'll break down the door."

"Please, don't do that." With shaky fingers, she unbolted the lock. Two large men pushed their way into the house, forcing her to step back quickly or get mowed over.

One was tall with thinning blond hair, the other was shorter and dark, with a military haircut and Latin features. They wore business suits, yet it was obvious they didn't belong in a corporate boardroom. Their eyes were hard and their faces were set in grim lines. Arms folded across her chest, she faced them. "What's the meaning of—of getting me out of bed at this hour in the morning?"

"We have reason to believe you are harboring an illegal alien at this address," the blond one answered.

"What reason?" she demanded.

"A report from the local police with regard to an attempted theft of a van belonging to the Light Street Foundation," his partner retorted.

Jessie swallowed as understanding dawned. She had Officer Waverly to thank for this! After the scene in the driveway, he'd checked out the vehicle registration and found out it wasn't hers. Then he'd alerted the INS.

Feigning a calm she didn't feel, she raised her chin and asked, "Can I see some identification?"

"Of course." The blond one reached into his pocket and pulled out a leather case, which he flipped open. Inside was a plastic-laminated card with his picture and name—Daniel Fader. The other one also produced his identification. He was Ramón Martinez. Undoubtedly his Spanish came in handy for interrogating suspects from south of the border. "And here's our warrant," he added, unfolding an official-looking piece of paper.

Switching on the light, she scanned the sheet, her pulse pounding as she tried to focus on the words. She was saved from her pretense at reading when she caught a flash of movement out of the corner of her eye. Turning, she found that Fader had already started down the hall to the back of the house.

"Wait, you can't—"

"I'm afraid we can," Martinez contradicted.

Without bothering to argue, she hurried to catch up with the agent, who was already poking his head into the den. When he found nothing, he continued down the hall to the bedroom where she and Miguel had been sleeping.

Worrying her lower lip, Jessie followed him into the room—and found that it was empty. The covers on the bed were pulled up, and the basket of laundry that she'd left to be sorted was dumped in a pile on the far side of the bed. Only one pillow—hers—showed the indentation of a head.

When Fader lifted the spread and got down on his knees to look under the bed, she cringed, remembering the gun. Apparently it was now gone, because the agent straightened and turned before trotting over to the closet and flinging open the door.

Stepping inside, he roughly shoved her clothes out of the way and felt along the back wall. Then he exited the room and joined his partner, who was inspecting the bathroom. The sink was clean. And only Jessie's toilet articles were in evidence. Even the towel Miguel had used the night before appeared to be missing.

With a shiver, she realized what he'd been doing while she slept—clearing all evidence of his presence, just in case. Had he been planning to leave all along, or had the agents made the decision for him?

The men exchanged glances, then moved back toward the front of the house. Martinez poked into closets, then opened the basement door and went downstairs to see if Miguel might be hiding behind the furnace.

Still on edge but feeling more confident, Jessie followed

Fader into the kitchen. The room was neat and orderly, with only one glass on the drainboard.

Martinez came back and held out his hands, palms up, indicating he hadn't found what he was looking for.

"When did he leave?" his partner growled.

"Who?"

"Your boyfriend, Miguel Diego."

Silently she cursed Officer Waverly and his damn report. "Miguel left a couple of days ago," she said, investing the lie with as much conviction as she could.

"To go home?"

She shrugged and leaned back against the wall for support.

"When are you getting together again?"

She gave another shrug.

"Let's have his address."

"I believe he gave it to Officer Waverly. I don't have the house number memorized," she retorted.

"According to Waverly, the two of you looked pretty friendly. Are you saying you hardly know him?"

"I don't have to answer questions like that," she replied evenly, wondering if it was true, wondering if these men had the power to arrest her. But for what?

Both agents gave her a long look during which she stood without moving.

"You're not exactly being cooperative," Fader said. "Are you trying to make us believe you have an intimate relationship with a man you hardly know?"

She stiffened, pretty sure that Waverly had described the passionate kiss in front of the window.

"Maybe I should call a lawyer before we continue this discussion," she answered, careful not to let her anger show.

The agent regarded her consideringly, probably trying to decide whether she was bluffing. Finally, he straightened. "Okay. That's all for now, but we may be back with some more questions."

Not trusting herself to answer, she simply nodded.

The two men wheeled, and she followed them down the

hall. When they'd left, she shot the bolt, then stood leaning heavily against the door, her body trembling in reaction.

Several minutes passed before she felt able to push herself away from the door. First she looked out the window to make sure the agents were gone. No one was out front, but they could be waiting around the corner to follow her when she left, she thought as she made her way back to the bedroom.

"Miguel?" she called softly.

No one answered. Still, she went methodically back through the house anyway, looking for—praying for—signs of his presence. Her heart squeezed when she saw a strand of dark hair on the floor beside the sink. Stooping, she gently picked it up and wound it around her finger as she wandered slowly back to the bedroom. Everything of Miguel had vanished. But as she looked around, she saw now that the bedroom window was not quite closed. When she peered outside, she spotted a pair of footprints in the dark soil of the flower bed. Luckily, Fader hadn't thought to make an inspection of the grounds.

With a little catch in her breath, she sank to the surface of the bed, rolled onto her side, and hugged her arms around her knees. Over the past few days, Miguel had been a constant presence here. Now there was a great cavity at the center of her world. Turning her face into the sheet, she breathed in his scent. They'd slept here together. Made love here. And it had been so good—so incredibly good that she'd dared to hope that it was the beginning of something important.

But what had it really meant to him? Would he even call and let her know he was all right? she wondered. Or was this the end? The very abrupt end. Like last time—only worse.

With a broken breath, she pressed her cheek against the pillow and wrapped her arms around her shoulders because he wasn't there to hold her.

The silence of the house seemed to press in upon her.

Chilled to the bone, she pulled the covers over herself and stayed there for a long time, trying to get warm.

But she couldn't hide forever. And anyway, she was making too many assumptions, she told herself with a kind of forced optimism. She didn't know what Miguel intended. Maybe he would contact her when he thought it was safe.

Clinging to that thought for dear life, she got up and began to get dressed. But whether she heard from Miguel today or not, it was Monday morning. This was one of the days she worked at the rec center, and she was better off going through her caseload than hanging around the house, brooding.

On the way downtown, she found herself thinking about detouring from her regular route and heading toward Miguel's apartment. Swerving onto a side street, she looked in the rearview mirror to make sure the INS agents weren't behind her.

That thought was pretty paranoid. But if they wanted Miguel badly enough, they might follow her. She didn't see any sign of them, but she wasn't going to take a chance on doing something stupid—this morning of all mornings.

So, after driving around the block, she pulled into a gas station and filled her tank, then headed straight to work. The blacktop parking lot was deserted as she pulled into her assigned space at the corner of the redbrick building that had once been a school. For a moment she couldn't figure out why no one else was around. Then it hit her. The men from the INS had barged into her house at dawn, and it was still pretty early in the morning. Glancing at her watch, she saw that nobody would be in the office for at least half an hour.

Well, that meant she could get more done, she decided as she cut the engine and climbed out of the car. Pulling her keys from her purse, she unlocked the padlock that secured the entrance. The heavy door creaked on metal hinges as she pulled it open. Over the rasping sound, she thought for a moment that she heard someone call her name.

Miguel?

Pivoting, she stared around the parking lot but saw no one. With a sigh, she told herself to stop looking for him around every corner as she turned back into the building. The interior was dark and silent, the hallway lit only by early-morning sunlight filtering through the dirty windows on either side of the door. To her right was the gym—a shadowy, forbidding cavern where an ax murderer might be hiding. When she realized she was standing with her back pressed against the door, she sighed. She was in a pretty fragile emotional state if going to her own office made her feel like the victim in a slasher movie.

To prove to herself that she wasn't spooked, she took a couple of deliberate steps forward and was relieved when nobody leaped out of the shadows. This wasn't a slasher film, she told herself firmly as she marched down the hall toward the office complex at the back. Even so, she found herself hurrying past the darkened doorways that loomed on either side of the corridor. And the sound of her high-heeled shoes clicking on the tile floor of the empty building created an eerie echo that made her feel as if she were being followed.

But she knew there was nobody here. For gosh sakes, the door had been locked when she'd arrived, she reminded herself. It was just that she was alone in the early-morning silence—and feeling vulnerable.

Yet all the logical reassurances in the world couldn't stop the hairs on the back of her neck from tingling. By the time she reached her office door, she was practically tiptoeing. Just as she was about to grasp the knob, a noise from inside made every muscle in her body go rigid.

My God, someone *was* here. Somehow, on an instinctual level, she'd known it all along, and she should have trusted her instincts.

Who was in there waiting for her?

For one joyful moment, she decided it was Miguel. Then a harsh voice speaking in Spanish brought her back to reality.

"Shut up!" The exclamation was followed by an epithet that made her blush.

"There's nobody here yet," another voice objected.

"They will be! *She* will be. She works here on Mondays and she gets here early."

Jessie's heart clunked in her chest, then started to beat in double time. She knew that voice. It belonged to Georgie, the leader of Los Tigres, the gang that had threatened her outside Miguel's. She'd seen the hatred in the kid's eyes when she'd made him back down. So much had happened since then, she'd forgotten all about him.

Her mistake.

With a silent prayer, she took a cautious step back—then another, moving inch by inch away from the door until she was six feet down the hallway. Eight feet. Afraid to run and give herself away, she kept up the slow, steady pace, until she was more than a dozen feet from the office door.

But she didn't realize she was angled toward the wall, and didn't know she was backing into a fire extinguisher until cold metal clunked into the hollow between her shoulder blades.

An involuntary gasp welled in her throat as she whirled around. The canister was supposed to be tightly fixed to a wall bracket, but somehow, the whole assembly was loosening from its moorings. Frantically she grabbed at the cylinder before it could clatter to the floor and give her away.

But it was already too late for stealth. When she turned with the fire extinguisher in her arms, she saw her office door ease open the tiniest crack as someone furtively peeked out.

In the next moment, the door flew open, and two youths wearing black and orange jackets barreled into the hallway—Georgie and one of the other gang members.

"It's her!" Georgie shouted as he hurtled toward her, his hands stretched in front of him like claws.

Whirling, Jessie ran. Her heart was in her throat, yet strangely her mind kept working. For a split second, she thought about turning and hurling the fire extinguisher at her pursuers. Then a better idea came to her as she remembered using the device in several practice drills.

Clutching the cylinder against her chest, she fumbled frantically with the seal on the top of the trigger as her feet pounded against the tile floor.

She'd had a few yards' head start. But she was never going to win this race—especially in high-heeled shoes and carrying fifteen extra pounds in her arms. Behind her, she heard the gang leader gaining. When she felt his hand on her shoulder, a scream tore from her mouth.

"Gotcha!" Georgie crowed.

"Let me go," she sobbed, her fear almost driving the remnants of rational thought from her mind.

"Not this time, *caramelo.*"

Georgie spun her around, his face a frightening mixture of anger and triumph. The other boy hung back, giving his leader first dibs.

"You're going to find out what happens when you mess with me," Georgie growled in a low, dangerous voice. One of his large hands dug into her shoulder while the other reached up to tangle in her hair. He jerked her hair back sharply, bringing a scream to her lips and a smile of satisfaction to his.

She didn't have to pretend utter and complete fear. For long moments she couldn't move, her fingers frozen on the canister's trigger mechanism.

"Look at me," he growled. "I want you to know who's playing with you." Yanking at her hair again, he pulled her chin up and lifted her face toward his. The look of pleasure in his eyes made her stomach cramp. It also banished the paralysis from her fingers. Blindly she fumbled with the catch.

A hissing noise filled her ears, and foam began to shoot from the nozzle in a cold cloud of white.

"Wha—" Georgie managed as she aimed the spraying hose at his face.

A fog of the white chemical hit him in the mouth. He grabbed for the canister, but she held tight, knowing she was fighting for her life as she raised the nozzle higher.

The spray hit his eyes, and he screamed, clawing at his face.

The moment his hands left her body, she jerked away. When she realized she was still holding the canister, she threw it at his chest. It bounced off his body and hit the floor, the clatter echoing in the darkened hallway.

As quickly as she could, she began to totter down the corridor.

Behind her, Georgie was cursing loudly in Spanish. "Get her! Get the bitch!" he ordered his companion. Instead, the boy ran in the opposite direction.

Somehow Jessie made it back to the entrance, pulled the door open, and staggered outside, blinking in the sunlight. She was halfway across the parking lot when she felt a hand tug at her arm. Georgie again! God, she'd sprayed his eyes, and now he was crazed with anger. On a sob, she wrenched herself away and tried to run.

Feet kept up with her.

"Senorita Douglas. Are you all right?" a high voice near her right shoulder questioned.

She didn't stop long enough to find out who it was.

"Senorita Douglas!"

The voice penetrated the fear that swamped her mind. Not Georgie. Looking down in confusion, she saw a small figure at her side. It was Luis.

"Are you all right?" he asked again as his fingers dug into her arm.

"Wh-what are you doing here?" she stammered.

His face contorted, and he hesitated for a moment before blurting, "I would have stopped you. But I didn't want anyone to see me. I can't get in trouble or he's going to beat me again."

She nodded, remembering what he'd said about his stepfather.

"Are you all right?" he asked once more, his voice high and urgent.

"Yes," she managed.

The sirens grew louder.

Then she heard the squeal of tires as a police car came to a halt a few feet from her.

Two uniformed officers jumped out.

"We got a call about some trouble at the recreation center," one of them said, addressing Jessie.

She struggled to pull herself together. "Inside. A guy named Georgie. The leader of Los Tigres. When I came to work, he attacked me."

"Okay. Clear the area," the one who had addressed her shouted, then spoke into the microphone near his collar. The transmission completed, he and his partner disappeared into the building, guns drawn.

All she could do was stand transfixed, staring at the door as it banged heavily on its hinges.

Luis pulled on her arm. *"Señorita, por favor."*

She took a step back just as another car pulled up, and out stepped Jim Alvarez, the recreation-center director. Slim, dark-haired and in his early thirties, Jim had grown up in the neighborhood and won a scholarship to the University of Maryland, where he'd gotten a master's in social work. He'd wanted to stay in the barrio, and the job with the Light Street Foundation had been perfect for him. Jessie admired his work, yet sometimes she found him a little hard to take. He was a stickler for rules and a traditionalist who could be hard on people when he thought they weren't living up to what he considered essential moral standards.

"What's going on?" he asked as he trotted toward her, his face contorted with alarm.

"What are you doing here?" she asked stupidly.

"I work here."

"Right," she replied with a little shake of her head. Probably it was late enough now that the rest of the staff would also be arriving.

Another police car came to a halt in the parking area, and two more officers dashed into the building.

MIGUEL WATCHED FROM the shadows of the passageway across the street, his hands clenched into fists as he studied Jessie's pale, pinched face.

Coward! he silently accused himself. Yet, after this morning, he knew very well what would happen if he showed himself. The police or the INS would grab him.

Without considering the consequences, he'd come to the center to see Jessie. But when he'd gotten here, he'd found Luis lurking in the passageway, pacing back and forth, looking scared. Luis had said that Jessie was in the building— and in trouble—but he couldn't go inside. His stepfather was back from the city jail again, and he'd already beaten the boy for not keeping his head down. So Luis had called 911, but the police hadn't come yet.

Miguel had started across the street to rescue Jessie when she'd staggered outside looking dazed but unhurt. Then the police cars had started arriving.

His hand stretched toward her, then fell back. He ached to comfort her, ached to assure himself that she was all right. But even that was denied him.

He cursed under his breath. She had saved his life, and all he could do was lurk in the shadows and watch the action when she needed to feel his arms around her. But if he went to her now, he would only make things worse—for both of them.

He closed his eyes, fighting a choking feeling of rage. Over the past few days, she had made him want to believe that he could live like a normal human being again. Even after the INS had barged in this morning, he had come back here to be with her, hoping, praying that she might offer him salvation. Now he silently admitted that he'd only been fooling himself.

"WHAT'S HAPPENING?" Jim demanded.

"Gang members broke into the building," Jessie answered. "Thank the Lord someone called the police," she added, then stopped short as she realized it must have been Luis. When she looked around for him, he had vanished again. The boy made a habit of stepping in, then disappearing when it was convenient.

A flicker of movement caught her eye, and she glanced up to see a uniformed policeman staring through the glass, looking directly at her. As she watched, he turned to speak to someone inside, then disappeared from view again.

Endless minutes passed during which she felt her stomach twist into painful knots. Then the policeman came to the door again. This time, he motioned for Jim to approach.

"I'm going with you," she said in a shaky voice.

"No. Wait here." He left Jessie standing in the parking lot and strode toward the door where he and the officer conferred. She saw them both looking at her and knew she couldn't simply wait to find out what they were discussing. Moving toward them, she glanced questioningly at the policeman; Officer Haroldson, his name tag read.

"What's going on?"

"The gang leader—Georgie Cota—says he broke into the rec center because he was looking for *you*," the cop said in a grim voice, his narrowed gaze giving the impression that she was the one at fault.

Her mouth went dry.

"Why?" Haroldson demanded.

When she didn't answer immediately, he persisted, "He's plenty angry with you. What's going on between you two?"

"I—I had a run-in with him a few nights ago when I came down here," she said in a halting voice.

"Here?"

"In the neighborhood."

"And you didn't say anything to me about it?" Jim interjected.

"I haven't been back to work since," she explained, remembering that Jim didn't like being out of the loop.

"Maybe you'd better tell us what's going on," the cop added.

"I—" She stopped, feeling trapped. If she revealed what had happened on her first meeting with Georgie, then she'd have to explain what she'd been doing in front of Miguel's apartment.

"He claims you had a gun."

Jim's head snapped toward her.

"Can you explain that?" Haroldson demanded.

She sucked in a sharp breath and let it out slowly. "Maybe I need to get some advice from a lawyer before we continue this discussion," she said, using the same line that she'd used a few hours ago with the INS agents.

"You have that right," the cop replied, his voice conveying disapproval.

Jessie had seen enough police dramas to know that the cops tried to get suspects to talk before they "lawyered up," as the phrase went. But she wasn't a suspect, she told herself. She hadn't done anything—except help Miguel and get herself assaulted.

Before the conversation could progress, the door opened again and two more officers came out, escorting Georgie Cota between them. The look he gave her made the blood in her veins freeze. She had bested him twice, humiliated him twice—first, in front of his gang members; and now, when he was in the hands of the police. The look in his eyes told her very clearly that if he ever walked the streets again, he'd kill her.

Chapter Eight

You thought you had your life all figured out. Then one day you woke up and realized that nothing would be the same again, Jessie mused as she stood in the lavishly appointed garden behind Cameron Randolph and Jo O'Malley's mansion.

Spring had given way to summer. Around her, flower beds overflowed with bright annuals, a string quartet played in the shade of a dogwood tree, and wedding guests chatted as they waited for the ceremony to begin.

Jessie smiled at the other guests and made the right responses in the flow of conversation. But it was hard to keep herself from tugging at the bodice of the pale peach dress that felt as if it were crushing her breasts into her chest.

Probably she should have bought something new for Kathryn and Hunter's wedding, but generating the enthusiasm to go shopping was simply beyond her. Showing up at work every morning and dragging herself through the day was about all she'd been able to manage recently. And it had only gotten worse since she'd confirmed her growing suspicions by taking a home pregnancy test. She was carrying Miguel's child.

From the other side of the crowded lawn, Erin Stone caught her eye, and Jessie tipped her chin up, manufacturing a fleeting smile to prove that she was holding up okay on this festive occasion. Erin was her boss at the Light Street

Foundation and one of the few people who knew what she was going through. She might be pregnant by Miguel, but she hadn't heard from him since the morning two months ago when he'd fled her bedroom through the back window.

Out of necessity, her other confidante had been Laura Roswell. Laura was a lawyer with an office at 43 Light Street. Jessie had gone to her immediately after the break-in at the recreation center. She'd needed legal advice, and she'd just plain needed someone to talk to. So she'd poured out the whole story of what had happened with Georgie and then found herself confiding about her relationship with Miguel. To her relief, Laura had advised her that she wasn't obliged to talk to the police about Georgie, although she'd pointed out that her failure to admit what he'd done to her might not be in her own best interests. Jessie had kept silent in order to protect Miguel.

Luckily, the police hadn't needed her to file a complaint to hang on to Georgie. He was being held without bail because he was already in trouble for several other offenses. But what if he came to trial and her testimony was crucial to keeping him locked up? The prospect of his being back on the streets terrified her. He would come after her again.

"Wow, this wedding is really something," her friend Noel Zacharias murmured, breaking into Jessie's churning thoughts.

She nodded in agreement, hoping her face didn't reflect the pain and confusion she had been living with for weeks. She'd almost stayed home today. A wedding wasn't the best place to contemplate single motherhood. Yet she'd wanted to be here for Kathryn and Hunter because they were two of the Light Street gang, and they meant a lot to her.

The music changed, and Cam Randolph and some of the other men moved through the crowd, asking everyone to take their seats. Jessica chose a chair at the back—praying that an attack of morning sickness wouldn't hit her in the middle of the ceremony. Why did they call it ''morning'' sickness, anyway, she wondered, when it could strike at any time of the day or night?

When everyone was seated, the minister, Hunter, and Cam, who was the best man, stepped toward the stunning bower of white roses that had been set up facing the assembly. Then the music changed to the "Wedding March," and Kathryn began to walk down the grassy aisle between the seats, holding tightly to her father's arm. Her steps were sure, and her eyes were fixed on Hunter as his were on her.

They were so fortunate! Their love for each other had helped them survive a terrible ordeal a year ago, and now they were standing up in front of God and their friends, pledging to share their lives.

Jessie's eyes misted as she watched the bride and groom and listened to the service, the familiar words taking on new meaning as she found herself wishing she and Miguel were standing in the sunshine making a commitment.

Commitment. The word sent a shiver through her. She knew she had no right to think in those terms. She had no claims on Miguel. They'd only spent a few nights together. Yet she'd sensed that what they felt for each other could have grown into something rich and lasting if they'd given it a chance.

The minister pronounced Hunter and Kathryn man and wife, and Jessie saw the joy on the groom's countenance as he faced his bride, his love for her shining out for all to see. Then his expression changed to a broad grin just before he lowered his lips to hers.

The spirited kiss drew clapping and lusty comments from the crowd, and when the groom finally lifted his head and looked around, Jessie had the feeling he'd forgotten that he and his new wife weren't alone.

"I think I was a little too enthusiastic," he whispered, his cheeks endearingly flushed.

His bride's face was radiant as she smiled into his eyes. "It's okay. We're among friends."

The observation drew a laugh from the audience, and Jessie found herself smiling, despite her own inner turmoil. Hunter had lived a lonely existence until he'd met Kathryn. But he'd been welcomed by the Light Street group, and now he was truly among friends who could make up for the childhood he'd missed.

As people began to head for the terrace where bars and buffet tables had been set up, Jessie hung back, letting the flow of the crowd pass by. The ceremony had made her feel happy for her friends, but now that people were getting into a party mood, she felt very much alone. She wasn't sure she could get through lunch and socializing when she wanted to be with Miguel so badly that her throat was starting to ache with the effort to keep from crying.

As she was slipping away onto a brick side-path, Katie joined her.

"How's everything?" Katie asked.

To Jessie's utter mortification the simple question triggered a spasm of misery. The tears she'd been struggling to hold back began to slide down her cheeks. Quickly she stepped around a boxwood hedge so that no one could see her. Katie followed.

"Oh, honey." Katie took a step forward and held out her arms. Jessie went into them, letting her head sink to her friend's shoulder as Katie patted her back. "It's okay," she murmured. "It's okay."

It wasn't. But the words and the comforting gesture had a soothing effect as Jessie struggled to get herself under control. When Katie handed her a tissue, she wiped her eyes and blew her nose.

"Want to tell me about it?" Katie murmured as she led Jessie to a stone bench enclosed on three sides by boxwoods.

Jessie sat down, giving herself some time to decide what she wanted to say.

Before she could speak, Katie answered her own question. "You're pregnant, aren't you?"

"How—how do you know?"

"I'm making an educated guess."

Unable to meet her friend's eye, Jessie nodded.

"You've been to a doctor? You're okay?"

Jessie managed another nod. She'd had her first prenatal appointment, and everything was progressing normally—at least with regard to the pregnancy.

Katie waited a beat, then asked, "So what's Miguel going to do about it?"

Jessie kicked at the brick below her right foot. "I don't know."

"My God, Jessie, you probably saved his life, and he's treating you like this?"

"My getting pregnant wasn't his fault."

"An angel of the Lord visited you after he left?" Katie asked in an acerbic voice.

Jessie flushed. "No. I mean, he would have walked away without letting things go that far. I forced the issue."

Katie's lips quirked. "You're saying you dragged him kicking and screaming to bed?"

"No," she replied in a small voice, her color deepening again as she remembered how it had been that night.

"And now he doesn't want to acknowledge his child?" her friend asked.

"He doesn't know about the baby."

"Why not?"

"Because he hasn't called me! He hasn't made any attempt to communicate," Jessie flung at her friend, venting her hurt and grief on the only person available. She'd kept her feelings bottled up for so long that she felt like a dam bursting. More anguished words kept tumbling out. "I waited a couple of days and went to his apartment, but the place was empty. He'd moved out without letting me know he was leaving. And nobody will tell me where he's gone. I guess I've got two choices. I can put an ad in the *Baltimore Sun* advising him that he's going to be a father. Or I just go ahead with my life like he and I never made love," she ended with a little gulp that held as much misery as bitterness.

Katie absorbed the verbal blows without comment, then reached to lay her hand gently on Jessie's arm. "I know you're hurting," she said in a voice that made Jessie's vision cloud again.

"But maybe you're not, uh, giving him the benefit of the doubt. He and I had a chance to talk when I was examining him. There were things he wanted me to understand about his being at your house. He was worried about you—worried that your association with him would get you into trouble. From his point of view, he turned out to be right. You got harassed by the police, a couple of agents from the INS and that creep Georgie."

"He's in jail now."

"Lucky for you."

The quiet observation hung in the air between them.

"Let's get back to Miguel," Katie said, her voice taking on a pragmatic note. "He has a right to know that you're carrying his child. If you don't give him that information, then he doesn't have a chance to respond."

Not trusting herself to speak, Jessie nodded again.

"Tell him," she urged. "Promise me you'll do him that favor."

"He might not think it's a favor."

"You won't know unless you try."

"Okay," Jessie managed in a small voice.

Katie squeezed her arm again. "Good." She hesitated for a moment, then asked another question. "Are you in love with him?"

For weeks, Jessie had considered that the most important question in the world. Now she tried to answer honestly. "I don't know whether I fell in love with him or with an image of him I made up. It would be easier to give you an honest answer if I could spend some more time with him."

"I shouldn't have pried."

"No. You were a big help."

"Then let's get back to the reception before they send out a search party."

"You go ahead," Jessie murmured. "I need a few more minutes."

CARLOS JURADO HAD always appreciated the finer things in life—and the simple pleasures, he thought with a self-satisfied smile as he stood beside the Vulcan stove, the show-piece of his country kitchen. Soon he would have to leave this cozy estate and fade into the jungle, where he would emerge as another person. All the plans were in place—had been in place for almost a year. And by the time he was ready to make his move, the last little impediment would be out of the way.

But for now, he could still enjoy the luxury of his palatial hideaway. With the practiced gesture of a master chef, he hefted the weight of a cast-iron skillet in his hand. Cast iron was the only kind of pan for searing fish properly, he mused as he added a generous dollop of butter and watched it melt into a pool of golden yellow. Then he added shredded leeks, carrots, garlic, serrano peppers, salt, and pepper.

Humming under his breath, he adjusted the gas flame. He had a houseful of servants and an army of bodyguards on the grounds of his estate. But there was nothing like the epicurean pleasure of cooking a simple but delicious meal for himself. A man who didn't stay in touch with his do-mestic side was missing a great deal of life, he mused.

When the vegetables had cooked down into a flavorful medley, he pushed them to the sides of the skillet and added a tender salmon fillet. He was going to enjoy it the way he'd had it in Madrid, seared on the outside and naturally pink in the middle.

"Sir?"

He deliberately waited several beats before looking up at Eduardo Sombra, one of his senior security men.

"I told you not to disturb me while I am in the kitchen," he said in a deceptively mild voice as he reached to turn down the heat under the salmon. His people had learned to fear that voice, and it gave him a glow of satisfaction to see the man cringe ever so slightly.

"You also asked to be informed if we had any more information on Miguel Valero. We have a dispatch from the States on him."

The announcement made Carlos turn from the stove. "You've found him?"

"A man using the name 'Miguel Diego' was spotted in Baltimore a few weeks ago," Sombra related with some satisfaction.

"A few *weeks*. And you're just telling me now?"

Sombra coughed delicately. "Well, there was your change in staff."

"Our new operative came highly recommended."

"There was also some ambiguity about Valero. I wanted to be accurate before I came to you."

Carlos waited with narrowed eyes.

"We have reason to believe that the individual in the report is Valero. He's working with the poor in the Spanish-speaking section of the city—giving medical advice without a license."

Carlos snorted. "He always had a soft spot for the lower classes."

Sombra nodded. "The man's size and build fit the description we have for Valero."

"Does he look like Valero—yes or no?"

"Not exactly. That was part of the confusion."

So the man was using a disguise. Apparently it had been effective. "Well, if he was spotted, what happened to him?" he snapped.

"He disappeared—went underground again. But I have a man on our payroll looking for him there."

"What man?"

"Someone with excellent connections." Sombra spread his hands as though offering a gift. "If anyone can find Valero, he can."

The sudden sharp smell of burning fish reached Carlos's

nose. Swearing, he whirled and snatched the pan from the burner and slammed it onto the stovetop. His lunch was ruined. Valero had ruined his lunch. But at least there was progress. He was closing in on the only man who had the power to wreck his carefully constructed plans.

"I want him brought to me."

"Brought here?" Sombra asked in surprise. "I thought you wanted him dead."

"I do. But he has been on the run for a long time. He might have talked about me to someone. I want to eliminate any possibility of detection. Do you get my meaning?"

"Perfectly," Sombra answered.

JESSIE PICKED HER moment carefully. In about a half hour, the evening staff would be taking over the rec center.

For the past week she'd been keeping track of Luis. He was often here in the late afternoon and still at the center when she left work. She had asked some careful questions about him and found out that he hung around to stay out of his stepfather's way. The man was brutal with him—which made it remarkable that Luis had taken the risk of threatening her with a gun. But he'd done it for Miguel. Probably Miguel was like a substitute father to him.

Today she found Luis standing near the soda machine in the hall behind the gym. Casually, she put in sixty cents. After the can of Coke clattered into the slot at the bottom, she lifted the door and handed the boy the soft drink.

He looked at her questioningly.

"I'd like to talk to you for a few minutes," she said, keeping her voice steady. He was just a kid, but an unpredictable kid. And he might hold the key to her future. So far, no one else would admit to knowing where she could find Miguel. Apparently there was an elaborate conspiracy of silence in the community concerning him. You wouldn't think a whole neighborhood could keep the secret of his whereabouts, yet they seemed to be doing it. But perhaps she could get Luis to give her the information.

"About what?" he asked, edging away.

"Nothing bad," she said quickly. "Why don't you come down the hall to my office."

He hesitated.

"It's okay," she said, trying to stay casual.

Reluctantly, he followed her, clutching the Coke as if it were a shield.

"Am I in trouble? Did Papa Roberto complain about anything?" he asked, his face tense as she closed the door behind them and sat down in one of the visitors' chairs so that the desk wouldn't be between them.

She looked down into his worried brown eyes, trying to put as much reassurance as she could into her own expression. "No, it's nothing to do with him. And you're not in trouble. But why don't you sit down so we can talk. I need a favor from you."

He perched on the edge of the other chair, his sneakers on the floor, still looking like he might take off at any minute. "What do you want?"

"I need to talk to Miguel."

"He left town," the boy replied without missing a beat.

Jessie felt her heart sink. Although she'd assumed the father of her child was still in the city, the answer made sense. Miguel's run-in with Officer Waverly and the visit from the two INS agents were good reasons for him to have moved on. Yet, even as she considered the boy's statement, she wondered if it wasn't a cover. When he'd said it, Luis hadn't looked her in the eye. Now he was staring fixedly at the Coke can in his hand and scuffing his foot against the tile floor.

"I know you're very loyal to Miguel. I admire that very much," she said softly. "But there's something important I need to discuss with him—if it turns out he's still in Baltimore."

"What?" Luis asked.

She shook her head. "It's something personal. Between him and me. Something that he needs to know."

She tried not to twist her hands together as she waited for the ten-year-old to make a decision. She wanted to say something more—argue that he owed her his cooperation since he had started things by threatening her with a pistol. But she sensed that she wouldn't help her case by leaning on him.

Finally he gave a quick nod, and she let out the breath she was holding.

"If I tell you where he lives, will you promise not to tell anyone else?"

"I promise not to reveal his whereabouts," she answered very formally.

Still, the boy hesitated. "He won't like you coming there. But he doesn't have a phone. You can't call him."

She shrugged. "I'll deal with that."

"What if he's mad at me?" Luis muttered, and Jessie had to clench her hands to keep from reaching out and shaking him. He had said he would give her the information. Now it looked like he was changing his mind. Still, she forced herself to answer calmly. "I won't tell him. If he asks, I'll make sure he understands that I put a lot of pressure on you."

The boy nodded, though his eyes still reflected hesitation. "If you go there, you must be careful. You must be sure nobody is following you."

"I will."

"The bad man is looking for him. He has spies around here—asking questions."

Jessie swallowed. Luis was being very cautious, but it was only to protect Miguel. "I promise. I'll be very careful."

"Okay. He's on Juniper Street. Just before the block with the warehouses. You go around the back—like at his other place."

Her brow wrinkled as she pictured the area. "Are you sure? I thought the houses down there were boarded up."

"*Sí.* He's in one of those, where the bad man won't look for him—I hope."

Jessie closed her eyes for a moment. She'd thought Miguel's former apartment was pretty bad. Now Luis was telling her that he was staying somewhere worse—in an abandoned building. No wonder he didn't want her to see him there.

"Which one?" she asked.

"It has blue paint on the bricks." The boy's eyes sought hers. "Remember, don't let anyone see you poking around there."

"Yes. I understand. Thank you for trusting me."

Still clutching the Coke, he stood and started to leave the office, then stopped abruptly in the doorway.

When he glanced uncertainly back at her, she rose and followed him to the door. Outside in the anteroom, she was startled to discover Jim Alvarez talking to Ramón Martinez, one of the INS agents who had come to her house looking for Miguel.

"Miss Douglas," the agent said, glancing up, his gaze zeroing in on her face. He looked pleased to have caught her by surprise.

She made an attempt to compose her features as she gave him a curt nod, then bent toward Luis who was still standing rigidly in front of her. "Thanks for talking with me. Go on back to your basketball game."

"*Sí.*" He gave her a relieved look as he made a wide circle around the men, then hurried down the hall toward the gym.

"Problems?" Jim asked.

"No. I thought he might know the name of a girl who talked to me on the street about some help."

"What girl?"

"That's the problem. I don't know her name."

Jim looked as if he didn't quite believe the explanation, and Jessie was instantly sorry she'd resorted to making up a story. Lying was so foreign to her. Yet she didn't know whether she could trust either one of these men.

The agent was inspecting her with what appeared to be

detached professional interest. "Have you seen that fellow who was staying with you—Miguel Diego?"

She raised her head and looked him straight in the eye. "Did you come down here to ask me about him?"

"That's one of my purposes."

"Then I'm sorry you wasted a trip. I haven't seen him."

"You don't want to get in trouble for harboring a fugitive," the man observed.

The advice made her angry. What right did this guy have coming to the place where she worked asking questions about Miguel or making remarks about her personal life?

Still, she kept the ire in check. Maybe he'd hoped he could get her going, and that she'd say exactly the wrong thing.

Instead of rising to the bait, she gave him a tight nod. "You're absolutely right," she agreed icily. "I wouldn't want to get in any kind of trouble."

He held her gaze for several more seconds, as if he were an expert in hypnotism and he expected his beady eyes would force her to speak some vital information.

When she didn't succumb to his mesmerizing stare, he gave her one last jolt of mental energy before turning back to Jim. "I have some other cases to check."

The staff had had requests like this before, and they had always complied—at least on the surface. It was a matter of playing ball with the feds or risk losing the government funding for some of their programs. So Jessie wasn't surprised when Jim led the way to the room where the files were kept.

As soon as the men were out of sight, Jessie ducked back into her office and flopped into her chair. She'd been in here pumping Luis for information right when Martinez had been in the building. What if he'd heard?

Panic rose at the thought. She forced it down, assuring herself that she was overreacting. Still, it was impossible to keep her hands from shaking as she straightened her desk.

She was heading for the ladies' room, when Jim came out of the men's.

He looked at her speculatively. "I didn't know you, uh, were friends with that guy Diego."

Jessie gave a little shrug.

"Martinez said he stayed at your house, that you're lovers."

She felt heat creep into her face. "That's a pretty personal revelation."

"He wants information about the guy."

"I'm aware of that."

"Are you in a position to give it to him? Because if you are, it would earn us some brownie points."

Jessie swallowed painfully. "I haven't seen Diego in months," she answered truthfully.

"Don't make Martinez mad. He could cause a lot of trouble for us. With our clients. And with the government."

"I understand," she replied stiffly, then pushed her way into the ladies' room so she wouldn't have to answer any more questions. When she finally emerged, she was relieved to find that Jim wasn't lurking in the hall. Quickly she left the building and headed for her car.

As she pulled out of the parking lot, she ached to turn right and drive directly to the block on Juniper Street where the boy had said she'd find Miguel. Instead she headed for a little restaurant in Fells Point where she sometimes went for lunch. Getting a table where she could watch the boats in the harbor, she ordered a Caesar salad with grilled shrimp.

Her raw nerves took away the taste of the food, and she sat there pushing romaine lettuce and shrimp around her plate as she imagined her reunion with Miguel. She wanted to tell him about the baby. But maybe she wouldn't tell him unless he seemed glad to see her. What if she revealed that she was pregnant, and he came back to her out of guilt? That would be worse than nothing.

Silently she clenched her fist under the table and blinked back the tears in her eyes as she vowed she wouldn't ask him for anything. She wouldn't put any pressure on him or turn this into a confrontation, or act needy. She would do no more than give him the information.

Still, her throat was so dry she could hardly swallow as she drove toward his hideout. To make sure she wasn't being followed, she kept glancing in her rearview mirror. As she made a right turn onto Juniper, she saw a kid in an orange-and-black jacket. One of Los Tigres!

Her hands gripped the wheel. She hadn't even been thinking about the gang. Since Georgie's arrest, everything had been quiet on that front. But she'd also been careful not to venture into the barrio alone. Thankful that she was driving her own car instead of the van, she reached into the glove compartment, pulled out the floppy sun hat she wore to protect her fair skin and jammed it down onto her head.

She made a run past the row of boarded-up houses, peering at them through the side window, finding the one with the blotchy blue paint on the bricks. It was the fifth from the right and had plywood nailed across the front door and the windows. Somebody had spray-painted obscene messages on the wood and on the brick walls.

Lord, what a place to live. Was Luis right—or was he deliberately misleading her to get off the hook?

Well, there was only one way to find out. After parking around the corner on a street where the dwellings were still occupied, she sat in the car for ten minutes, watching for any further sign of gang members. When none appeared, she quickly made her way around the corner to the row of houses. Unlike the place where Miguel had been living before, there was no convenient passageway between the buildings. So she walked to the end of the block, then up the alley behind.

Glad that she'd worn low-heeled shoes, she picked her way gingerly along the broken pavement, her eyes darting from side to side as she scanned the deserted landscape. The fifth house had a back fence made of wooden boards that looked like they might blow away in a strong wind and a gate hanging drunkenly from one hinge. Slipping through the opening, she found herself in a yard filled with refuse. Old tires, cereal boxes, discarded clothing and other trash were mounded in piles, making the place look like an outpost of the city dump. Great camouflage for a hideout—if Miguel was really living here.

Under more ideal circumstances, she would have stationed herself just inside the fence and called out his name. She knew, though, that it would be a mistake to alert anyone else to her presence, so she began to make her way cautiously across the area, heading for a stairwell that was similar to the one outside his former apartment.

The evening was warm, the air humid. As she picked her way across the mess, she felt sweat collect at the base of her neck and trickle down her back. Wishing she had a stick to poke through the litter, she skirted a pile of ashes that might have been the remains of a vagrant's cooking fire.

Then, reaching a clear area in the middle of the yard, she climbed over a low concrete wall and started across a stretch of flat ground. After a few steps, she realized that the dirt hid a layer of old wooden boards. They creaked under her, and she caught the smell of dampness wafting up from below.

Better go back, she thought, stopping short. This thing wasn't safe. But as she took a tentative step to reverse her course, the surface below her feet gave way with a sickening crack. In the next moment, she felt herself plunging through a thin veneer of earth into a dark, yawning cavern below.

Chapter Nine

A scream welled in Jessie's throat, even as her arms flailed. In the grip of panic, she tried desperately to stop her fall. When her hand hit the concrete rim, she automatically closed her fingers and clung. But with her body already tumbling through the air, she couldn't hold herself up with only one hand.

All she could do was break her fall. Her fingers tore loose from the concrete, scraping her skin, making her scream again as she slipped downward into a dank, darkened pit that had been concealed by the boards.

Seconds later, she landed on an uneven dirt surface, barely managing to stay on her feet. She flung out her arms to steady herself against the curved wall as she struggled to collect her wits. When she could think clearly again, she took stock of the situation. Her hand was scraped, but she hadn't fallen far. Moving her arms and legs, she decided nothing was broken.

But she couldn't stop a surge of maternal fear from shivering through her. Her hand was trembling as she brought it to the barely rounded swell of her abdomen. There was nothing she could really tell by feeling the contours of her tummy, but she considered it a good sign that she wasn't experiencing any cramping.

You're lucky, she thought, then castigated herself for putting her baby in jeopardy. Craning her neck, she peered up at the broken boards above her. They'd been covering this...this... She didn't know what to call it. It was too wide for a well and not nearly deep enough. And it was too crude to be one of those bomb shelters that people had dug in their backyards in the early sixties.

But it was definitely man-made—and, unfortunately, too deep for her to climb out of. Cautiously she began to explore her prison. The walls were cement. Too bad there were no convenient handholds.

Lord, now what?

She had vowed not to call out to Miguel. Now she had no choice. She tried his name in a raspy voice that she could barely hear over the pounding pulse in her ears, and then louder: "Miguel!"

The sound reverberated around her, and she realized with a shudder that she should have stuck with her original resolve. Shouting from down here was dangerous. What if one of Los Tigres heard her?

The thought of the gang members cornering her here brought a wave of nausea roiling through her. Georgie might be in jail, but his friends wouldn't let an opportunity like this pass.

That scenario was terrifying. Others weren't much better. Like, what if someone had heard her and called the police—and that led to Miguel's hiding place being discovered?

Tears of fear and frustration welled in her eyes, and she sank to the ground, her arms hugged tightly across her middle. Nobody but Luis would know where to look for her when she turned up missing. What if he didn't tell anyone because he was afraid of getting into trouble?

She wasn't sure how long she sat there. Finally she realized that the daylight above her was starting to fade. If she didn't want to stay here all night, she had to find a way to get out.

MIGUEL AWOKE COVERED with perspiration. He had been dreaming again. Another nightmare. Only this time, Jessie had been there. At the clinic. He'd heard her scream, then call his name, and her voice had jarred him from sleep.

He swiped a hand across his face, then lay very still in the darkened room, listening. The only sound was the drip of water from the old faucet that wouldn't turn off.

He'd been in this place for two weeks. He didn't know how much more he could take. But Bernardo Contrares had told him he and his friends would find him another dwelling soon. Something better.

He had saved the life of Bernardo's wife by diagnosing her bacterial endocarditis. And Bernardo had been grateful, like so many of the other people in this little community who lacked the money for proper medical care.

So Dr. Miguel wasn't cleaning offices anymore; he was taking care of patients. It might not be legal, but it gave him a great deal of satisfaction. He had bonded with these people, and they were an important part of his decision to stop running from Jurado. He'd decided that if he wasn't safe here, he wasn't safe anywhere.

A gun rested beside him on the sheet. He tucked it under the pillow and lay in bed for a while longer, thinking of Jessie, missing her, wondering what she was doing. He spent a lot of his free time that way. Sometimes he pictured himself phoning her. Or knocking on her door. The closest he'd come was standing in the shadows of the garage across from her Light Street office—where he could watch her arrive and leave. Otherwise, he'd stuck to the promise he had made to himself; he wouldn't put her in danger again because of his own needs.

Heaving himself out of bed, he stretched the kinks out of his muscles and went into the bathroom. The sink had a working tap, but he had to flush the toilet by filling a bucket of water and pouring it into the bowl.

After shaving with cold water, he stripped and stood in the shower, grimacing as he washed with another bucket of water. Maybe he'd ask to take a hot shower somewhere later, he thought. And maybe one of the families would offer him a meal.

JESSIE SWIPED A DAMP lock of hair away from her face, then began to search over the ground, looking for something—anything—useful. The best thing she found was a three-foot-long piece of board that had tumbled down with her. Perhaps she could use it as a shovel. If she could pile up enough dirt, maybe she'd raise the ground level enough to be able to jump up and reach the top.

Plunging the board into the ground, she came up with a couple of cupfuls of soil. The wood rubbed against the scraped skin of her hand, making her wince, but she kept working, building a hill at the side of the shaft nearest the fence.

It was growing dark when a sound from above made her go rigid. Footsteps—moving toward the top of the pit. The steps stopped, and she breathed in a little sigh. Nerves. It was just her nerves. Tight-jawed, she dug the board into the ground and loosened another couple of inches of dirt.

The steps came again. Nearer.

"Who's there?" a harsh voice demanded.

She didn't move, didn't speak, praying that the darkness would hide her—until the beam of a strong flashlight angled downward, hitting her squarely in the eyes. With a gasp, she threw one arm across her face.

"Jessie?" The voice above her had changed from sharp to incredulous, and now she knew who was there.

"Miguel! Thank God, Miguel!" she cried out, stretching her arms upward toward him, even as she closed her eyes against the brightness of the light.

"Jessie. What are you doing down there?" he demanded, moving the beam away from her face.

"I fell through the rotten boards up there," she managed, her breath catching.

"Are you all right?" he asked urgently.

"Yes. I think so."

"Thank God."

"Wh-where am I?" she asked. "What is this place?"

"It is an old cistern—where they used to collect rain-water."

He set the light on the concrete rim so that it shone partially on the ground above and partially into the pit—but out of her eyes. Then he began to pull at the remaining boards, wrenching them apart and flinging them out of the way before throwing a leg over the side of the concrete and jumping down. With a cry of joy, Jessie threw aside the board she was still clutching and launched herself into his arms. He took the impact of her body and pulled her close so that she melted against him.

Until that moment, she hadn't let herself admit how much she had missed his embrace, missed the strength of his arms around her, the warmth of his body, the familiar scent of his skin. Closing her eyes, she simply clung to him, letting his presence wipe away her terror—and all the long lonely nights when she hadn't been sure if she would ever see him again. She felt his lips skim her hair, the side of her face as she tightened her grip around his waist.

"Thank you for finding me," she breathed. "But—but how are we going to get out of here?"

"We can worry about that in a minute." He held on to her as if he would never let her go again, then continued in a choked voice, "I came outside to go to work and heard someone down here. I didn't know it was you."

She nodded against his chest, too overwhelmed with relief and joy to say more. She was hardly aware that they were standing in a hole in the ground. As long as she could hold on to him, she knew everything was going to be all right.

He didn't kiss her. And she wanted that, too—so much. To feel his lips move against hers. To taste him. She was tipping her face toward his when his voice turned stern, bringing her back to reality. "This place is dangerous. You should not have come here."

She looked away, remembering where they were and how she had gotten herself into this mess. "I came to see you."

"Are you sure you are all right?" he demanded, his hands moving over her back and shoulders, then more carefully over her arms. He knelt and probed her ankles. "Nothing hurts?"

She held up her hand. "I scraped myself when I tried to grab the concrete."

She heard him swear under his breath. Taking her hand, he turned the palm up and moved it into the light. Then he brought the injury to his lips for a quick kiss. "It hurts. But it's not serious. You should put some antiseptic on it."

"I know."

"How long have you been down here?"

"About an hour. Maybe a little longer."

He turned toward the pile of dirt she'd accumulated. "What were you doing?"

"Trying to make a place to stand where I can reach the top."

She saw him inspect her work, then shake his head. "I'll get you out of here."

Moving away from her, he flexed his knees and jumped, his hands catching the ledge above them so that he could pull himself over the side and onto solid ground.

She stared up at him, awed by the athletic performance. Apparently he'd gotten his health back after the bout of malaria. "I'm afraid I'm not quite that strong," she told him.

"You don't have to be. I'll be back as soon as I can with a ladder or a rope or something. Wait there."

"Do I have a choice?" she asked with a shaky laugh.

He made a low sound, then turned and trotted off.

She leaned against the wall, folding her arms across her chest, paying attention to her body. Maybe she shouldn't have done all that frantic digging, she thought with a little shiver of worry. Yet she seemed to be okay, and she'd been keeping herself in good shape—doing exercises recommended for pregnancy a couple of times a week. After she told Miguel about the baby, he could make sure that everything was all right.

He was gone for a long time. When she finally saw light at the top of the pit, she turned her face upward expectantly.

"Did you find a ladder?"

"No." He sounded exasperated. "I'm going to try something else." Leaning over, he adjusted the flashlight, then motioned her to stand back.

She followed orders, and he gently tossed a wooden crate down onto the dirt. As soon as it landed, he rejoined her, then stepped on top of the box. Flexing his knees he tested the surface before bracing his back against the wall.

"I'll lift you up so you can pull yourself out," he said, beckoning her to join him on the box.

Snatching up her purse from where she'd dropped it on the ground, she slung it across her back. Miguel reached for her, boosting her to his level so that they were standing on the box—face-to-face, the position both awkward and intimate.

She heard him swallow.

"Miguel?"

"*Querida.*" His hand flattened against her back, pressing her breasts tightly to his chest. Her breath caught. So did his.

She waited for his lips to capture hers. Instead, he turned his head to the side. "I must get you out of here," he said thickly. "While I can still remember what I am supposed to be doing."

"Okay," she managed, reminding herself why they were standing like this.

"I am going to lift you—now," he said, moving his hands to her waist and thrusting upward. But he hadn't counted on her dress sliding up as he lifted her, halting her progress. She stopped several feet short of her goal, breathing hard.

For just a moment, she allowed her fingers to tangle in his hair. She heard him make a low, muffled sound. Then, shifting his grip, he pushed the fabric out of the way and cupped her hips and bottom. Before the touch could turn into a caress, he gave a mighty thrust upward with his powerful arms.

"Yes!" she exclaimed as she worked her elbows over the concrete edge. When he gave her one more push, she toppled onto solid ground.

As she lay there, he vaulted up and flopped down beside her, breathing heavily. "Did I hurt you?" he gasped out.

"No." She reached for his hand, knit her fingers with his. For long moments she lay in a patch of weeds, feeling their scratchy stems against her legs and arms. And yet, the darkness and her mood had transformed the scraggly yard into a magical place. A soft breeze had sprung up, and it sifted through her hair like caressing fingers as she stared up at the sky. It was absolutely cloudless, and the canopy of stars spread across the heavens was like diamonds on a field of black velvet. Had they ever before sparkled so brightly here in the city? she wondered as her hand tightened on Miguel's.

"Thank you," she whispered. "I was so frightened down there. And then you came, and everything was all right."

He didn't answer at once. When he spoke, the words were clipped. "It was nothing."

The flat tone of his voice sent a little shiver over her skin. Her hand tightened convulsively on his.

Stiffly, he pried his fingers free from hers and stood, making a production of brushing the dirt from his slacks.

"Miguel?" she questioned, pushing herself to a sitting position.

When he didn't respond, she tipped her head up questioningly. He'd held her, rescued her, acted as if he cared. But now…

The feeling of magic had evaporated. Standing, she stared at the lines of his face. In the beam from the flashlight, they had turned as harsh and uncompromising as those of an ancient Mayan sculpture, and she was struck by the sudden sick feeling that nothing between them would ever be the same again.

"How did you know where to find me?" he asked, slipping his hands into his pockets.

"I—" She gave a little shrug. Reaching down, she took off her shoes and shook out the dirt that had accumulated inside, using the interval to collect her scattered wits.

"Was it that little snitch, Luis? He thinks—"

"What does he think?"

When he didn't reply, she responded to his earlier comment. "He's not a snitch."

Miguel sighed. "It wasn't his place to say where I was."

"I was persuasive," she managed. "I made it sound important."

Holding her breath, she waited for him to ask what had been so urgent. But he stuck with his own agenda. "Coming here was a foolish thing to do," he chided. "You fell into that damn cistern. What if someone else had found you?"

"They didn't."

Glad that the darkness hid the sudden desolation in her features, she reached out, laid a hand on his arm. "I needed to talk to you."

"About what?" he finally asked, his voice sharp, almost angry.

She had come to tell him she was carrying his child, but as she stood there next to him, she felt the words sticking in her throat.

"Jessie, I am very grateful to you for taking me in when I was sick," he said, making it sound like that was the sum of their interaction.

She swallowed painfully. "I thought there was a little more to it than that."

"You tempted me to do something that, to be blunt, shouldn't have happened."

His answer stung her like a lash raking across her skin. "You're wrong!"

He ignored her and went on. "It was a mistake. I was lonely, and a man has needs."

At the merciless words, she gasped and tried to drag in a

breath, but an enormous weight was constricting her chest. For a long, terrible moment, she thought she was going to suffocate—or faint and give herself away.

She clenched her fists, her nails digging into her palms. The light-headedness passed, and she gasped in air. It seared her lungs like an inhalation of fire or ice.

"I thought that making love meant something to you," she whispered.

He didn't answer, and she finally understood that she had been deluding herself all along. She had been imagining a future for the three of them—herself, Miguel, and the child they had made together. But she had simply been a convenience for him. The time he'd spent with her meant no more to him than a respite from the bleak life he had been leading.

And the baby?

She simply couldn't bring herself to tell him that his reckless interlude with her had created a new life.

He stood with his arms folded across his chest, unreachable, unapproachable.

"Miguel." His name was a choked whisper.

This time she didn't expect an answer. In fact, she didn't even know why she had spoken. Sharp, searing pain knifed through her—pain more deep and lasting than any physical blow. Wincing, hoping the pain didn't show in her face, she took a quick step back, then another, before turning and stumbling across the uneven ground. All she could think was that she had to get away from this man who had hurt her in ways she hadn't imagined possible. She almost fell, caught herself, and hurried to get out of the yard—and away from him as fast and as far as she could.

HE STOOD LIKE A MAN turned into granite, watching her—wanting desperately to go to her, to catch her in his arms, pull her to him. But he didn't allow his body to act on the strong image in his mind. Instead, he stood and suffered her pain while he watched her leave. As she disappeared through the fence, he felt part of himself dying.

He had hurt her with his sharp words. The ploy had been ruthless and deliberate, because he knew that the only way he could force her to give up on the two of them was to make her think that he didn't want her.

It wasn't true. He wanted her more than he wanted his freedom; needed her as much as he needed air to breathe. Sometimes, alone at night, thinking about the time with her was the only thing that kept him from going insane. Yet he had already made too much trouble for her—with the police and the INS and Los Tigres. And the trouble would only multiply if he let things go any further.

His ears strained as he listened to her footsteps pound down the alleyway. If he hurried he could stop her. Yet he knew in his soul that sending her away was the best thing to do.

He let himself follow her only as far as the fence, shouldering his way through the boards, watching to make sure that she made it to the street with no trouble.

When he heard the sound of a car starting, he sprinted down the alley in time to see her car pull away from the curb with a jerky motion. He could see her behind the wheel, her face white, her eyes fixed straight ahead with an expression that caused a razor-sharp twisting in his gut.

Yet he told himself he had done the right thing—the honorable thing. His life was in danger. And hers would be as well if he let her get close to him again. So he stood with his insides bleeding, staring at the rapidly diminishing taillights of her car and feeling as if everything that made life worth living was fading as those lights disappeared.

Chapter Ten

As soon as she got home, Jessie called her gynecologist and told him about the fall. After a quick examination in the hospital emergency room, he assured her it looked like no damage had been done. But she still spent the next few days watching anxiously for signs of trouble. When none appeared, she finally breathed a sigh of relief. She hadn't hurt the baby with her dumb stunt.

Yet her life was hardly back to normal. She went to work and did her job. She dutifully cooked meals and ate them because she had to nourish the child growing inside her. She went through the motions of living. Yet she felt numb inside. In a way, that was a blessing. It was better than the raw pain she had felt before she'd turned and staggered away from Miguel.

Sometimes she could stand outside herself and analyze what had happened to her. She had invested too much hope in the idea of finding Miguel. She'd thought he cared about her—that he'd care about the baby. In her fantasies, she'd figuratively sung herself to sleep with a lullaby about the three of them living happily ever after. But he had shattered that lullaby as easily as he'd shattered her heart.

She'd been so terribly wrong about his feelings, and the realization was crushing. But, really, if she were brutally honest, she couldn't blame him. The time they had spent together was so short—not long enough for him to have bonded with her.

It was different for her. She had a reason to feel connected to him. But he didn't know about the baby, and she wouldn't try again to tell him—at least not until after the child was born. Then he would have a right to know that he was a father.

She should be making plans for the future, she knew. Yet she found she was incapable of anything beyond simple day-to-day survival. All she could do was get herself through each twenty-four-hour period, wondering how she was going to face the next one.

Inevitably, the days slipped past, and her body changed. By the end of the summer she was wearing extra-large-size clothes and feeling fluttery little movements inside her tummy that must be the baby kicking. They made the pregnancy take on a new kind of reality. In another four and a half months she was going to be totally responsible for another human being, and she'd better start making some important decisions.

FAR TO THE SOUTH, in San Marcos, gray clouds hung low, forming a thick, wet blanket over the landscape. And rain fell in a steady downpour that beat against the tin roof like a thousand fingers drumming in sequence. It was a warm rain that brought no relief from the endless heat. Carlos Jurado dragged a handkerchief across his damp brow, then swore softly as a fly that had worked its way through the window screen circled around his head. He swatted at it with the handkerchief and missed.

Damn insects. Damn heat. Damn rain.

He hated this place—especially his new living quarters. Yet he had chosen them for their geographic location—and for their isolation. This was where he needed to be while he prepared for his new life.

Two weeks ago he'd moved far from his comfortable estate to a backwater province near the southern border. The whitewashed stucco buildings of the jungle compound were cramped and dark. Electricity was provided by a generator that ran only eight hours a day. And drinking water had to be trucked in.

There were none of the luxuries that he appreciated so much. But it was the best accommodation he could find in a region where most of the natives lived in huts with walls of bamboo stakes and roofs of woven palm fronds. And the move was a necessary step in the process of turning himself into another man.

Ironic, he thought. He was following the example of Miguel Valero. Pulling the doctor's file from the plastic case he kept with him at all times, he riffled through the pages. A few months ago, he'd gotten his hopes up. It seemed the lead hadn't panned out; his agents hadn't found Valero yet.

But they would. Soon. The bastard couldn't hide forever.

And then Carlos Jurado would be free to disappear for good. And another man would come back to life—a man who had died ten years ago.

JESSIE WAS AT HER Light Street office when Erin Stone appeared in the doorway. Coming into the room, she closed the door behind her. The gesture was so unlike Erin that Jessie felt a tingle of alarm.

"What's wrong?" she asked.

Erin let out a long breath as she stood with her hands clasped, her back to the door. "I was just on the phone with Jim Alvarez. Has he, uh, said anything to you?"

"About what?"

Erin shook her head. "He wants me to fire you."

"What?" The paper cup Jessie was holding slipped from between her fingers and landed on the desk, splashing water all over the computer printout unfolded across her blotter. She stared down helplessly at the spreading pool.

Erin hurried forward and grabbed a wad of tissues from the box on the filing cabinets. Together she and Jessie dabbed at the water.

"What a mess," Jessie murmured, glancing quickly at her friend. From Erin's expression she knew that neither one of them was referring to the water.

"Yes." Erin wadded up the tissues and threw them into the trash.

Finally, Jessie cleared her throat. "What, uh, specific reason did he give?"

"He said you're a bad example for the women of the community."

Jessie felt her jaw clamp tight.

"You know what he's like. He's the kind of guy who insists on what he calls 'traditional values'—even when they don't quite fit the reality of today's society."

"Yes. He can be judgmental. Come to think of it, I caught him staring at me yesterday. I bet he gave you a very fulsome description of my dumpy body."

Erin laughed. "How did you guess?"

"I've heard him do it before when he was picking apart an unwed mother. Funny how a married woman never looks quite so distasteful."

A flicker of apology crossed Erin's features. "Uh, probably you should have told him you were pregnant, instead of—you know—letting him hear people gossiping about you."

Jessie sighed, knowing Erin was right. "I didn't want to talk to him or anyone else about the baby," she whispered.

"I understand. And I know what you've been going through. But he doesn't."

"And he wouldn't care if he did!"

Erin nodded. "Yeah. He reminded me that you're scheduled to teach another course for teenage girls on 'Just Saying No.' He asked me how an unmarried pregnant woman could possibly take on that assignment."

Jessie looked down at her hands, which were clasped so tightly on her desk that the knuckles were white. "I guess I don't have an answer to that," she said in a small voice. "I wasn't thinking about the course. I was trying to get through my life—one day at a time.''

Erin moved forward and put a gentle hand on her shoulder. ''I know you've been doing the best you can in a bad situation.''

''Apparently the best I can isn't good enough. I—'' She stopped, her voice cracking as she steeled herself for yet another upheaval. ''I'll give you two weeks' notice. Or you can have my resignation today, if you prefer.''

''Oh, honey, I didn't come here to get your resignation,'' Erin answered instantly. ''I just want things to work out for you. I was thinking that maybe we'd pull you out of the rec center for the time being and have you work up here at the Light Street office full-time.''

Jessie swallowed, unable to raise her eyes. She knew that if she looked into Erin's face, she'd start to cry.

''Unless you want a confrontation with Jim,'' Erin added.

Jessie shook her head, made an effort to compose herself. It was several moments before she could speak again. ''I've put you in a bad position,'' she said in a thin voice.

''I don't see it that way. You're one of our best social workers.''

''And you'll be pulling me off my cases.''

''Jessie, tell me honestly. Do you want to quit? I mean, are you finding that working full-time and being pregnant aren't compatible?''

She sighed, pushing away a lock of hair that had fallen across her face. It slipped back into its previous position the moment she moved her hand. ''It's not easy. But working keeps my mind occupied—even if I haven't exactly been giving you my best.''

Erin's hand tightened on her shoulder. ''Despite what you think, you've been doing a good job.''

''Thank you for saying that—even though I know it's not true.''

''I wouldn't lie about it. You hold yourself up to a pretty

high standard. When you slip, you slip to the level of the average office worker.''

The words were meant to be kind, but they still cut Jessie to the quick. She sat up, squared her shoulders. ''Well, I'll get back up to my previous level. I promise.''

Erin gave her a reassuring squeeze before withdrawing her hand. ''So maybe you can straighten out the mix-up with Mrs. Vargas's child-support payments. The court can't find the records.''

''Do you want me to go down there and do battle with the clerk?''

''Would you?'' Erin asked gratefully.

''Of course.'' Jessie slipped open her bottom-right desk drawer and pulled out her purse. She'd been in the dumps for the past few months. Now she vowed to get back on track.

ONCE, MIGUEL VALERO HAD been a civilized man. Now he functioned on a more primitive level, like an animal constantly on guard—even in sleep. He came awake suddenly, instantly alert as he lay in his narrow bed in a room where heavy shades blocked out the light. His eyes went to his watch. Three in the afternoon. Nobody from the barrio would come at this time.

He lay without moving, waiting. He had changed his lair twice since the night Jessie had given away the location. This week he was living in a building where the rat population was minimal. So that was probably not the source of the noise outside.

When a man-shaped shadow flickered on the other side of the window shade, Miguel's hand reached for the gun that lay beside him. Tensely, he waited for the intruder to make himself known.

''Dr. Miguel?'' a small voice called out in Spanish.

The tension eased. It wasn't a man out there. It was a boy—his head and shoulders magnified in the shadow on the shade.

There was a tap on the window. "Dr. Miguel?"

Sighing, he got up and went to the door. When he opened it, Luis darted into the room, his face partially obscured in the dimness.

"Do not sneak up on me like that! You could get hurt," Miguel advised mildly.

The kid nodded tightly, but otherwise he didn't move. Miguel motioned him closer.

"Is someone sick?"

"Not sick…"

Jurado's men had found him, he thought with a stab that was part alarm, part resignation. He'd known he shouldn't have stayed in Baltimore. But the community had kept him anchored here—and the woman he had hurt. He hadn't talked to her in months, hadn't even gone downtown to watch her from the shadows, because that would have been too painful.

His eyes focused on Luis and he saw the uncertainty on the youthful features. "I heard something today," the boy said in an almost-inaudible voice.

"Better tell me," Miguel said gently.

Luis swallowed. "It's about Senorita Douglas."

Every cell in Miguel's body was suddenly on the alert. "Is she in trouble?"

The boy shook his head, looking miserable. Obviously he didn't want to be here delivering this news. But he had come anyway, and that meant the situation was urgent.

"What?" Miguel demanded, barely restraining himself from reaching out and digging his fingers into the kid's shoulder. "Say it, whatever it is."

"I was hanging around near the offices. I heard the director talking on the phone about her to Senora Stone. He was angry." Luis swallowed, then continued, his gaze focused on a spot somewhere over Miguel's left shoulder. "He said she's setting a bad example for the community."

"A bad example? She's an angel. How could she set a bad example?"

"He said—" The boy stopped, his face bright red, then whispered, "He said that she's—she's *encinta.* And she shouldn't be working with young, impressionable girls."

"She is pregnant?" Miguel heard the shock in his own voice.

"*Sí.* Senor Alvarez said people are wagging their tongues about it. Now I know why she looked so sad."

Miguel cursed under his breath. He knew exactly when he'd made love with Jessie. In April. Four and a half months ago. Long enough for a pregnancy to be showing. Long enough for her to have told him about it—if the child was his.

He caught himself up short. Of course it was his!

A lump filled the cavity of his chest as he remembered the night almost two months ago when she'd shown up at the abandoned house where he was hiding. She'd said she'd come to talk about something important, but she'd never told him what it was, and he had assumed she'd made up an excuse to contact him. Now he pictured the stricken look in her eyes when he'd made his voice hard as stone and told her that making love with her had been a mistake—implying that he'd only been using her as an outlet for his sexual needs.

God. He had known he was hurting her by pretending he didn't care. He hadn't known exactly the degree of cruelty he'd wreaked on her. Of course, she hadn't tried to get in touch with him since then; she was carrying his child, and she thought he wouldn't give a damn.

He ran a hand through his hair. "Where is she?"

"Senor Alvarez said he didn't want her at the center. Maybe they fired her."

"Oh, no." All she had done was try to help, and he had betrayed her in the worst way a man could betray a woman.

"She could be at the other office. The one on Light Street."

He nodded, already pulling on his shoes. It was a dangerous time for him to be on the street, but the danger was secondary now. He had to go to Jessie.

"THERE'S A CALL FOR YOU or Jessie. It's urgent," Jenny Brisco said as she buzzed Erin's line.

"From the court?" Erin asked.

"No, the city jail."

"I'd better take it," Erin said, punching the button on the phone. "This is Erin Stone. Can I help you?"

"This is Craig Martin at the Baltimore City Jail. We've, uh, we've had a slipup down here, and we want to notify you."

"About what?" Erin demanded.

"Georgie Cota was accidentally released this afternoon."

"Georgie Cota. The gang leader who broke into our recreation center?"

"Yes. You might want to put on some extra security."

Erin's hand tightened on the receiver. "I can't believe this. Are you sure?"

"Unfortunately, yes."

"He was supposed to be held without bond until his trial. How was he released?"

"We're, uh, checking into that," the nervous voice on the other end of the line related.

"Maybe you want to station an officer at the center," Erin suggested.

"You'll have to speak to the police about that."

"Yes, well, thanks for the information." She hung up and reached for the phone again, hoping she could get in touch with Jessie, warn her to be careful.

Fifteen frustrating minutes later she learned that Jessie had probably left the courthouse. They thought she was on her way back to work, but they weren't positive.

MIGUEL CALLED IN A FAVOR and borrowed a van that had been brought in for repairs to the Fells Point gas station where Bernardo Contrares worked. The owner of the vehicle had been short of cash and had left it taking up space in the crowded parking area behind the station.

"Sure, you can borrow it," Bernardo told him. "Just bring it back in good shape."

"Don't worry," he replied, skidding out of the lot and heading for the garage across the alley from where Jessie worked.

After finding a parking space, he took the back elevator to the third-floor offices of the Light Street Foundation. When he stepped into the waiting room, he found a short dark-haired woman pacing back and forth.

Her head jerked up when the door opened, her expression hopeful. It changed to disappointment when she saw him.

"I'm looking for Jessie Douglas," he said.

Her eyes narrowed as she gave him a more thorough inspection. "You're too old to be one of Los Tigres. Why are you looking for Jessie?" she inquired.

He had become skilled in evading answers to direct questions. "I need to find her," he said carefully.

"Why?" The clipped syllable gave away the woman's tension, and he realized evasion wouldn't work.

"Did she talk to you about Miguel Diego?" he asked.

Her eyes narrowed. "Are you Diego?"

He gave a tight nod.

"I told myself I'd choke you if I ever came face-to-face with you. Now I don't have the time."

"You know," he said simply.

"Of course I know! She's my friend. And I also know that the city jail called an hour ago to warn her that Georgie Cota, the leader of Los Tigres, was released by accident."

He felt the hairs on his arms stand on end. "The one who attacked Jessie when she came down to help me? The one who was waiting for her at the center?"

The woman's eyes narrowed. "You know about that?"

"Yes."

"Why did you break her heart?" she asked suddenly.

He swore. "I thought I was protecting her."

She looked startled, and he knew that Jessie hadn't talked about his background.

"From what?"

"From the man who is trying to kill me. People who get close to me tend to end up dead," he said in an even voice, giving away too much. At the moment, it didn't seem to matter.

"I didn't know. I... Maybe I misjudged you."

Again, he found himself explaining. "I learned about the baby today. I came to tell Jessie I love her, that I would never have left her on her own if I had known."

"Yes. She needs to hear that." To his surprise, the woman held out her hand, and he took it. She cleared her throat. "I'm Erin Stone. If you could help me find Jessie, I'd be very relieved. She isn't at the courthouse—where she went a couple of hours ago. And she didn't go home. I left a message on her answering machine there, but I'm hoping she comes back here. We've got to get her off the streets until they take Georgie into custody again."

Well, he knew all about hiding, but he wasn't sure where to start looking. "I will get the people in the neighborhood searching for her."

"I'll go with you," Erin volunteered.

"No. You stay here in case she comes back. Keep her in the office, and tell the police. I'll check with you as soon as I can."

She raised her hand toward him, touched his arm. "We'll find her."

"Yes," he answered, but his hands clenched in frustration. Maybe this was his punishment for what he had done to the woman he loved. Before Erin could see the depth of his anguish, he turned and hurried out of the office, his mind already working on the problem of Georgie Cota. Would the bastard stop to catch his breath after his escape from the law, or would he go after Jessie the moment he had his freedom? Miguel didn't know. His only option was to get to Jessie first, he thought as he waited impatiently for the elevator to arrive.

It appeared to be stuck on a lower floor. With an angry curse, he headed for the back stairs and took them at a driving pace. In one fluid motion, he sprinted from the stairwell to the back door of the building, not even sure where he was going, where he would look, how he would protect his woman.

He spotted her as soon as he ducked under the cement ledge. She was getting out of a blue Dodge.

As she turned toward the exit, he was granted a split second of relief. "Jessie!"

She looked up, saw him, stopped in midstride, her face registering shock at his sudden reappearance in her life.

"*Querida.*" His heart was threatening to pound its way through his chest as he took a step toward her, wondering what she would say, what she would do when the look of shock faded.

But he never reached her. From the shadows, a flurry of orange-and-black-clad bodies converged on her, surrounded her, pushed her back into the car.

Chapter Eleven

He stopped dead, uncertain what to do. Every instinct urged him to leap forward, to throw himself at the car. But he couldn't stop a speeding vehicle with his body; he'd only get run over, and Georgie would make a clean getaway—with Jessie.

Jessie. His heart was pumping so wildly in his chest that he could hardly breathe as he pivoted and sprinted toward the borrowed van.

Jumping inside, he gunned the engine, planning to cut the car off before it could exit the garage. But he was too late. Or maybe Georgie had figured out his intentions. The car did a wild turn like a vehicle hitting a patch of ice.

Miguel slammed on his brakes and held his breath, praying that the car would crash against one of the concrete posts so he could get to the driver. When the vehicle spun in the opposite direction, he cursed, and cursed again as it shot the wrong way out of the entrance ramp, narrowly missing a Camaro that was about to turn into the garage.

All Miguel could do was follow, probably giving the Camaro's driver a second heart attack as he hurtled by, the paint on the two vehicles almost exchanging colors.

Unfazed, Georgie barreled down Light Street, turned left at Pratt, heading for the neighborhood, Miguel supposed, as he kept pace with the fugitives. The van didn't have as much power as the car, or as much maneuverability. But for once the rush-hour traffic was a blessing. It slowed Georgie down, and Miguel was able to slip through a light that turned red, thanking Providence that there were no traffic cops on the scene.

As they made a quick turn onto Princess Street, he studied the car and its occupants. He could detect only three people inside. Jessie sat rigidly between Georgie and another man.

When Miguel imagined her terror, his hands clenched convulsively on the wheel as if they were closing around Georgie's scrawny neck. Yet his anger was as much for himself as for the gang leader. Jessie's problems had started when she had come to his room to help him. He had brought this one on her, and he would save her now or die trying.

Did she know he was right behind her? "Jessie, I'm coming," he chanted, trying to send her a telepathic message. He doubted she was receiving it, but it helped him to keep saying it anyway. God, if he lost her now, he would go insane.

No. He couldn't think that way. He would get her back. That was the only option. But at least he knew Georgie was worried. He could see the bastard's eyes constantly flicking to the rearview mirror.

Miguel's foot pressed the accelerator to the floorboards, and he gained another few yards on the Dodge. Ahead of him, tires squealed as the car turned onto a side street lined with abandoned warehouses where there was almost no traffic, and Miguel cursed as he realized he was going to lose them if they picked up any more speed.

Again Georgie was watching his rear, not the road ahead. Too late, he snapped his attention back to his driving and had to turn the wheel sharply to the right to keep from hitting a ruined tire lying in the street. His front wheel went up on the curb, and Miguel took advantage of the precarious position to pull alongside them, crowding the Dodge farther onto the sidewalk.

He looked toward Georgie, and their eyes locked with the hatred of mortal enemies. The two were so focused on each other, that neither of them saw the low pile of boxes ahead on the sidewalk until the front end of the car was almost engulfed.

Georgie slammed on the brakes, but it was too late to stop. The Dodge struck the barrier with a shattering crash, slowing momentarily. Perhaps he thought he could plow through like a stunt driver in an action/adventure movie. Unfortunately for him, the boxes hadn't been put there by an accommodating movie crew. On the other side was a concrete barrier. The car struck it, and jolted to a halt.

Heart in his throat, Miguel was out of the van even before the vehicle had come to a complete stop. Dashing to the car, he grabbed the handle and pulled the driver's door open. Georgie was leaning over the wheel; Jessie was on the floor below the seat. The other gang member had flown forward and struck the windshield with his head.

Georgie looked dazed—probably still trying to comprehend what had happened. It seemed, however, that he was functioning well enough to reach for a gun he'd slipped onto the floor near his left foot. Before the weapon came into firing position, Miguel leaped forward. They struggled, but the younger man was in no condition for hand-to-hand combat.

Miguel wrenched the gun from his grasp. For a split second, blinding rage almost swept away his sanity and he came close to shooting the bastard at point-blank range. But somehow, rationality prevailed. He had to get Jessie away from here. That was the important thing.

Instead of shooting Georgie, he brought the butt of the revolver down on his head, punctuating the blow with a oath. Before the gang leader could slump forward over the wheel again, Miguel pushed him onto the sidewalk, then dived into the car.

"Jessie?"

She didn't answer. Tenderly, carefully, he scooped her up. She made a terrified sound when she felt his hands on her, and he soothed her with reassuring words as he lifted her from the car.

"Miguel?" She blinked at him.

"Yes. I have you. Everything's all right now."

To his relief, she relaxed against him.

He wanted to make sure she was uninjured. But not here. Somewhere in the distance he could hear police sirens. Maybe they weren't headed in this direction, but he couldn't take a chance. All he knew was that he had to get her away from the scene of the accident before the cops started asking questions.

"Miguel. Thank God," she whispered.

Cradling her in his arms, he hurried back to the van, part of his mind registering astonishment that he hadn't bashed the fender when he'd screeched to a halt. He gave a short, barking laugh.

"What's so funny?" Jessie asked in a shaky voice.

"I was thinking that maybe I'll get this vehicle back to the gas station in one piece after all."

Opening the passenger door, he laid her carefully on the middle seat. "Do you feel okay?" he asked.

She nodded uncertainly, her hand going to her head.

He moved her fingers aside and probed the spot. There was a slight bump but no bleeding. "Did you black out when the car crashed?" he asked.

"No."

"That is good," he said with heartfelt relief. Very good. It was unlikely that she had a concussion.

Moments later he was back in the driver's seat and heading down the block at a pace that wouldn't get him arrested. Jessie was still huddled on the middle seat when he pulled into the alley behind the row house. He lifted her into his arms again and took her to the basement apartment.

If ever he was granted a normal life, he'd build a house without a basement, he thought as he shifted her weight so that he could find his keys.

Inside the one room, he laid her on the low bed. He

wanted to stay with her, hold her, check her condition. But it was much too dangerous to leave the van like a beacon in the alley.

"Will you be all right for a few minutes?" he asked. "I cannot park by the back door. If Georgie sends Los Tigres looking for the van, they will find us."

"Yes. I understand," she whispered.

He would have liked to take the vehicle back to the gas station where it belonged—where no one but Bernardo would know it had been missing. That would be safest. But he wouldn't leave Jessie for that long. He settled for moving the van into a garage he knew was empty on the next block.

He ran all the way back, his breath coming in gasps as he stepped into the room. Jessie was lying on her back, staring at the ceiling, her hand flattened over the small mound of her abdomen. The hand jumped away when she heard him, but their eyes met, and he knew she knew he had seen the protective gesture.

He'd been so focused on rescue, that he hadn't thought about the reason he'd sought her out in the first place. Now he stared at the evidence of her condition. She was carrying his child. The realization slammed into him with enough impact to knock the breath from his lungs.

She sat up and turned, her features taut. He came down on his knees beside her, gathered her close, feeling fine tremors racing across her skin as she let her head sink to his shoulder.

"How do you feel?"

"Shaky," she murmured.

"You are safe here," he murmured, his hands stroking over her back, his lips moving over her hair. He wanted to turn her face, find her mouth, kiss her until both of them were gasping for breath. Instead he simply held her.

"I'm scared," she whispered. "For—for the baby." Her breath caught, and her hand went to her middle again. "This is a great way for you to find out," she said in a barely audible voice.

He drew back, his eyes finding her. "Luis told me about the phone call Alvarez made to Senora Stone."

"He did?"

"That was how I knew about Georgie. I came to your office. I came to you as soon as I knew."

A wealth of emotions flickered in her eyes—hope, relief, anger. They were banished by a kind of resignation that made his throat ache. He had driven her away, and she thought he had only come back for her because of the child.

"You are wrong," he declared.

"Wrong about what?" she demanded with a bleakness that tore at him.

"About my motives."

"I'd understand them better if you hadn't said that making love with me was a mistake," she answered in a voice edged with tears.

The accusation was like a body blow. "It was a lie. I did it—for you."

She took in the clipped explanation with a doubting expression. Wearily she said, "We can talk about it later."

"Jessie, please—"

"Miguel, I was just in a car crash! What I want from you right now is to tell me the baby is all right!"

He made an effort to pull himself together. He might be eaten up with guilt, but he understood her fear—a mother's instinctual fear for her child. He was less worried about the pregnancy than she was, because he knew that a woman's body was designed to protect her unborn child under all but the most extreme circumstances. His fingers tightened reassuringly over hers. "Chances are that everything is all right."

"Please, I have to be sure!"

"Okay. But first I have to see how *you* are."

"I don't care about that!"

"Yes, you do. Any problems you have, put the child at risk."

She nodded tightly.

He got up, retrieved the medical bag from one of the boxes on the other side of the room, feeling a bubble of anxiety grow inside his chest. He had told himself there was nothing to worry about. Now he needed to make sure. Methodically checking her helped him to stay calm. First he examined her eyes, then her reflexes as he asked her questions that would pinpoint the extent of her injuries. To his relief, she seemed in remarkably good shape.

"The baby. What about the baby?" she demanded.

"No cramping or bleeding?" he asked, his breath catching as he waited for her answer.

"No cramps. And I checked for bleeding while you were gone."

He felt as if a weight had been lifted from his chest. "Good. Lie down so I can examine you."

"An internal exam?" she asked in a shaky voice as if the intimacy would be unbearable.

"No. Just your abdomen. Lie down."

She let out a little breath as she eased back on the bed, then looked away, her bottom lip between her teeth, as he rolled up her dress and pushed down the waist of her panties, his fingers barely touching her as he moved the clothing out of the way. Yet he was vividly aware of every brush of his fingertips against her soft flesh—and of the rounded swell of her abdomen.

His child was there—in her body. A wave of tenderness and longing swept over him. He wanted to mold his hands to her in a possessive caress. Instead, he tried to remember that he was a physician with a job to do.

"Relax," he murmured. Yet he felt the unaccustomed tremor in his own hand as his palm settled over her. He hadn't been with her in months, and the lack of her had left a cruel gap in his life. Now he was touching her with an intimacy he knew she wouldn't have permitted under any other circumstances. She was letting him do this because she wanted his reassurance that their baby was unharmed.

Reverently, he moved his hands over her. Somewhere on

his long journey from San Marcos he had started to doubt the existence of God. As he touched Jessie's warm flesh, he felt a resurgence of faith. With a tremendous effort, he kept himself from lowering his face to her abdomen and kissing it. For long moments he was so choked with emotion that speech was impossible.

"Is...is everything all right?" she asked in a quivering voice, reminding him that he was supposed to be examining her—not marveling over the miracle of the new life growing inside her. A life the two of them had created together in passion—and love.

"I think everything is fine," he answered thickly, his palm flattened against her.

She gave a little nod. "Thank you."

The baby chose that instant to kick. They felt it simultaneously, their gazes colliding. For several heartbeats, neither of them spoke, yet there was no need for verbal communication. They shared this child, and he couldn't let her carry the burden alone. Tenderness overwhelmed him—a tenderness so achingly sharp that his vision blurred.

Her hand came up; her fingers slid along his. He took a steadying breath, then made the declaration that had been bursting inside him since he'd learned about the child: "We must be married."

He hadn't known the words would shatter the spell.

She sat up, pushing his hand away as she yanked down her skirt. "I'm not going to marry a man just because he has some macho idea that he has to do the honorable thing."

"That is not the reason!"

"It looks that way from here."

"I want to give the baby my name. But it is much more than that. I want both of you."

"I don't think so. I kept waiting for you to call me, and you didn't."

The hurt in her voice flayed his flesh to the bone.

"Then when I came to you—" She stopped, sucked in a strangled breath and started again. "When I came to tell you

I was pregnant, you sent me away. You made it very clear that you didn't want a relationship.''

Frustrated, he tunneled a hand through his hair. ''I was lying! I had to lie.'' When she wouldn't meet his gaze, he put his hand on her chin and tipped her face toward his. ''I wanted you with me. Every day, I have thought about being with you, holding you, making love with you. But I was afraid that something bad would happen to you if you stayed close to me.''

She stared at him. ''I don't want to argue. All I want is for you to be honest with me, for once. Are you going to tell me why you're in trouble? Are you going to tell me what's between you and Carlos Jurado?''

He felt as if he were standing on shifting sand. ''I can't.''

JESSIE LOWERED HER EYES, unable to cope with the intensity of his dark gaze. He wanted to keep her safe, keep the baby safe. She believed that much. But that was only part of the equation. He had sent her away—and come running to find her only when he'd learned she was pregnant. Apparently his code of ethics demanded that he take responsibility for his child. But he still didn't really want to be a husband.

She wasn't in good enough shape to cope with the wounded look on his face, so she stood on shaky legs and crossed to the only door in the room. Luckily, it led to a bathroom.

The space was tiny, with cracked tile on the floor and a permanent stain in the bottom of the sink. But it was clean and very neat—like the apartment where she'd gone to help him. She used the toilet, then she washed her hands and splashed water on her face before inspecting her pale image in the cracked mirror. Her eyes were red, and she looked like she'd been through the Battle of Baltimore, she thought, as she pushed her hair out of her face. It needed a good combing.

Her comb was in her purse. And the purse—

With a moan of panic, she burst out of the bathroom.

Miguel stopped in the act of pacing the room, his expression going taut.

"Are you all right?" he asked anxiously. "Did something happen?"

"My purse. It must be in the car. Georgie—"

"You dropped it in the garage," he said. "I—I couldn't stop to get it. But we can call your friend, Senora Stone."

"Yes!"

He nodded in agreement. "I can call her from the corner store—let her know you're okay."

"Yes, thanks." She wrote down the number on a piece of paper he handed her.

"There is running water here, but no electricity," he told her, sounding as if he hated to leave her in such a place.

"I'll be fine."

"Do not open the door," he warned as he folded the paper and stuffed it into the pocket of his jeans. "Pretend you are not here."

"Okay."

She watched him shift his weight from one foot to the other. Then he reached under the pillow and pulled out Luis's gun. "Do you know how to use this?"

"Yes."

"Good."

She felt goose bumps sweep over her skin as she looked from him to the gun. "You think I need this?"

"I hope not. But I think it will make us both feel better."

Not her, and not now, she thought as she laid the weapon beside her on the bed and pressed back against the wall.

As she waited for Miguel to return, scenes from the past months crowded in upon her. She wanted to make sense of them, to put them all into a nice neat pattern. But it was like a box of puzzle pieces from several different sources. And they didn't all fit together.

She felt again the raw pain she'd known when Miguel had sent her away. Still, as soon as he'd learned about the baby, he'd come to find her. And he'd risked his life to snatch her away from Georgie, she reminded herself.

Did he have feelings for her? Or was he simply trying to protect the mother of his child?

She sat there, in a kind of numb haze, until the sound of a voice reached her through the door. Blinking, she realized that it was almost dark in the room—and she hadn't even noticed. When Miguel called her name, she set down the gun with a little sigh of relief.

He came through the door, accompanied by two men she'd seen around the recreation center. One was Bernardo Contrares who coached the ten-year-old boys' basketball team.

Picking up a large camp light from the floor beside the bed, Miguel turned it on and set it on the table. Then he put the gun away.

Jessie sat up straighter, tugging at the hem of her dress, which had ridden above her knees. She could picture how she must look—with her swollen belly and her hair a mess. And sitting on Miguel's bed.

The men inclined their heads politely, and she pretended she wasn't upset at being seen like this.

"Bernardo and Ernesto are going to help us," Miguel told her.

"Thank you," she managed.

"Senora Diego," Bernardo said, nodding at her deferentially.

She blanched. Had Miguel told her they were married? Or was Bernardo simply being polite?

Her eyes locked with Miguel's for a moment, but he didn't correct the false impression.

Instead, he pivoted back to his companions, and the three of them began a conversation in Spanish—most of which was too low and too quick for her to follow. But she gathered several things. These men thought a lot of Miguel, they wanted to help him, and they were going to organize an extensive search for Georgie.

Turning to her, Miguel outlined the plan. "They will find out where Georgie is hiding. Bernardo will tell us when he is safely in custody again."

She nodded, not trusting herself to speak. She wanted to make some things very clear to Miguel, but she wasn't reckless—or unfeeling—enough to challenge him in front of these men. So she waited, her stomach churning, while they completed their discussion.

The moment they left, she stood, hands on her hips. "I'm not your wife!"

"You will be. Very soon," he informed her.

"That's a pretty arrogant assumption on your part. Did you tell Bernardo we were married?"

"No. But he knows me well. He made the *assumption* that I would take care of my woman and my child. Which I am going to do, whether you like the idea or not," he added with a gritty rasp.

"Is that a promise or a threat?"

"I have a duty to you and the baby."

"So it comes back to the pregnancy changing things in your mind," she said, hearing her voice crack. "But not enough."

"What do you mean by that?" he asked, his voice barely under control.

She raised her chin, feeling infinitely weary. "Okay, I'll spell it out very clearly, if that will make a difference. If you want to marry me, you have to tell me why you're in trouble. And you have to let me help you get your life back to normal. Otherwise, we don't have much of a future, and I might as well leave right now."

His face twisted into a complex mixture of pain and determination. There was torment in his eyes—torment that almost undid her. Yet his words offered no comfort, no compromise. "I can't! I know what Carlos Jurado will do to you if he finds you with me."

She had to look away from him. "So what kind of a marriage did you have in mind? Long-distance?" As she crossed to the door, she wondered where she would find the strength to leave him—and wondered how she was going to get home with no money and no credit cards. Yet she knew she couldn't remain here under his conditions. With a heavy heart, she opened the door and stepped into the twilight. She hadn't been lying—or bluffing. If he couldn't share his problems with her, then they had nothing to talk about.

Chapter Twelve

Jessie was halfway out the door when she felt his hand on her shoulder.

"Wait!"

Turning back, she lifted questioning eyes to him—hoping against hope.

His clipped words dashed her hopes. "I won't let you leave until I know that it is safe!"

She lifted her chin. "You can't keep me here."

"I can if I have to, but I am hoping that you are smart enough to wait. If you want to risk your own life, that's one thing. The baby is quite another."

Anger almost choked her. "Where do you get off telling me what to do for the baby?"

"It's my child as much as yours."

"Technically, maybe. But I've been dealing with the pregnancy on my own for months!"

His face contorted. "I came to you as soon as I knew," he said sharply, then added gently, "Come in. At least until we know what is happening out there."

He was right. She was so upset that she wasn't thinking straight, but she couldn't knowingly put their child in danger. Reluctantly she stepped back into the small room. It was a very small room indeed, she thought as she and Miguel eyed each other.

"You should sit down," he muttered.

There was a table with one chair, and the bed. Before she could make a choice, he pulled out the chair and sat down at the table.

Shrugging, she went back to the bed, sitting with her back against the wall again. Figuring she might as well be comfortable, she kicked off her shoes.

After several long minutes of silence, he said, "Jessie, I am trying to do the right thing."

"I know," she answered softly.

"Then you'll let me do what is best for you?"

"Only if I get to participate in the decision."

He swore, adding a couple of choice phrases to her Spanish vocabulary. "Did anyone ever tell you you were stubborn?"

"Yes. You did. The night I brought you home. Did anyone ever tell you you were a male chauvinist?"

"No."

"Somebody should have."

The silence stretched again, and she found herself twisting the edge of the sheet in her fingers. There was more she could say. She could tell him she hadn't been able to stop herself from falling in love with him. She could tell him how much she'd missed him or that she wanted their child to know and love his father. But the words were too dangerous to speak. They would only give him power over her, so she kept her lips pressed together.

When she saw him slump in his seat, she wanted so much to go to him. She stayed where she was, feeling tired and defeated. The nervous energy that had propelled her toward the door had evaporated. Now she was wrung out. From under lowered lashes she looked at Miguel. It was difficult to sit so close to him and still be apart. He was a good man, and she knew she was hurting him.

More than anything she wanted to feel the security of his arms around her. And she wanted to hold him tight. But she couldn't give in to that weakness—not on his terms. Marriage was a partnership, not a caretaker relationship. Unless he was willing to share everything with her, she knew she wouldn't be happy. So that she didn't have to watch him suffer, she leaned her head back and closed her eyes.

A low knock on the door made her jump, and she realized she must have fallen asleep. When Miguel opened the door, Bernardo stepped back inside. To Jessie's surprise, Erin Stone was right behind him.

"Erin? What are you doing here?"

"I couldn't just sit around the office doing nothing. I got Laura to wait there. Then I came out to look for you. Bernardo came to the recreation center to check in with the people there. I, uh, persuaded him to bring me here. Blind-folded, of course."

"'Blindfolded'?"

Erin laughed. "Well, not quite as cloak-and-dagger as that. But almost." She looked from Bernardo to Miguel, who stepped forward stiffly.

"Senora Stone," he said.

"I was worried about Jessie."

"She is fine."

"And safe from Los Tigres," Bernardo added. "We found Georgie and gave him a ride to the police station. The cops were very glad to see him again."

Miguel breathed out a deep sigh. *"Gracias."*

Bernardo nodded in acknowledgment. "We have put out the word that anyone who harms the *señora* will be dealt with by us," he added.

As he said *"señora,"* Erin's eyes questioned Jessie.

She shook her head. "You'd better tell them I'm still using the name Senorita Douglas," she said to Bernardo before turning quickly away to find her shoes.

"I need a ride home," she said to Erin, glad that the little room was so crowded. She was pretty sure that Miguel wasn't going to make a fuss in front of their visitors.

And she was right. Yet the brooding look in his eyes told her that he wasn't happy about being manipulated. She moved toward him and laid a hand on his arm. "We'll talk," she said in a voice meant only for him.

He answered with a curt nod. Then he reached for her and pulled her to him. Again, because there were people watching, she didn't protest. In fact, she used the excuse to hold him tightly for several heartbeats, closing her eyes and molding herself to him. He could alter her whole life now, she thought almost frantically—willing him to change his mind. But he didn't receive the silent message. Sadly, she was forced to ease away.

"Thank you," she whispered.

"Keep yourself well—and safe," he said, his voice thick.

"I will," she answered, her throat tight with pain, moisture swimming in her eyes as she eased away from him.

Jessie managed to keep from crying until she was safely inside Erin's car. Then the tears began to fill her eyes and run down her cheeks.

"I'm sorry," Erin said, finding a tissue in her purse and handing it to Jessie. "What can I do to help?"

"Just drive away before Miguel or Bernardo comes outside and sees me doing this waterfall act."

As Erin started the car and eased away from the curb, Jessie sat beside her, sobbing. It was several minutes before she could make the tears stop.

"Are you and the baby okay?" Erin asked gently. "Do you want me to take you to the emergency room or anything?"

"Miguel checked me. I'm fine," she managed, then had to stop talking because she was afraid she'd start to weep again. "I love him," she finally said in a voice that broke before she got through the short sentence.

"And he loves you."

"How do you know?"

"It's pretty obvious."

"Because?" she prompted.

"The way his voice goes soft when he talks about you. The way he looks at you. The way he held you when you said goodbye.'' Erin took her eyes from the road for a moment. ''Not to mention the way he dashed off to find you when you were in trouble.''

Erin's assessment made her heart swell.

''Besides,'' her friend continued, ''he told me.''

''He did?''

''We had a pretty intense five-minute conversation when he came to the office. I know that he's being chased by some kind of killer. I know he's afraid that you'll go down with him.''

Jessie nodded. Miguel had been surprisingly frank with Erin. ''I don't suppose he gave you any details about the man who's after him?''

''No.''

''Well, I don't know much more than you do. Miguel won't let me help him, and that's not…acceptable.''

''He's trying to protect you.''

''I know,'' Jessie practically shouted in frustration. ''That's what he keeps saying. But I can't marry him under his conditions.''

''He proposed to you?''

''Well, it was more like an order,'' she said with a little snort. ''He didn't tell me what was supposed to happen after the ceremony.''

''Why don't you ask him?''

''He won't discuss his plans. He comes from a country where the guys make the decisions, and the women live with them.''

Erin covered her hand for a minute. ''I know you're seeing this in black-and-white terms. But cut him some slack. He just found out about the baby today. And I gather he got you away from Georgie. Then he organized a citizens' patrol to get the guy off the streets. He's been busy. Maybe he hasn't thought any further ahead.''

Jessie nodded, feeling a tiny stirring of hope.

They turned into Jessie's driveway, and Erin went around

to the back of the car and unlocked the trunk—from which she pulled Jessie's pocketbook.

"You found it!"

"It was right where you dropped it."

Jessie took out her keys and unlocked the door. "Thanks for bringing me home."

"I don't know about you, but I could use a cup of herb tea," her friend said.

"Well…"

"Sit down and relax, and I'll get us each a cup."

"I don't need to be pampered," Jessie protested.

"Of course you do. You've had a hell of an afternoon. You want cranberry, right?"

"Yes," she answered as she dropped onto the sofa, leaned her head against the cushions, and closed her eyes. She could hear Erin in the kitchen, and for just a moment she let herself indulge in the fantasy that it was Miguel out there. The weak, scared part of her wished she could simply have accepted his terms. But that wasn't the kind of relationship she could live with—not after the disaster of her first marriage.

Her friend came into the living room with two mugs of tea. Jessie cradled the warm cup in her hand, absorbing the heat into her fingers. Erin took several sips, then proposed, "Why don't you take it easy for a couple of days? Take some sick leave," she suggested.

"No. I'll go crazy. Maybe I can sleep late tomorrow and come to work in the afternoon."

"How are you going to get to the office?" Erin asked.

Jessie stared at her friend, then pressed her fingers against her mouth as she remembered that her car had plowed into a cement wall. She made an unladylike exclamation. "You're right, I don't know if my car is in working condition. Or if the police have it. I guess I need a rental. And I need to contact my insurance company."

"So take tomorrow off," Erin suggested again, "and get things straightened out."

"We'll see."

"Just remember that your friends are here for you any way you need us," Erin told her.

Too overwhelmed to speak, Jessie nodded her thanks.

THE CAR HAD BEEN TOWED to the police lot, and the insurance company declared it totaled. Jessie used some of her trust-fund money to replace it with a Volvo, figuring a nice sturdy car would be safest for the baby.

As Erin had predicted, she had a lot to keep her occupied. But a kind of compulsion was forming in her mind and wouldn't let go. Miguel didn't want to burden her with his problems. What if she could learn something on her own? If she came to him with what she knew, he'd have no reason for secrecy. He'd have to let her help him get out of trouble.

The thought rattled around in her mind, filling her with hope and a kind of sick dread. Suppose it turned out that Miguel had been lying to her all along? Suppose he was a criminal, and he was afraid that she'd get him arrested?

It couldn't be true, she told herself. She knew him too well. He was honest and honorable, and he was caught in a terrible situation that wasn't his fault. She wanted that to be true—so much. Yet, at the same time, she was angry with him for deserting her.

If things had been different, she would have turned to her friends at Randolph Security—Jed Prentiss, in particular. He'd been to San Marcos, and he had contacts down there. Yet she didn't want to share her doubts with him, and she found she was too proud to let anyone know how much she was suffering over Miguel's rejection.

So she needed another source of information. She wasn't sure what it might be until she remembered Donna Russell. Donna had been a Spanish major with her at university and had taken a job at the Organization of American Nations in Washington, D.C. Perhaps she'd know how to get some information.

"Jessie!" her friend said when she got her on the phone.

"This is a nice surprise. I haven't heard from you in months. Are you in town?"

"No. I'm in Baltimore."

"Still with the Light Street Foundation?"

"Yes."

"Everything going okay?"

"Fine," she managed, knowing she wasn't emotionally strong enough to bare her problems at the moment. Instead she paused and took a steadying breath. Making up stories went against her principles, but she knew she had to be circumspect. If she asked for information about Miguel, it could direct attention toward him. She could try another approach, however. "I was wondering if you can do me a favor. And keep it confidential."

"What kind of favor?" Donna asked cautiously.

"I need some information on a man in San Marcos. Carlos Jurado."

"In what context?"

"One of my clients mentioned him. I think she, uh, had some trouble with him before she came to the States. And I'd like to find out about the man."

There were a few moments of silence at the other end of the line. "His name doesn't ring a bell right offhand. But I can do some research."

"I'd appreciate it."

"I'll send you what I dig up. Or you could come to D.C. and have lunch with me," Donna suggested.

The offer was tempting. She liked Donna, and it would be good to get away. But then her friend would see that she was pregnant, and it would be impossible to avoid questions. So she begged off, and they chatted for a few minutes before she hung up.

Donna faxed her some material later in the day at work— newspaper articles and a listing in the San Marcos equivalent of *Who's Who*.

Jessie's hands were shaking as she sifted through the stack of papers. Jurado must be important or there wouldn't have been so much information on him that Donna could put her hands on so quickly.

Apparently he was a businessman, now in his early fifties, who had cultivated a wide range of interests in San Marcos and in other Latin American countries over the years. He was from a wealthy family, and, at first, he had let his father run the show. But in his thirties Carlos had fought the older man for control of the Jurado interests. He had won, and the elder Jurado had died of a heart attack a few months later.

After that, Carlos had gone about systematically taking over other companies. Sometimes he dismantled them. Sometimes he ran them into the ground. Sometimes he sold them at a profit.

There was no editorial comment in the newspaper stories, but Jessie gathered that the man was ruthless. Several articles from a magazine published in Florida speculated that Carlos might have invested some of his fortune in the drug trade. From San Marcos sources she learned that he had dropped out of sight almost a year ago. There was speculation that he might have been murdered.

Jessie felt the hairs on the back of her neck stir. Had Miguel killed him, and now Jurado's friends were after him? But in her heart she knew Miguel wasn't capable of murder.

Sighing, she told herself that she was letting her imagination run wild. She had been hoping for some startling revelation about Jurado, but she knew little more than she had at the very beginning. Jurado must have a secret that Miguel had found out. But what could it be?

Feeling defeated and alone, Jessie sat staring into space. She'd just wasted a bunch of time on speculation that could lead nowhere. And she was no closer to knowing what had happened to Miguel.

The next morning she made a concerted effort to focus on her job. But right after lunch she was distracted again by a list of requests for data on students who had applied for Light Street Foundation fellowships.

The information was in the files at the recreation center.

Knowing she was too restless to sit at her desk, she decided to go over and pull the folders herself. But as she drove toward the neighborhood, her stomach began to do a nervous little dance as she pictured herself running into Jim Alvarez.

When she parked and walked to the door, she saw a car pass on the street and recognized Bernardo. She had noticed him behind her several times since the kidnapping—him and several other men. Either Miguel had asked them to keep an eye on her, or they had taken it upon themselves. But she didn't know for sure, because nobody had told her. Certainly not Miguel. She hadn't heard from him since the day he'd found out about the baby, and the silence was driving her crazy. She'd thought he'd make another argument for marriage. Instead, he'd let her stew—which was turning out to be an all-too-effective tactic.

She tried to drive him from her mind as she pushed open the door of the recreation center. Inside, a girl named Maria was just stepping out of the gym.

"Senorita Douglas. Where have you been?"

"Working at the Light Street office."

"We miss you."

"I miss you, too."

Maria's gaze dropped to Jessie's belly, which was now the most prominent part of her anatomy. "Are you going to have a boy or a girl?"

"A boy." In fact, she'd had a sonogram appointment this week. For the first time, she'd asked the baby's sex. So now she knew, and she longed to tell Miguel about his son. But she wasn't going to use that as an excuse to get in touch with him. She'd gone that route once. And once was enough.

She didn't realize her face had twisted into a grimace until Maria's expression filled with alarm.

"Are you all right?" the girl asked anxiously.

"Yes."

"Well, good luck."

"Thanks," she answered, thinking that the girl didn't

seem particularly disturbed by her marital status. Maybe Jim had had a chance to get used to the idea.

Still, she was unable to shake the feeling of being an intruder as she opened a file drawer and began to search for names on the list of candidates. She had been working for about twenty minutes when she sensed that someone was standing behind her. Turning, she saw Jim filling the doorway, his gaze far from friendly.

"What are you doing here?" he asked.

She took a step back, resisting the urge to fold her arms protectively across her middle. "I'm getting some materials I need, so Erin and the committee can make scholarship recommendations."

"You could have called over and had the folders sent."

"Since I know the filing system, I thought it would be more efficient to do it myself."

He shifted his weight uncertainly from one foot to the other. "I assumed you wouldn't be back."

"I've been busy since you contacted Erin. But I've been thinking that we do need to talk," she answered.

He had the grace to look uncomfortable. "About what?"

"About your trying to get me fired."

He straightened his shoulders. "I wouldn't exactly put it that way."

"That was how Erin related your conversation to me," she replied in a sharper voice than she'd intended.

The color in his cheeks heightened, and she realized that she'd made a mistake. She hadn't wanted to be so confrontational, but the words had slipped out.

"Jim, I—"

He cut her off before she could say anything more. "Well, since you insist on putting it in those terms, I'd like to clarify my position. I know you think I'm the bad guy here, but I was hired by the Light Street Foundation to serve this community, and I've done that to the best of my ability. That includes making staff recommendations. Everybody here is a role model first and foremost. Each of us has to set an example for the community, and unfortunately, your unmarried pregnancy sends a message to our young, impressionable girls that having a baby out of wedlock is a perfectly acceptable alternative to the traditional family.''

''There's a big difference between a responsible adult and a teenage girl,'' she told him.

He dismissed the argument with a wave of his hand. ''I happen to think that children raised by a single mother lack the stable environment provided by a two-parent family. And that isn't even taking economic hardship into consideration.''

''My child won't suffer any economic hardship,'' Jessie retorted.

''That's only part of the problem,'' Jim countered. ''The moral example is far more relevant.''

Her face stung—from the tone of his voice as much as from his words. Looking away, she focused on the folders in her hand.

Before she could come up with a response, he added a piece of unsolicited advice: ''If you know who the father is, you should ask him to marry you.''

''What do you mean—*if* I know?'' she managed, so stunned that she could hardly think.

''Of course she knows,'' a voice came from behind her— a voice edged with outrage.

''Miguel!''

She hadn't seen him in days, and the reality of his presence made her knees weak. He had told her he didn't go out during the day. But he had done it again—for her. He was here, at the rec center—a place he had avoided for months.

He stepped into the room, his eyes glittering as he moved to Jessie's side and put his arm protectively around her, declaring without words that this was his woman.

Jim stared at him, his face taking on a speculative look. ''Dr. Diego. I haven't seen you recently.''

''I have been around.''

The two men regarded each other across several feet of charged space.

Miguel's free hand tightened into a fist, and Jessie remembered yesterday that she'd been wondering if he'd done something to Carlos Jurado.

"Don't," she whispered, her fingers closing on his arm, tugging gently.

She held her breath, feeling his anger radiate through the room. Then he turned dismissively away from the other man, his expression softening considerably as he looked at her. "You don't have to stay here and listen to him insult you."

"I guess not."

"Come on."

She let him lead her toward the door, then out of the building where the sunlight made her blink. Without hesitation he steered her toward her new car. Either he'd seen it before, or Bernardo had described it to him.

"Give me your keys."

"I can drive."

"I know. You are very independent. But it is easier for me right now if I don't have to give you directions," he said in a tight voice.

Fumbling in her purse, she found the keys and handed them over. "Where are we going?"

"Where we can be alone."

She wanted him to explain, but he was absolutely silent, his face grim as he drove out of the parking lot. All she could tell was that he was holding his emotions under tight control.

She had assumed he would be heading to the house where he'd brought her the week before. Instead, he drove several miles in the other direction and turned into an alley behind a row of well-kept brick houses. After pulling into a garage and locking the car, he led her across a large patio bordered by flowers and through a back door.

"Where are we?" she asked as she looked around at the expensively remodeled kitchen. Whoever owned this place had money.

"At the home of a friend, Tony Marco. He's away on vacation—which is lucky for us."

Miguel methodically locked the door behind them, then stood very still, his hands clenched at his sides as he stared out.

She felt as if the silence in the room might shatter her. "Miguel?"

When he turned toward her, she saw the look of desperation on his face.

"I tried to do the right thing," he said thickly. "But I need you. More than you can ever know."

Chapter Thirteen

His words as he reached for her were soft and pleading. "I love you. Was it wrong to try and protect you from the danger of getting too close to me?"

She didn't know how to answer the question—not when his face was so full of sadness and longing. "I'm already close to you. And you know it." Trembling, she held out her arms to him.

With a low sound of need, he gathered her to him, rocked her, held her tightly.

"My love. Oh, my love," she murmured, the words ending in a broken sob as she laid her head against his shoulder, letting go of the worst of the tension that had tied her in knots. Finally he had made it safe for her to say what had been locked in her heart for so long.

"I don't think I can go on without you. Do not leave me again," he gasped out even as his arms tightened around her.

"No. No, I won't."

He lowered his mouth, kissing her with a hunger she felt to the marrow of her bones. His hands shook as they caressed her back, combed through the blond strands of her hair. And hers were no steadier as she touched the corded muscles of his arms, buried her fingers in his shaggy dark hair. She still could hardly believe this was happening, and yet the feel of his hard body anchored her to reality.

"Holding you again is like being in heaven," he told her in a hoarse whisper, his hands making small circles on her back.

"Yes."

"I almost went crazy when you walked away from me."

"So did I."

He cradled her hips against him, and desire rose within her in a sharp, swift tide, like a river overflowing its banks. She heard herself moan as his hands cupped the weight of her breasts. When he found their hardened tips with his thumbs, she thought she would go mad with the pleasure of it.

"You want me," he growled, the satisfaction in his voice pulling her back toward sanity.

"Yes."

He took her hand and led her down the hall to a small den furnished with a comfortable-looking daybed. When he started to pull her onto the bed, she stopped him with as much conviction as she could muster.

He raised his head, his eyes questioning hers.

"Miguel, I'm not going to let either one of us duck the important issues. We're going to talk—really talk—before we...before we do anything else."

"Is that what you want?" he asked in a gritty voice.

"No." She managed a regretful little smile. "But that's the way it's going to be."

The tone of her voice must have convinced him, because he signed in resignation. "All right. But don't deny me the comfort of holding you close to me."

She couldn't deny herself that comfort, and she knew he saw the acquiescence in her face.

He lay down, moving so that his back was against the bolsters as he held out his arms to her. She lowered herself beside him, burrowing into his warmth, pressing her lips against his neck and then his cheek.

His hand slid possessively over her abdomen, his palm cupping their child with a tenderness that made it impossible for her to draw in a full breath. Gently, in response, she covered his hand with hers, holding his palm against her through the thin fabric of her dress.

"God, I wish I had known," he whispered, his voice husky. "You must have had a bad time—alone, carrying my baby. Dealing with people like Jim Alvarez."

"Most people aren't like Alvarez. My friends have been very supportive."

"I should have been standing beside you all these months.... I would have—"

"You would have come for me?"

"Yes." There was conviction in his voice. Remorse.

Under his hand, the baby shifted in her womb, and she heard Miguel's uneven breath catch in his throat.

"I found out this week, we're going to have a boy," she said.

"You are giving me a son!"

"Would you have been disappointed with a girl?"

"A son means a great deal to me, but I would have loved a daughter, too."

"Next time," she answered.

When he tipped her head up and moved his lips back and forth against hers, she gave a shuddering sigh. Then he angled his mouth, tasting her more fully, his hand moving upward to find her breast, and she realized she was in serious danger of postponing their discussion.

She loved him too much, though, to let it happen. She had to know what had turned him into a fugitive, and she had to change the way he thought of their relationship. They had to be partners, equals, if they were going to survive this crisis and build a life together. So she folded her fingers around his hand, brought it to her lips, and kissed his fingers before murmuring, "Tell me what happened to you. I mean, tell me why you're in hiding."

His eyes blinked open, met hers. "You can be cruel."

"We'll both be glad when we get the telling over with," she replied.

"Maybe." He shifted them to a sitting position, so that her back was to his chest and his arms were around her. Dragging in a sharp breath, he let it out in a rush like a man resigned to his fate. "All right. Do you know I am a plastic surgeon?"

She shook her head, hardly daring to breathe. Was he finally going to tell her the truth?

"Last year I operated on a man who told me he was being hunted by government agents for something he didn't do. He said the only escape for him was to change his face. He brought me a sketch of the way he wanted to look. It was a picture of his cousin who had died a year earlier. He said he could pass for this relative—assume his identity."

"You operated on him?" she asked.

"Yes. At my clinic. It was in a nice secluded location in San Marcos. Rich people from Central America and Mexico and even the U.S. came to me to be fixed up. I charged them big fees and used the money to finance the treatment of some charity patients. But I also had a very comfortable lifestyle."

"There's nothing wrong with being comfortable."

"I enjoyed my success. I enjoyed my skill. I thought I was set for life. Then, three days after the operation on—"

"You already told me his name. Carlos Jurado."

"Yes. I did not know it when he came to me. I found out later."

When he didn't continue, she prompted, "'Three days after the operation—'"

His fingers clamped on hers in a death grip as he spoke again. "He came back to the clinic with a squad of men and murdered everybody in the compound. My staff. My sister, Anna, who was working for me. My patients. Anyone who might have seen him—before and after. I was picking up a shipment of medicine from the airport, or I would be dead, too."

She shifted in his embrace, turning so that one arm could tighten around him while she tunneled her other hand through his hair, cradling his head against her breast as she struggled to take it in. "No," was all she could manage.

He was shaking now. When she raised her head, she saw that his face was a mask of pain and horror—a mirror of the pain and horror he must have felt on that terrible day.

"Oh, God, it must have been unbearable. Coming back to that."

He pressed his face into the back of her neck, and she knew he must be trying to blot out the terrible vision.

"You still dream about it, don't you?" she whispered, remembering his fevered nightmares during the malaria attack and wishing she could do more than simply hold him tight. Now she understood.

After a long time he said, "I got away. Sometimes I think I should be dead, too. It was my fault, my arrogance that killed all those people."

"No!"

He ignored her and went on. "Other times I tell myself I have to stay alive so I can make Jurado pay for what he did."

She wanted to tell him he was safe here. She didn't know if it was true. Jurado was a powerful man. She had learned that from her reading.

"His men followed me north. They almost got me in Mexico. After that—" He stopped again, gulped in air. "After that, I operated on my face."

"You what?"

"I changed the way I look," he said, his voice low and even.

"Miguel!" She heard the words, but had trouble taking in their meaning. She'd known he was on the run; she hadn't guessed the level of his desperation—or his resolve. Her hand went to his cheek as she tried to see what he had done to himself. When she couldn't discern the results, she stroked her fingers gently against his flesh, as if her touch might still be painful. "How could you do that to yourself? Didn't it—" She gulped. "Didn't it hurt?"

He gave a curt nod. "It was painful but necessary. It threw them off my trail for a while. They were looking for me in Florida, but they didn't know it was me. Then I found out Jurado's agents were talking to people I had known in the Washington, D.C., area. And to men who had gone to medical school with me. He offered a lot of money for information. He could have someone in Baltimore right now. He has been hunting me for almost a year. I do not think he is going to give up."

"But why? You're out of his way."

He swallowed. "I have had a lot of time to think about it. If he simply wanted to disappear, that would be one thing. He must have some public role in mind. And the only person who knows about his new face is a fool of a doctor named Miguel—" He paused, his eyes burning into hers. "Miguel Valero. That is my real name. No one else in Baltimore knows it, but I am telling it to you."

She nodded slowly, overwhelmed by the act of trust. "It's a good name."

"I'm afraid it has also become a dangerous name." She saw him swallow. "I long to give my son that name. But I think I will not be doing him a favor."

"Yes, you will!"

His dark gaze bored into her. "You sound so positive. Does that mean you will marry me?"

She had spoken without realizing the implication of her words. Now she felt a shiver race over her skin. "You came back to me because of the baby."

His eyes never left her as he said, "Yes. I walked away from you because I knew I was making you vulnerable to Jurado. Then I found out about the baby, and I was happy that I had an excuse to marry you. When you turned me down, I…I almost went out of my mind. I want to make you an honest woman. But I want a lot more than that. I need you more than I need air to breathe. Without you, I have been only half alive."

The words wrapped themselves around her, sank into her heart. "Yes," she said, meaning the same thing.

"If...if you did not carry my child, would you still want to marry me?" he asked in a low voice.

"Yes. I love you."

"But you have seen me at my worst!"

She stroked her fingers against his cheek. "Yes, I saw you at your worst—when you were sick. But I've also seen your best qualities, your sense of honor and duty. Your warmth. Your loyalty to the people. Every time you have a choice, you put others before yourself."

There was still tension in his arms and shoulders. "Not always. My motives toward you weren't so pure. I was reckless with you," he ground out. "I knew making love without protection was taking a chance. But I did it anyway. I wanted you too much to stop."

"That's not all *your* fault. I was taking the same chance," she replied, her eyes steady on his. "What happened between us five months ago was very intense. Not just making love—all of it. But I kept being afraid that you were going to walk away from me." She swallowed, determined that she would be completely honest. "Maybe in a tiny corner of my mind I was thinking that if I got pregnant, you'd have to stay."

His expression eased a little as he considered that.

"And it turned out all right," she said in a shaky voice.

"Truly? You are happy to be carrying our son?"

"Yes."

The look of love on his face touched her soul, and she felt the last barrier between them drop away. He folded her close, gave her a fierce kiss that might have started as an act of possession. It quickly changed to passion. His hands moved greedily over her, caressing her breasts and the gentle curve of her abdomen. Her own hands were no less ravenous. It had been so long since she'd touched him like this. She couldn't stop herself from running her fingers over his face, the hard muscles of his arms, his back.

He tossed the bolsters onto the floor to make more room on the bed, then sighed in pure pleasure as he brought her down to lie beside him.

"*Querida.* My angel," he gasped out as he undid the top button of her dress so he could press his lips to the warm hollow at the base of her throat. She murmured his name, her voice high and breathless as her body tuned itself to his touch. Yet, when he undid the rest of the buttons and started to pull the dress upward, her hand caught his.

His eyes questioned hers. "You don't want to?"

"Miguel, you haven't seen me in months. My body's changed a lot. I look—" her gaze slid away from him "—like a whale. And my nipples are so dark."

He planted a light kiss on her lips. "To me, you look very beautiful." His mouth traveled to the vee between her breasts. "Very feminine." His head turned one way and then the other, kissing the inside curve of each breast. "Very desirable." Hooking a finger under the edge of her bra, he pushed one cup out of the way, baring her nipple, which he delicately circled with his tongue.

"Oh!" she cried out as a small shock wave rippled through her.

When his lips closed around her and he began to suck, she cried out again as the ripples came faster, higher.

"I need more of you," he said in a thick voice. "Twice as much."

She could deny him nothing. At her little nod, he pulled her up, eased the dress over her head, and tossed it onto the brass railing at the end of the daybed. Then, while she was still leaning against him, he unsnapped the clasp of her bra and pulled it out of the way.

She wanted to stay close against him, but he eased her back so that he could take the weight of her breasts in his hands, stroking them as he bent to bring his lips first to one distended nipple and then the other.

"You look like an ancient goddess," he murmured, his voice rough as he pushed her panties out of the way. Then his lips were on the swollen mound of her abdomen, kissing her there as his fingers drifted lower to find the moist heat at her center.

She arched into the caress, helpless to stop herself from crying out at the pleasure of his touch.

When he raised his head, his eyes burned into hers. Then he stood to quickly discard his own clothing. As he turned to face her, she saw very clearly that her body pleased him.

Handling her like fragile silk, he stretched his length along hers and gathered her to him. "To be with you like this again is a miracle," he murmured.

"Oh, yes," she said, watching as his hand moved over her lovingly, touching all the places that kindled a fire inside her.

She felt the hunger in him when his mouth came back to hers. Yet he was gentle, oh, so gentle, as he drove her upward to a higher plateau of pleasure.

"Please, I need you," she gasped.

"Yes." Rising above her, he positioned himself between her legs. Then, slowly, carefully, he eased inside her, supporting his weight on his elbows as he gazed down at her.

"All right?" he asked.

"Perfect," she answered, looking up at him, reaching to tenderly touch his lips with her index finger.

She shattered almost as soon as he began to move within her, then climbed with him again—up, up, up and over the moon. She cried out his name as she shattered once more into a shower of brilliant shooting stars, then felt him follow her into the heavens, felt his body stiffen as he shouted out his satisfaction.

EXHAUSTED, JESSIE SLEPT, coming back to consciousness only when Miguel got up to bring a quilt and cover them. Then she nestled back into his arms, finding his hand and holding it tightly.

It was dark when she finally awoke, disoriented until she felt him beside her.

He turned his head to kiss her.

"Have you been awake long?" she asked.

"Long enough."

She sensed the disquiet in his voice. "What's wrong?"

"I was lying here thinking."

When he offered no more, she found his hand under the covers again. "Tell me," she whispered. "Whatever it is, we'll face it together."

She heard him swallow in the darkness as his thumb stroked her palm. "Being like this with you is like a dream come true, but if something happens to you and the child because of me, I will never forgive myself."

"Nothing's going to happen!"

"Jessie, I have been living like a fugitive for a long time. I know that at any moment Jurado's men could find me. If they do, and you are with me…" His voice trailed off.

"That sounds like you're getting ready to leave me again," she said with a catch in her voice. "I thought we agreed to get married." Sitting up, she fumbled for the brass lamp she'd seen on the table beside the bed. When she switched it on, they both blinked against the light.

"Jessie, I want you as my wife. But if you live with me, Jurado will be after you, too. I can't risk that. Or risk the child."

She swallowed. "What do you have in mind?"

"I did some research on marriage licenses," he said. "We must get married in a small county—far from Baltimore, where the records will be buried. Then you will live as you have before, as Senorita Douglas. And I will come to you when I can." He sighed. "I do not like it. I want the world to know that you are my wife. But I cannot see an alternative."

She didn't like it, either. But for the time being, she knew he was right. "We have to find out what Jurado is up to—and have him arrested."

He laughed harshly. "That will be difficult. If I set foot in San Marcos, I am the one who will be arrested—or killed.

He made it look like I was responsible for the massacre at the clinic. I read the story he planted in the papers. It told how Dr. Valero got mixed up in the drug trade and ordered a cover-up.'' He finished with a sound that was half curse, half snarl.

Her hands tightened on his arms. "That's crazy."

He shrugged. "He has great wealth. He can buy reporters as easily as he can buy a new face."

She struggled to keep her voice calm and reassuring, even as she wavered between optimism and despair. "Remember when I first brought you to my house, I told you that I had friends who could help? Well, it happens that one of them is a man named Jed Prentiss. He's been to San Marcos. At one time, he trained troops for General Sanchez. Then he and my friend Marci had to escape from the general. Jed knows his way around your country—I mean, he knows the geography and the politics. And President Palmeriz owes him a favor. If you can't go down there, he can."

Miguel stared at her as if he had trouble comprehending.

"It's true," she whispered. "He can help get Jurado arrested."

The expression on his face made her chest tighten. He looked as if he was afraid to hope, yet he wanted to so badly.

"Jed works for Randolph Security," she continued. "And so do some of my other friends. They've pulled off some pretty tricky operations."

"They would help me?" he asked in a gritty voice.

"Yes. The sooner I call them, the sooner we can get something going." She started to climb out of bed, then remembered she was naked. Her dress was where Miguel had draped it over the railing at the edge of the bed. Slipping it on, she made a stop at the bathroom, then called Jed.

"He'll meet us tomorrow afternoon. At my house," she said. "So we have a lot of time between now and then to make love."

His eyes glittered. "Do we?"

"Yes. But your pregnant fiancée has to eat first. Did the guy who lent you this house leave any food?"

Miguel laughed. "Tony's refrigerator is kind of bare—except for beer. But one of the women from the neighborhood gave me a chicken casserole when I took care of her little boy."

She tipped her head to one side. "The women feed you?"

"Sometimes."

"Well, you'll have to tell them your wife is taking over the job."

"Yes. My wife," he said with a thickness in his voice that made her forget about eating and reach for him.

JED AND HUNTER BOTH came to Jessie's house the next afternoon. She watched Miguel size them up, then, with a little encouragement, relate the same story that he'd told her. The men were more thorough about getting pertinent details than she had been.

"It sounds as if Jurado is up to something big," Jed agreed with Miguel's assessment.

Hunter silently nodded.

"I, uh, had a friend of mine, Donna Russell, who works at the Organization of American Nations look him up," Jessie interjected. "There wasn't any hint of what he's planning."

All eyes swung toward her. "You did not mention that before. When was it?" Miguel demanded in a sharp voice.

"After Georgie. When you still wouldn't tell me anything. I thought if I could find out something for myself, I could get you to tell me the rest."

Their eyes locked. "I would have appreciated knowing," he said, his words clipped.

"I didn't learn anything significant," she answered. "He's a businessman who pushed his father out of the management of the family company. And he may be involved in the drug trade, according to a magazine published in Miami."

"An excellent way for a man like him to invest his money," Miguel observed with an edge in his voice.

"I can go down there at the end of the week and start poking around," Jed volunteered, and Jessie was grateful that he had stepped back into the conversation.

Miguel looked uncomfortable. "Until I can get to my bank accounts, I don't have the funds to pay for a trip like that."

"We've got discretionary money we can use."

When Miguel tried to protest, Jed shook his head. "There's other stuff we should discuss. Like, for example, it complicates your situation, being in the country illegally. If the INS finds out where you are, they can send you back to San Marcos—where you'd be vulnerable to Jurado."

"Technically, I am not illegal," Miguel said. "My mother was an American. So I am an American citizen."

"Thank God for that," Jessie breathed.

Miguel gave a little shake of his head. "The problem at the moment is that I can't reveal my true name. And I can't send to Santa Isabella for any of my records."

Still, Jessie felt a sense of relief. "Can you get a copy of Miguel's birth certificate while you're in San Marcos?" she asked Jed. "And other papers that would prove his identity, like his driving record or credentials from the medical society?"

"I hope so."

"Good."

Hunter cleared his throat. "Do you have any proof that you operated on Jurado and changed his appearance?"

"You do not believe me?"

"Of course I do," Hunter said evenly. "But I'm not the one you have to convince."

Miguel closed his eyes and rubbed his fingers wearily against the bridge of his nose. "I had proof at the clinic. Before-and-after pictures. I am sure that if he went to the trouble of killing everyone in sight, though, he would also have destroyed the photographs."

Jed nodded as his pen hovered over a blank page in the notebook he'd brought. "I'll check, just in case. Give me the location of the clinic."

They went on to explore other options for proving Miguel's claim, but nobody could come up with an easy answer. At the end of the meeting, Miguel thanked the men. When they had left, however, she found him staring at her with an expression that made her feel uncomfortable. "You should have told me about your friend," he said.

He didn't have to clarify the observation. She knew that he was talking about Donna. "It didn't seem important."

"It was important," he disagreed, emphasizing every word carefully.

"I meant, because I didn't find out anything."

"Jurado has considerable resources. He may have an informant at the OAN. Or he may be watching for his name to come up in any unusual context. I told you, he had men looking for me in Washington, D.C."

Jessie's bottom lip quivered. "You didn't ask for the information. I did."

"How do you know this person—Donna Russell?"

"She's a friend from college. I told her one of my clients—a woman—might have been mixed up with Jurado in San Marcos."

He took in the explanation with narrowed eyes. "What if they trace the request back to you—and then to me?"

She stared at him helplessly. "Isn't that pretty farfetched?"

"I've been through a lot on Jurado's account. And I have come to expect the unexpected from him. You should have talked to me before doing anything that rash."

"You were the one who wouldn't talk to *me*," Jessie protested defensively. "I didn't know what to think. I couldn't just sit around waiting for you to change your mind about trusting me. I had to do something."

He nodded tightly. "Have you done anything else that might compromise me?"

Hurt welled up inside her. "Besides getting pregnant?"

He didn't answer, and she didn't want him to see the tears clouding her vision. Stiffly, she turned and walked down the hall to her bedroom. He didn't follow.

Chapter Fourteen

Jessie sat on the bed with her fist pressed against her mouth, her teeth digging into the side of her finger as she struggled for control, but she couldn't keep tears from trickling down her cheeks. She had thought she and Miguel had come to an understanding. Now it seemed that understanding was just wishful thinking. Or were they simply living in two separate fantasy worlds?

All at once she heard Miguel's voice from down the hall. She thought he was speaking to her and hastily wiped her eyes. When she didn't hear his footsteps outside the bedroom, she realized he was on the phone—and speaking too low for her to make out what he was saying.

When all was silent again, she rolled onto her side, her hand cradling her child protectively through the fabric of her summer dress. She wanted to be strong for the baby. Instead, she felt fragile. Brittle.

''Jessie?''

Miguel's voice made her stiffen. Hastily she pushed herself up and ran a hand through her hair. ''Come in,'' she called softly as she slid her feet to the floor.

He filled the doorway, and she tangled her fingers in the bedspread, needing to hold on to something solid as she waited for him to step into the room. He did, but he didn't come over to her. Questioningly, she raised her eyes to his.

''I have to leave, Jessie.''

"Not yet. We need to talk," she managed, glad that she somehow kept her voice from cracking.

His face contorted. "We cannot do it now. When I checked with Ernesto, I learned there is a woman who is very sick. I must go and find out what is wrong."

She wanted to beg him to stay so they wouldn't part with this uncertainty between them, but she knew he took his obligations seriously. "When will I see you again?"

"I cannot say, exactly. I will come at night, when it is safest. Later in the week. The best thing is not to keep a regular schedule, so no one will know where I will be next."

"Will you be at the house where you took me yesterday?"

"Only for tonight. Then Tony will be coming home. I must move again. Probably to a place that isn't quite so nice."

"Is there a phone number where I can reach you?"

"The gas station where Bernardo works." He gave her the number. "But do not use it unless it is very important. It is safer if I contact you," he said wearily.

She gave a little nod, not particularly liking the feeling of being caught in the middle of a spy movie. Yet she couldn't suggest a better alternative to his carefully worked out arrangements. He was still in danger. Maybe she really had made things worse by her hasty call to Donna Russell.

She swallowed painfully. "Miguel, I'm sorry about calling my friend at the OAN."

"You did what you had to do," he answered in a gritty voice.

She looked down at her hands. A few hours ago she had felt so comfortable with him. Now they were both on edge. Uncertain.

"I didn't consider there would be any consequences," she whispered.

"I've been living like this for a long time. It's hard for you to get used to it." He paused for a moment. "If *I* need to get a message to *you*, I will call Mrs. Stone—if you think she won't mind."

"I'm sure that's okay."

A knock at the back door of the house made them both jump.

"See who it is," he said brusquely, then followed her down the hall and waited while she cautiously pulled aside the curtains. Bernardo was outside.

"He'll be there in a minute," she told him, then went back to Miguel. Swiftly she put her arms around him and clasped him tightly. His hands came up to cup her shoulders, but she felt the stiffness in his embrace. She wanted to beg him to stay, so they could feel easy with each other again.

"I love you," she whispered.

"I love you, too."

His words sounded mechanical. When he pulled away, she searched his eyes, not finding any comfort in their veiled depths.

She couldn't think of anything more to say, so she let him go, feeling a giant fist squeezing her heart. Tears welled in her eyes, but she managed to hold them back until he had gone to the door and slipped outside.

EDUARDO SOMBRA STOOD in the hallway outside the closed study door, weighing his options. As the Americans liked to say, he had good news and bad news for Carlos Jurado. He had learned that it was profitable to make the most of good tidings. In the same way, he had observed that a messenger with bad news was likely to be shot. And he wasn't using the expression simply as a figure of speech.

On the other hand, there was also danger in withholding information—the danger of arousing Jurado's fury if he found out. Sombra took a handkerchief from his back pocket and wiped his perspiring brow. Then he schooled his features carefully before knocking deferentially on the door.

"Enter."

"I have a communiqué from the States. Valero has made

a mistake!'' He saw the eager expression flash across Jurado's face and hurried to explain. ''We have positive proof that he is in Baltimore. He has been in hiding, never coming out during the day. Yesterday we had a report that he showed himself at a local recreation center.''

''Why didn't our agent grab him?'' Carlos demanded, looking as if he wanted to personally do the job himself.

''Unfortunately, there were too many witnesses in the building. Before our man could make other arrangements, Valero slipped away again.''

Jurado cursed loudly. ''He could be in San Francisco by now, for all you know.''

''He isn't going anywhere.''

''Oh?''

''We know from the incident yesterday that a woman named Senora Jessie Douglas is carrying his child.''

A slow smile spread across Jurado's face. ''He's been…imprudent.''

Sombra laughed, relaxing several degrees.

''Too bad for him that he's an honorable man. He won't leave her. Keeps her under constant surveillance. She will lead us to him. And then we can finish them both off.''

He took a step back. ''If you have no further need of me, then I will get back to my duties.''

''Yes. Go.''

Not until he had closed the door behind himself did Sombra breathe a sigh of relief. He had gotten through the interview in good shape. Now he had to consider what to do with the communiqué he had received from one of his informants in Washington. Out of the blue, an employee at the Organization of American Nations had done a search for information on Carlos Jurado. Was it a random event? Or was Miguel Valero getting ready to strike back?

Either way, Jurado would see it as a failure of his intelligence team. But what if that didn't matter? Eduardo asked himself. If he took some initiative on his own, the situation at the OAN could be nullified.

He looked at his watch. Plenty of time to make a call to Baltimore.

WITH A SMALL SOUND OF frustration, Jessie heaved her awkward body out of bed. She wasn't hungry, but she knew that she had to eat. So she padded down the hall to the darkened kitchen to fix herself some dinner.

On the way, she stopped in the living room, thinking that she should close the blinds and turn on some lights. But when she reached the window, she stopped. Across the street, moonlight gleamed off a parked car. As she watched, a match flared, presumably because the person inside had lit a cigarette.

Her skin prickled as she wondered how long the watcher had been sitting there. Was he one of the men Miguel had asked to keep an eye on her? She hadn't seen Bernardo or Ernesto smoke. But maybe they were being considerate of her condition when they'd been around her.

Pulling the blind shut, she went to another window and stood so that she could look out without being observed. The moon had slipped behind a cloud, and all she could see of the interior of the car was the red glow at the end of the cigarette. Could it be one of Los Tigres? she wondered suddenly. They'd been warned to leave her alone. But what if some enterprising member of the gang had changed his mind and tracked her down?

The number Miguel had given her was written on the pad next to the phone. She dialed it, and a man picked up. He told her Bernardo would be back later—then hung up when she said she wanted to get in touch with Miguel.

Jessie peeked out the window again. Now the car was gone. Craning her neck, she looked up and down the block but didn't see the vehicle. She managed to convince herself she'd been getting all worked up about nothing. There was no reason to suppose the man in the car had been watching *her*. He could have come to visit a neighbor, found the person wasn't home, and waited for a while. That explanation made as much sense as anything else.

Her steps lighter, she returned to the kitchen and fixed a can of split-pea soup. Then she took a quick shower, checked the window one more time, and went to bed.

At first she lay sleepless under the covers. But the events of the day had been too much, and finally her body gave in to exhaustion.

Even in slumber, though, her mind wasn't going to let her relax. Not long after she'd drifted into a restless slumber, she found herself caught in the grip of a nightmare.

Strangely, she knew she was dreaming. And she knew that her subconscious was playing a continuation of the day's anxieties, twisting them into a different form. Unfortunately, that knowledge didn't help. She was powerless to wake herself up.

In the dream, she was pregnant—more pregnant than in reality. Her enormous belly rode in front of her like a giant beach ball. Filled with dread, she looked around at an unreal landscape. She was in a warm and sunny place overflowing with lush greenery and bright flowers. Colorful birds hopped about and sang in the branches of the trees. She was walking barefoot up a flagstone path toward a charming white stucco building that should have been inviting, but her sense of unease increased with every step she took.

She tried to hang back, yet her feet kept carrying her forward.

The farther she traveled into the dream landscape, the more frightened she became. Something was wrong here—very wrong.

Then, all at once she knew where she was. Miguel's clinic. He had told her about it, and she had come to see for herself. Yet she didn't want to see. She didn't want to be here.

''No!'' she gasped out.

No one answered.

An ugly lizard skittered across her path, then a large black spider. She tried to drag her feet, but she couldn't stop herself from stumbling toward the open door that loomed like the mouth of a skull. She grasped the doorframe with desperate fingers. But it was no use. Some invisible force tugged on her, pulling her forward until she had stepped from sunlight into shadow.

At first she could see nothing except the vague outline of a car shining in the moonlight—the same car that had been sitting across the street from her house. It dissolved into vapor, and the real contents of the room swam into focus. A scream ripped from her mouth as she saw the first body sprawled in a pool of blood. Another body lay farther into the room. And another. Two men and two women.

She knew their names because Miguel had told her. Tony and Paco, Anna and Margarita.

As she watched in horror, they all rose up to a sitting position, their movements jerky like marionettes attached to strings.

"Join us," they chorused.

"No!" The protest tore from the depths of her soul. She wanted to back away, but she was frozen to the spot.

They blinked their large eyes and looked down at the round red holes in their chests. Then, in unison, they jerked to their feet, wavering unsteadily as they started to move. One flailing arm knocked a vase of flowers off a table and it crashed to the floor with a shattering of glass.

The noise freed her. On a sob she turned and fled, hearing their footsteps tap, tap, tapping behind her as she ran down the path as fast as she could. But her enormous belly hampered her, and she couldn't make much speed. The zombies behind her were catching up. She heard their feet, which were somehow making the flagstone path creak like old floorboards. A skeletal hand clasped her shoulder from behind, the force of it finally catapulting her out of the terrible dream.

Disoriented, drenched in freezing sweat, she lay in a tangle of sheets, her breath coming in little gasps. She was in her own bed, she told herself. She was safe. It was only a dream of San Marcos and Miguel's clinic. She had made him relive the horror of it, forced him to share the pain; now she had been helpless to stop herself from visiting the place where he had almost been killed.

"Oh, Miguel," she murmured. She wanted him with her now. She wanted to comfort him, and wanted him to tell her everything was all right. But she was alone, and she would have to deal with her worries on her own, the way she had dealt with so many other things over the past few months.

Pushing herself up, she wiped a sleeve of her nightgown across her clammy forehead and looked toward the hall, thinking that a glass of water might help. Then she thought she heard a sound somewhere at the other end of the house, and a new sensation of cold skittered across her skin.

A floorboard creaked, and she realized she must have heard it earlier and made it part of the dream. Like the sound of breaking glass, she thought with alarm, as the last of the fog cleared from her brain. She was wide-awake now, and she was sure someone else was in the house.

Her gaze shot to the phone on the bedside table. Calling the gas station was a waste of time. Even if Bernardo was there, he couldn't get here in time. Neither could 911.

God, now what was she going to do? Her mind flashed back to the evening when Luis had been creeping toward her office at the Light Street Foundation. Only she was pretty sure the stalker wasn't a little boy this time.

Clenching her fists, she willed herself to steadiness. Thankful that the darkness offered some protection, she pushed herself up and slipped as quietly as possible from the bed. Could she make it out the window before the intruder got to the bedroom? Probably not, in her condition. Wishing she had a weapon, she looked frantically around the room. Then she remembered the wooden baseball bat propped up in a corner of the closet. Someone had overlooked it at the Light Street picnic a couple of months ago, and she'd brought it home, intending to take it into the office so the owner could claim it. But she'd never managed to remember it.

Tiptoeing across the room, she slipped into the closet, leaving the door partly open. At first she couldn't find the bat. Then her frantic hand knocked against it, and it started to fall. Grabbing for it, she repressed a little sob as her fear-stiffened fingers slipped on the wood surface. Somehow she averted disaster.

With a silent prayer of thanks, she closed her fist around the wooden shaft, then carefully raised it above her head, bracing the top of the bat against a row of blouses as she waited with her heart pounding in her ears.

Almost as soon as she was in position, she heard stealthy footsteps right outside the bedroom door. In the next moment, a figure glided into the room. Straining her eyes in the darkness, she made out the form of a bulky man wearing dark slacks and a dark T-shirt. He looked strong and menacing, and she knew she was only going to have one chance to save herself from him. Silently she counted off the seconds, waiting for him to get close enough for her to land a solid blow on the back of his head.

As he crossed the room, she shrank against the clothes in the closet. Then a flashlight beam cut through the darkness, the light hitting the bed. When the intruder saw that it was empty, a low curse broke his lips. For a long moment he stood very still. Then he turned, swinging the beam in an arc that probed the far corners of the room. It glanced off the chair, the chest of drawers, the dressing table.

God, what should she do? Charge out and hit him? It was too risky. He'd hear her coming long before she reached him. But hiding in the closet was a risk, too. If he found her, she was trapped.

Clamping her teeth together to keep them from chattering, she waited, hoping against hope that he wouldn't discover her hiding place.

In the next moment, the flashlight beam hit her feet.

"Ah. There you are."

The light stopped, moved to waist level, spotlighting the rounded bulge of her belly.

He gave a satisfied chuckle. "What have we here? Come out of there, *señorita*, so I can get a better look at you."

Chapter Fifteen

"You'll have to come and get me," Jessie answered, projecting her fear into the quaver of her voice. It wasn't difficult to appear terrified when the blood in her veins had turned to ice water.

"Do not be afraid. I am not going to hurt you. I only want some information."

Yeah, sure, she thought. *You're here to recruit me for the neighborhood safety patrol.*

His face was hard and confident as he stood facing her, blocking any chance of a pregnant woman's escape. His hair was dark. So were his close-set eyes. She'd never seen him. But he looked too old to be one of Los Tigres. So that left Jurado. Miguel had warned her, and she hadn't wanted to believe him. Now she knew that she'd been playing out of her league all the time. But at least she was up at bat.

Purposefully, the intruder began to saunter forward, sure that he had the situation under control. The breath frozen in her lungs, she held her ground as she tried to calculate precisely the right moment to strike.

Only one chance. She had only one chance, her mind chanted. *If she fumbled it, she was dead.*

As he reached to pull her from the closet, his expression changed from complacency to anger, and she knew that he must have finally noticed the baseball bat she was holding above her head. Even as he sprang toward her, she brought the club down with every bit of strength she possessed, changing the angle of her blow to compensate for the change in his position. She cracked him on the head, but not with the fat end of the bat where it would have done the most damage.

Strike one!

He staggered back, but the blow didn't bring him down.

"*¡Puta!*" he gasped in Spanish, reeling like a drunk in a bar brawl. Maddened, he sprang forward again, his big hands reaching for her.

Two chances, she amended, as she kicked upward, aiming for his crotch. She felt her foot impact against a man's most vulnerable anatomy.

He yowled in pain, then cursed in gutter Spanish as he momentarily forgot about her and grabbed for his injury.

A home run! On a surge of adrenaline, she ducked around him and ran as fast as her pregnant body would allow toward the kitchen door. Still, she couldn't make much speed. Terror racked her as she heard shuffling steps coming out of the bedroom. In her mind, she pictured a wounded bear bent on destruction.

When she reached the kitchen, she bolted through the swing door and resisting the urge to look behind her, flew across the tile floor to the back door. She fumbled with the lock until the key finally turned, and she threw herself outside, almost at the end of her strength. A stone stabbed the sole of her bare foot, and she gasped but kept moving.

Her nearest neighbor was some distance away, and with her lungs burning and her body feeling as if it were weighted down with rocks, she knew she couldn't keep this pace up for long. If she could only get out of sight, she might have a chance. Along the side of her neighbor's detached garage were evergreen bushes so thick that kids liked to disappear behind them. If they made a great hiding place during the day, they should be even better at night.

Putting on a desperate burst of speed, she made it to the

dense shrubs and plunged between the branches, scratching her face and arms as twigs and needles slapped her sharply.

She pressed back against the rough brick wall of the garage and tried not to gasp for breath. Screened by the bushes, she heard her attacker charge past.

How long before he came back? Should she stay here or try to make it to a house? Either course carried grave risks. But her pregnancy settled the question. She simply couldn't run any farther.

She waited for aeons, her skin stinging from the thrash of the branches and her chest aching from the exertion. She was beginning to wonder if her attacker had given up, when she finally heard him coming back.

He was walking slowly now. She could hear him stopping to beat at the bushes along the way, and she saw the beam of the light winking at her through the branches. All she could do was wait and silently pray for invisibility.

Her heart stopped as he paused beside her hiding place, shining his flashlight back and forth into the greenery. But the thick branches kept their secret.

With a snarl, he kicked at the lower limbs, then moved on. Again she waited in the darkness, but this time he didn't return.

Was it safe to come out, or was he trying to trick her—make her think he'd given up? Unwilling to take a chance, she stood there in her nightgown, pressing against the brick wall, locking her knees to keep from toppling over.

Her legs and back began to ache. She wanted to sink to the ground, but she forced herself to stay on her feet. Finally she saw the darkness around her begin to brighten and knew that dawn was breaking. Still, she remained where she was— half dozing in her exhaustion, rousing slightly when she heard a phone ringing somewhere nearby.

She was jerked awake again by a loud curse and the sound of running feet. Not one man, but two—or maybe three. The runners dashed past her hiding place.

''Get him!'' someone shouted in Spanish.

Her heart leaped when she realized the voice belonged to Miguel.

"Jessie. Jessie, where are you?"

"Here! I'm here." Hoarsely calling his name, she gathered herself together and plunged through the bushes, falling into his embrace and clinging with what little strength she had left.

He grasped her and swung her up into his arms. "Jessie. Thank God." His lips skimmed her face as he carried her toward the house. She hung on to him, hardly able to believe that she wasn't dreaming of his arms around her.

Inside, he set her on a kitchen chair, then hunkered down beside her to examine her cuts and scrapes before washing them with warm water and soap.

"Did he hurt you?" he asked urgently, touching the skirt of her gown where she hadn't even known it had torn. "Did he do anything to you?"

"No. No. I got away," she answered, still in a kind of numb shock.

"Thank God," he murmured again, then brought a bottle of antiseptic from his medical bag. "This may hurt a little."

She winced as the cold liquid stung her skin, but it brought back reality. Miguel was here. He and another man had come back for her. And she was sitting in the kitchen wearing only a thin cotton nightgown that revealed quite a bit of her pregnant shape.

Miguel must have realized the same thing. When he was finished tending her scrapes, he strode down the hall and came back with her robe. "Bernardo will be coming inside," he said.

She nodded, slipping her arms into the sleeves and pulling the robe closed as best she could. When she looked back at Miguel, his face was etched with agonized lines. "I am sorry."

"It wasn't your fault."

"Of course it was! I never should have left you alone."

"You didn't know something like this would happen."

"Stop making excuses for me."

"How did you know I was in trouble?"

"Bernardo came back to the gas station, and Humberto finally remembered that some woman had called for me," he said, his voice grating. "We called here. When nobody answered, we came to check on you."

"I heard the phone!"

Before he could add anything else, Bernardo knocked on the door.

"Come in," Miguel called.

"He got away," Bernardo said in Spanish as he entered. Miguel nodded tightly.

"He broke into the house," Jessie told them. "I hit him with a baseball bat and kicked him where it would hurt. Then I ran and hid. I was afraid to come out. I was afraid he was still here, waiting for me."

"He was," Miguel said. He sucked in a sharp breath and let it out quickly. "I will help you pack your clothes."

"Why?"

"You cannot stay here. Jurado must know that you and I are…together."

"Yes," she acknowledged in a low voice. She hadn't understood the danger—not until she'd awakened to realize someone was in her house.

"Did you recognize him?" Miguel asked.

She shook her head.

"There will be others. We must leave quickly." He led her into the bedroom and closed the door behind them, then whirled to catch her in his arms.

"Jessie." He swept her close, held her to him, his hands moving over her in a kind of gentle frenzy. "If I had lost you, I would be wandering in hell," he gasped out. "Forgive me, angel. Please forgive me."

His pain was almost too much to bear. "For what?" she managed.

"For getting angry with you. For holding you to an impossible standard."

"I should never have called Donna," she admitted shakily. "It was a dumb thing to do. That's probably how they found me."

"You didn't know. You have not been living like an animal in hiding for almost a year—calculating every move you make to keep yourself out of Jurado's clutches."

She closed her eyes and held him tight, thankful that he had learned to adapt, yet knowing that the way he lived had exacted a terrible price. She hadn't comprehended his situation—not really. All along, she had expected him to act like a free man who could choose to stay with her or choose to leave. She finally understood that he was far from free. And she also understood that she had laid a terrible burden on him. He had been responsible for his own life. Now he felt responsible for hers and the baby's, as well. Until this morning, she hadn't really "gotten" it. She had been pressing him to work out their relationship, when her needs had only added to his agony.

"All those months ago, I should have let you go." She uttered the words that filled her mind. "I should never have taken you to my bed. I've forced you into a terrible position."

He shook his head, clasping her closer. "No. Loving you kept me sane. Kept me human. When I wanted to give up, I remembered the sweetness of making love to you. I vowed to find a way to come back to you when I could."

"But you weren't counting on keeping a pregnant woman safe."

She saw the anguish—and the naked longing—in his face. "A pregnant *wife*," he said with such feeling that she felt her heart almost bursting inside her chest.

THEY WERE MARRIED a few days later in a small Methodist church in Princess Anne, a town on the eastern shore of Maryland that had been founded before the Revolutionary War. Now many of the Colonial and Victorian homes had been restored to their former elegance, giving the small community an ambience that charmed Jessie and made up for some of the other decisions they'd been forced to make—like choosing a place, time and church to minimize chances of detection.

The Methodist ceremony was a compromise, since Miguel was afraid that getting married by a priest could give them away. And the only friends in attendance were Cam and Jo and some of the men from Randolph Security, who functioned as bodyguards.

Cam and his men went in first to check the church for intruders. Jessie and Miguel waited in the parking lot in the Blazer that was one of the standard Randolph Security vehicles. When Hunter came out to tell them everything was ready, they entered the church together, holding hands tightly. Jessie carried no bouquet and she was wearing the one good maternity dress she'd bought. Miguel didn't even have on a suit, because he didn't own one. Still, he looked devastatingly handsome, Jessie thought, in a crisp blue shirt and dark slacks.

The tall, thin Reverend Carter had never met the happy couple before, but the Light Street Foundation had made a sizable contribution to his youth fund, so he only glanced once at the bride's rounded middle before casting his eyes upward. Probably he assumed that this was some kind of shotgun wedding, Jessie surmised.

She stopped worrying about what he thought when he began to lead them through the words of the marriage ritual.

"Do you, Miguel, take this woman to be your lawfully wedded wife?" Reverend Carter asked the age-old words.

She stole a glance at Miguel's face. It held so much love, so much hope, so much commitment that she could barely catch her breath. If she had ever doubted that he wanted this marriage—heart and soul—she had no doubts now.

She didn't realize that she had whispered his name until his fingers tightened on hers and he gave her a heart-melting smile. And when he slipped the ring on her finger, she felt to the marrow of her bones that she was bonding herself to this man for all time.

The service was over quickly, and it was followed by a kiss so tender and sweet, Jessie felt her vision blur.

"I love you," she and Miguel both said as their lips parted.

They stood looking at each other for several moments, forgetting their surroundings, until Cam cleared his throat. "We'd better stay on schedule."

Miguel nodded tightly. "Thank you," he said, shaking hands with all of the men.

Then the wedding party climbed back into the Blazer and returned to the Baltimore area—to the modest furnished house that Laura Roswell had hastily rented for Jessie on a quiet street in Pikesville. Half a dozen more friends had come and set out deli trays and a small cake from a local bakery. It wasn't the wedding day or the reception Jessie had dreamed of, but she was following Miguel's rules now. They could do nothing that would call attention to themselves—including hiring a caterer or filling the street with cars.

"We'll have a big party at our house in your honor when things calm down," Jo told them as the wedding guests sat rather awkwardly around the living and dining rooms eating corned-beef sandwiches and potato salad.

"You could combine it with a baby shower," added Hunter, whose background didn't include schooling in the social graces.

Despite herself, Jessie laughed. "Not a bad idea!"

Before anyone else could comment, Cam stood to toast the bride and groom. The guests raised their glasses of champagne, Jesse, her sparkling cider.

"To Jessie and Miguel," Cam offered. "Every happiness. Every good thing in life."

Jessie felt Miguel's hand tighten on hers. He was trying to look as if he believed in miracles. She clasped his hand with all her strength, trying to let him know that she would be beside him, whatever happened. But she had turned into a realist. She knew they would have to wait for their day in the sun until after Carlos Jurado was apprehended. She prayed it would be soon—or at least, before the baby was born.

IT WAS LATE, BUT Eduardo Sombra sat at his desk studying the report he had received from the States two weeks ago. It was a profile of Jessie Douglas, starting with her childhood in Chicago and covering her college days, her marriage, her return to graduate school, and her life in Baltimore. It was all there, in great detail. Her sex life. Spending habits. Favorite foods. Vacation preferences. Personality profile. Comments from friends and teachers who thought she was being investigated for a sensitive government job.

His boss had paid a great deal for the report. Now he was demanding results. Unfortunately, the chronicle ended abruptly in August, when Valero and Douglas had gone underground after he'd miraculously saved her. For a moment, Eduardo couldn't hold back the panic that always seized him every time he remembered that fiasco. Then he got a grip on himself. Jurado didn't know about that screwup, and there was no way for him to find out.

Eduardo made a low sound of mixed anger and frustration. The escape in Baltimore hadn't been his fault! Valero was like a cat with nine lives. At first he had been lucky; now the life of a fugitive was second nature to him. But the doctor would stick close to his pregnant woman. That was his fatal flaw.

His spirits rising, Eduardo skimmed back through the dossier, focusing on Jessie Douglas's character traits and the report on her call to the OAN. She had been reckless when she was desperate to help the man she loved. She would be reckless again—if she were pushed in the right direction.

Reaching for the phone, he called his chief informant in Baltimore and issued terse instructions.

JESSIE SIGHED AS SHE washed her face and got ready for another night without Miguel. She never knew when she was going to see him, and tonight, hope had faded as a December ice storm had started to beat against the windowpanes.

He had known their life together was going to be difficult. She'd been more optimistic. Their hopes for a quick resolution to their problems had dimmed, however, as the weeks wore on. Jed was trying his best to dig up something useful on Jurado in San Marcos. So far, all he had learned was that the man was in deep cover. And the body count was higher than they'd originally thought. It seemed he'd also executed the hit squad who had carried out the raid on the clinic. The news was chilling—and confirmed Miguel's assumption that the man wasn't going to give up his quest for Dr. Valero.

The tension put their marriage under a good deal of strain. Jessie wanted Miguel to hole up with her in a small town out of state until it was safe to come out of hiding. He told her that he'd go crazy with nothing to occupy his time. In addition, he was unwilling to leave the community that had come to depend on him and that had shown him such loyalty.

But he wouldn't allow his wife to participate in the nomadic existence that had been forced upon him by Jurado's relentless pursuit. So Jessie stayed in her furnished rented house, where Cam Randolph installed a state-of-the-art security system and a special secure phone line to connect her computer to the system at work.

From the hook on the closet wall, she took her nightgown and paused for a moment to stroke the fabric with her fingertips. Before they'd gotten married she'd slept in plain-looking, utilitarian gowns. Now she always wore the silk and lace Miguel liked, because she loved to see his eyes light up when he saw her in them—even now, when she was eight months pregnant.

Just as she had slipped her latest purchase over her head, she heard Miguel's special knock. Quickly she crossed to the dresser and ran a brush through her hair as his footsteps approached from the ground floor.

There was a charged moment as he entered the bedroom. Other wives might take their husband's homecoming for granted. To Jessie, it was always an occasion for giving thanks.

"How are you?" they both asked at the same time.

"Fine—now."

The question and answer had turned into a little ritual between them. Although Miguel looked tired as he stood in the doorway of her bedroom, his face took on a warm glow when she came toward him.

All the lonely days that he'd been away and out of communication evaporated as he took her into his arms and bent to cover her lips with his.

The kiss was long and hungry, growing more urgent as his hands moved over the ripe contours of her body, caressing her through the silky fabric. They had only each other, and their time together was always much too short.

He was breathing raggedly as he lifted his mouth from hers.

"You must have a thing for fat women," she said with a breathy laugh.

"The only woman I have a thing for is you." He caressed her tummy, then slipped his hands upward to cradle the weight of her breasts.

She marveled that he still wanted her. Then she stopped worrying about how she looked as he eased her onto the bed. Gently, with great care for her condition, he transported her to a place where only love and pleasure existed.

Afterward they lay naked together, his palm flattened against her abdomen as they savored the afterglow of lovemaking.

"I miss you so when I have to be away," he whispered.

"Yes. So much." She snuggled closer. "I want to hear what you've been doing."

He told her about a family where the mother could hardly

care for her children because she had mononucleosis. Miguel had sent her to a hospital clinic, and now she was recovering. As he talked about the woman and the other people he'd helped over the past few days, his voice took on an enthusiasm that made her chest tighten with mixed emotions. She knew he was putting himself in danger by seeing patients. Yet he needed to help people—as much as he needed her.

"What about you?" he asked.

She made a clucking sound. "Well, Jim Alvarez is still trying to speak to me in person," she reported. "He's desperate to apologize for being so mean to me."

"I don't trust him!"

"Neither does anybody else. He's not going to get near either one of us."

Miguel nodded.

They talked long into the dark winter night, neither of them willing to surrender to sleep.

Jessie burrowed her fingers through the hair on Miguel's chest as she asked about one of his favorite subjects—the clinic he was going to build when he came out of hiding. She knew he had a location all picked out—an old warehouse only a few streets off Broadway.

He had told her many times about his plans, but she let him tell it all again because she knew he needed to focus on that dream for the future.

Then they switched topics to something a bit more controversial—baby names.

"You still don't like Esteban?" she asked.

"It is not American," he repeated his earlier objection. "If you like Esteban, we can call him Steven."

"What about naming him after you? Michael."

"I want him to have his own name."

Shaking her head, Jessie reached for the stack of baby-name books on the bedside table. She knew that Miguel was keeping the argument going partly to take their minds off more sinister problems, and she was willing to go along with him.

The peaceful interlude was shattered by the ringing of the phone. Both their gazes shot to the clock beside the bed. It was after 1:00 a.m.—hardly the time for a friendly intrusion.

"Who is it?" Miguel asked, his voice taut, and again she realized how fragile their hold on happiness was.

With a shaky hand she reached for the small caller-ID box, then breathed in a little sigh as she saw "Randolph Security" on the display.

It was Hunter, who wanted to know if she could contact Miguel. When she started to hand him the phone, she found he was already striding naked to the office where he snatched up the extension.

"What is it?" he demanded without preliminary. "Good news or bad?"

"We had a message from Jed."

When Jed had initially gone down to San Marcos, they'd all been confident that he could get the information they needed on Jurado. As the weeks had worn on, they'd only discovered how well Jurado had used money, intimidation tactics and murder to cover his tracks.

Even more chilling, Jed had found that Miguel's past was just as inaccessible. His birth certificate had disappeared from the Santa Isabella bureau of records. His medical license was no longer on file and his tax records were missing.

Frustrated, Jed had vowed to unearth *some* information— on either Miguel or Jurado.

"What do you have for us?" Miguel asked.

"Jed got a tip that set him working on another angle. What do you know about a general named Juan Escobar?"

"He's called the Che Guevara of San Marcos," Miguel answered promptly. "Ten years ago he was sent by the president to aid the rebels to the north. But it was a trap to get rid of a political rival. He led his 'freedom brigade' into an ambush in the jungle. They were all killed—or died in prison."

"Jed's sent pictures of the men in the brigade. They've just arrived by courier, and you need to take a look at them."

"Why?"

"He thinks it's possible you might recognize somebody. Can I bring them over now?"

Jessie glanced again at the clock on the bedside table. It was the middle of the night, yet there was an urgency in Hunter's voice. "Yes," she told him.

She and Miguel got dressed quickly and silently, both of them keyed up. To give herself something to do, she made a pot of hot chocolate—the old-fashioned kind, the way Hunter liked it. She'd discovered he had a real sweet tooth, and she enjoyed feeding it.

While she measured cocoa and sugar, her husband paced to the window and looked out for the fifth time.

Hunter arrived twenty minutes later, with copies of old military records from San Marcos.

While she and Hunter sipped mugs of chocolate, Miguel flipped through the material. He stopped short when he came to a man named Andrés Cuento.

"That is him!" he exclaimed. "That is the face I gave Jurado."

"Are you sure?" Hunter asked.

"Positive."

They all read Cuento's dossier. He had an excellent education and a good military record. According to the official account, he had been killed in the jungle ambush.

"Jurado had me turn him into Cuento. That is why nobody can find him," Miguel muttered. "But what is he up to?"

"Now that we have a name to put with the face, we should be able to figure it out," Hunter said.

They talked about several possibilities, and when Hunter left, Miguel was in a very positive mood. He rarely allowed himself to be hopeful. For Jessie, it was a pleasure to see him so optimistic.

In the morning, she awoke to hear him talking on the phone. Then he came back to the bedroom with a broad grin on his face.

"Pack an overnight bag," he said as he began to get his own clothing out of the bureau.

"Where are we going?" she inquired.

"You need to get out of the house, so we're going on a short trip."

"Did you clear it with Randolph Security?"

"Of course."

After breakfast, he led her toward a luxury sedan that one of his friends had rented for them at an agency outside the beltway.

When Jessie tried to get him to reveal their destination, he only smiled mysteriously as he headed south, past D.C. and into the rolling Virginia countryside. He'd done some very specific research, she realized, as he pulled up in front of a warm and cozy bed-and-breakfast in Charlottesville, far enough away from Baltimore that the chance of being spotted was tiny. Still, he registered using a driver's license and a spare ID he'd acquired since they'd met.

They ate dinner at a small restaurant, made delicious love in a soft Victorian bed, and enjoyed breakfast propped against a nest of pillows. Then Miguel surprised her with a trip to a giant shopping mall where they filled a cart to overflowing with all the baby clothes and accessories she'd been longing to buy—including a small crib that folded flat and went easily into the enormous trunk of their car.

He even gave her half an hour alone in a men's specialty shop where she bought him some Christmas presents—a soft wool sweater and a warm terry-cloth robe.

It was almost possible to forget that they were a couple of fugitives—except that she knew Miguel was constantly alert to the people around them. And when he left the mall, he took a route that led through several residential neighborhoods to make sure they weren't being followed.

Still, it was a memorable outing, and it gave Jessie a taste of what life might be like if her husband were a free man.

On the way home, she fell asleep in the sedan's comfortable leather seat and didn't awaken until they came to a stop in the driveway. As her eyes came open, she gazed at Miguel's profile, seeing a vulnerability that made her heart squeeze. When he caught her watching him, he quickly adjusted his features.

"Did you have a good time?" he asked.

"You know I did. Thanks for the nice surprise."

His fingers closed over hers. "I wish we could do things like that more often."

"We will," she promised. She was reaching for the door handle when Miguel hissed, "Get down!"

"What?"

"Get down," he repeated, a pistol suddenly in his hand. "There's a car behind us blocking the driveway."

Jessie felt the blood in her veins turn to ice as she tried to force her bulky body below the dashboard. *God, no!* Jurado's men had finally found them.

Chapter Sixteen

Miguel slipped his door open, and she heard heavy footsteps coming rapidly up the drive. Trapped. They were trapped because they had let themselves enjoy a few hours of normal life.

And now her husband would defend her with his life. When he made a strangled exclamation, her heart leaped into her throat. She wanted to hide, to bury her face in her hands, but that would only postpone the inevitable. Lifting her chin, she followed the direction of his fierce gaze.

Seconds later, a large male shape loomed beside his window. Confused, she watched Miguel lower his weapon.

When the man bent down, she saw that it was Hunter.

The breath whooshed out of her lungs in a great sigh.

"Where were you?" he demanded. "You left the bed-and-breakfast before lunch. We thought something had happened. I've been here all afternoon."

"I'm sorry," Jessie managed. She and Miguel had been so blissfully wrapped up in each other that they hadn't checked in during their shopping trip, and Hunter had been waiting in the cold for hours.

His gaze went to her as she tried to hoist herself from her undignified position on the floor. "We were worried," he said in an apologetic voice. "I didn't intend to frighten you."

"It wasn't your fault," she answered quickly.

"You need to talk to us?" Miguel asked as he helped Jessie out of the car.

Hunter nodded. "Inside."

From the sound of his voice, it seemed that he didn't have good news.

Silently, they trooped into the house. "What has happened?" Miguel demanded as Hunter closed the door.

"After you identified the picture of Andres Cuento, Jed was able to start making inquiries about him. It seems Jurado—as Cuento—has told a few influential people about his 'miraculous escape' from captivity. He's allied himself with the most powerful political party in San Marcos. And he's let it be known that he'd humbly accept their nomination as a presidential candidate. According to Jed's sources, he has a good chance of going the distance."

Miguel snorted. "So now we know why he wanted to assume the identity of a dead war hero."

"Unfortunately, there's more." Hunter gave them an apologetic look before continuing. "He's going to campaign on a law-and-order platform. And he's starting with a personal tragedy. The story is that a Dr. Miguel Valero murdered his cousin, Carlos Jurado, over a drug deal gone bad. He's offered a reward for information leading to Valero's capture and he's circulating a drawing of your new face."

Jessie gasped. Miguel cursed softly.

"At least he doesn't have a photograph," Hunter offered.

"You need to prove that you operated on Jurado—that you made him into Andres Cuento," Jessie said.

"I can't!"

"There must be a way. What about DNA evidence?"

"You need cell samples for that." Miguel closed his eyes for a moment. Then he grabbed Cuento's file again, shuffling to the medical records, which included a dental chart. "What about this?" he asked in a gritty voice as he studied the notations. "Jurado had several teeth that were capped and plenty of fillings. They won't match Cuento's dental work."

Hunter nodded. "We can check it out, if Jurado hasn't assassinated his dentist."

The men talked long into the night. Jessie sat in the living room with them, listening. Once she asked why they couldn't send anonymous articles to the newspapers in San Marcos telling the story of what had happened. Hunter told her they'd already thought of that, but Jed had said that Jurado had too firm a hold on the press for the scheme to work without proof.

That was the crux of the problem. They needed some kind of proof—of Jurado's identity and Miguel's. Since Miguel couldn't prove who he was, he was in danger of being deported at any time. And until they pinned down Jurado's masquerade and got him arrested, Miguel's deportation to San Marcos would be fatal.

Finally, around 3:00 a.m., Hunter left. In bed, Jessie sought Miguel's warmth, and he held her, kissed her, told her that everything was going to be all right. But she knew he didn't believe it inside, where it counted. Because he'd dared to be optimistic, she was sure that the news from San Marcos had left him more frustrated than ever.

The next morning, when he said it would be safer for her if he left, she really wasn't surprised by the announcement. Yet she tried to lift his spirits.

"What about the dental records?" she asked softly. "Won't they make a difference?"

"Yes, maybe we will get lucky this time," he muttered, but she knew he couldn't let himself believe it. He'd learned all too well to adapt to the role of fugitive.

As they talked across the breakfast table, she realized there was nothing she could do to help him—except let him believe he was keeping her safe by staying away.

So she kissed him goodbye, and sent him off with a smile. As she watched him drive away, she told herself that a man with less strength would already have cracked under the strain. But that wasn't much consolation.

After putting the dishes in the dishwasher, she sat with

her fingers pressed against her mouth, trying to think of what to do. The last time she'd gotten involved, she'd only made things worse, she silently acknowledged as she remembered the episode with her friend Donna at the Organization of American Nations. Jessie had been too impulsive, and she wasn't going to make that kind of mistake again.

Still, the anxiety had become intolerable—for both her and Miguel. No matter how much he kept saying he loved her, the bottom line was that she saddled him with a wife and a baby on the way, which made everything worse for him.

She wanted with all her heart to make the nightmare vanish, but she couldn't come up with any way to help. Then, two days after he'd delivered his "bombshell," Hunter stopped by with copy of a hospital birth certificate that Jed had faxed from San Marcos.

As she scanned the official-looking document, her hope surged. This piece of paper bore Miguel's real name, as well as his mother's and father's, and his birth date, plus facts like his birth weight and length.

She let her excitement build—until she tried to figure out what it really proved. All the document said was that a baby had been born in San Marcos thirty-two years ago, and that his mother had been an American. Unfortunately, there was no way to connect the infant whose birth had been recorded with the man who had become her husband, now that his parents were dead.

Or was there? she wondered, as a plan began to form in her mind. Carefully she examined all the angles. She'd made a mistake before when she'd called Donna, and she wasn't going to do it again. But she was so worried about Miguel. She simply couldn't sit around and let the man she loved suffer when she might be able to help him.

By the afternoon, she was convinced she knew what she was doing. After donning a huge ski jacket that she'd gotten from a secondhand shop, she pulled a winter hat down over her hair. The outfit was one of several that she wore when she went shopping at grocery stores remote from her neighborhood.

Driving to a shopping center on Liberty Road, she dialed a number she'd gotten from the phone book. It was for the local field office of the INS, and the very thought of contacting them made her throat clog. Yet who else was in a better position to tell her how to prove a person's identity and U.S. citizenship? And what was the risk in calling from a pay phone at a shopping center?

Still, she felt her heart pounding inside her chest as she asked the secretary to connect her with one of the agents.

"Can you state the nature of your business?"

Jessie gave a brief summary of her reason for calling.

"Just a moment," the woman said.

The agent who came on the line next was Ramón Martinez, one of the men who had been notified by Officer Waverly and then had hounded her at the recreation center. When he identified himself, she almost dropped the phone. Then she cleared her throat and asked if anyone else was available. Unfortunately, the rest of the staff was out of the office. It was Martinez or nothing—and she was too keyed up to wait another day.

Figuring it didn't make a difference whom she talked to, she took a deep breath and tried to come across as matter-of-fact—like a customer calling an appliance repair service. "I have some questions about a man who is suspected of being an illegal alien."

"You have some confidential information for our office?"

She kept her voice steady. "No, that's not what I meant. I want to find out how someone goes about proving that he is—in fact—an American citizen when he wasn't born in this country."

"Does he lack proper documentation?"

"He ran into some unusual problems in the country where he was born and had to, uh, leave suddenly."

"He broke the law?" Martinez asked bluntly.

"No. He was framed for a crime he didn't commit."

"Um."

"I'm sure people tell you that all the time," she answered defensively. "In this case, it's true!"

"Well, it sounds like a rather complicated case," the agent replied, his voice becoming a bit more sympathetic.

Jessie sighed. "Yes."

"Are we talking about a man from an Asian country, or Eastern Europe, Latin America, or the Middle East?"

"Is that relevant?" she asked.

"It could be."

"I'm not sure I should go into that."

"Okay. What is your relationship to this guy?"

"I'm his wife."

"And you are an American citizen?"

"Yes."

"And you're afraid that he will be deported if we catch up with him?"

She swallowed and said, "Yes,"

His next suggestion put her on guard. "Why don't you come down to the office so we can discuss it?"

Sure, she thought. *And why don't I give you his name and address while I'm at it?* "I don't want to do that," she answered.

"I'm trying to help you."

"Maybe you can't." She started to hang up.

"Wait!"

The urgency in Martinez's voice stayed her hand.

"Wait... Ma'am, are you there? Ma'am?"

"I'm still here."

"Don't hang up. It sounds like you need advice, and I have a suggestion. I realize this is a very emotional issue for you. Also, you're worried about giving away your husband's identity because you don't know if you can trust me. And you're right, of course. I'm a federal agent, and I have to act in accordance with the law.

"Why don't you think a little more about what you want to tell me. And...I'll also think about *my* options. If your husband could offer me information that might be useful to the U.S. government, that would count in his favor. But we'll both be better prepared if you call back tomorrow. If you phone me about the same time, I'll make sure I'm in the office and available to you.''

She thought for a moment. "I... All right."

"Why don't you use a code name, in case you need to leave a message for me?"

"What do you mean—a code name?"

"You could be, uh, Mrs. Jefferson, and I'll know it's you. That way, you won't have to give your real identity."

"All right."

"If you need to get in touch with me at any time, use that name."

"Thank you."

After replacing the receiver, she stood staring out at the passing traffic. Nobody paid her any particular attention. The only risk she was taking was leaving the house, she told herself. Martinez didn't know who she was. In fact, he'd been sympathetic, although she knew she'd be crazy to trust him. Still, there was no way he could get to Miguel through her unless she gave away too much. And she wasn't going to do that.

JESSIE SPENT THE REST of the day alternating between feeling hopeful and worried. Once she picked up the phone to discuss her strategy with Randolph Security but changed her mind. They had been working on this for months, and Miguel was no closer to freedom. She was trying something else, and she was desperate enough not to want any negative opinions of her plan.

The next morning, she spent half an hour trying on and discarding several disguises and finally settled on a long tweed coat, high black boots and a wool scarf that went over her head and tucked inside her neckline. She would have added sunglasses, but when she came out she found that it was snowing, although it wasn't sticking to the roads.

She eyed the sky with misgiving. Yet she'd worked herself into a state where she felt it was imperative to talk to Martinez, and she knew she couldn't do it from home. So she drove slowly toward the Old Court Shopping Center on Reisterstown Road. By the time she got there, the flakes were thicker, and the parking lot was starting to fill with shoppers panicked over getting snowed in without necessities. She'd better confer with Martinez and get right home.

This time, he came on the line almost immediately. "Mrs. Jefferson?" he asked, using the name they had agreed on.

"Yes." The phone clicked, and she thought for several seconds that they had been disconnected. "Are you still there?" she asked anxiously.

"I'm right here. We've been having some trouble with the phones. I apologize. But I've been thinking about our previous conversation, and I've got a couple of options for you."

"Thank you," she answered, then caught her breath as her stomach clenched. Lord, all she needed right now was stomach problems. Her hand tight on the receiver, she waited for the spasm to pass.

"Is something wrong?" Martinez asked.

"No. I'm fine," she lied.

"Okay, I need more information before I can make any sug—" There was static on the line, and she waited tensely, hoping she wasn't going to lose him.

"Sorry," he said as the noise cleared and the volume increased several notches. "I guess the storm must be interfering with the phone connection."

Jessie made a small noise of agreement as she looked toward her car. In the few minutes since she'd gotten out, a blanket of white had covered the windshield. At least she was standing where the overhanging roof of a grocery store sheltered her from the worst of the snow. Still, she had started to shiver from the cold. Reaching into her pocket, she pulled out a pair of gloves and slipped them on as she kept hold of the phone.

"Are you living with your husband?" Martinez asked in a businesslike tone.

She hesitated. "Not exactly. He visits me when he can."

"But you're in communication with him?"

She lowered her voice as a harried-looking shopper rushed past. "I wait for him to contact me."

Martinez went on to another topic. "Does he have relatives living in the U.S.? Is he staying with them?"

"He has relatives here. He hasn't called them." Miguel had told her he had an uncle and aunt and several cousins in the D.C. area, although he hadn't contacted them because he didn't want Jurado's men coming after them. She told Martinez that they were living in another state.

"Have they met him as an adult? Could they vouch for his identity?"

"I don't know," she replied, thinking that she didn't know much about her husband's background.

Martinez kept on with a string of questions, sometimes interrupted by crackling on the line as if the phone signal were getting stronger and then weaker again.

Whenever she thought the response to a question might betray Miguel's identify, she said that she couldn't give an answer. Each time that happened, Martinez immediately dropped the subject and went on to something else. But finally, she began to get the feeling that he was simply trying to hold her on the phone for as long as possible. As that thought surfaced, she felt goose bumps rise on her arms. Maybe contacting the INS had been a bad idea, after all. Perhaps her innocent answers were somehow incriminating.

"I have to hang up," she said suddenly.

"Please, Mrs. Jefferson. I can't help Miguel unless you give me your full cooperation."

"Miguel?" she gasped.

On the other end of the line, Martinez made a low sound that might have been a curse. Jessie slammed the receiver into the cradle and turned toward the parking lot.

In the twenty minutes she'd been standing there, the

snowy pavement had been trampled by a mass of footprints as shoppers hurried in and out of the store. Making her way past empty carts, Jessie hurried toward her car. But the pavement was slippery, and her foot slid out from under her as she took a step toward the curb. Arms windmilling, she tried to stay upright. But her center of gravity had shifted, making it hard to keep her balance. She lost her battle with gravity and crashed to the sidewalk, landing hard on her bottom. For a moment she simply sat there, too stunned to move. God, what if she'd hurt the baby?

"Let me help you."

At the sound of a stranger's voice, Jessie cringed. Then she looked up and saw a gray-haired woman who had just come out of the store. Abandoning her grocery cart, the lady reached down to give her a hand.

"Thanks." Jessie heaved herself to her feet and took stock of her condition. She was shaken up but otherwise seemed okay.

"Are you all right?" the woman asked.

"I think so. But I have to go." All at once, the tension of the morning—the tension of her life—was too much, and she felt tears welling in her eyes. She'd tried to help Miguel, but it looked like she'd made a bad mistake.

"Are you sure you're not hurt, dear?" the woman asked anxiously. "Your baby must be due soon."

"I'm fine. It's my husband. He's in trouble," she blurted, part of her shocked that she was revealing so much to a stranger.

"Oh, you poor thing," the woman said, her gaze fixed on Jessie's protruding belly.

It was then that she saw a man striding purposefully toward her down the sidewalk. It was Martinez, momentarily stalled as a shopper pushed a cart into his path.

Oh, Lord. He'd zeroed in on her location by tracing the phone call. She reached out and grabbed the woman by the hand. "Please, you've got to help me. This is an emergency.

Call the Light Street Foundation. Tell them Jessie Douglas is in trouble. Tell them where I am.''

''What?''

''Please. Please, just tell them!''

Whirling, she crossed the strip of dry sidewalk and sprinted through the door into the crowded store. If she could lose herself in the throng, she could get away.

Inside, breathing hard, she darted down the first aisle she saw. With a sick feeling, she thought about how she'd been tricked. All the time she'd been talking on the phone, Martinez had been tracking the call. That had to be illegal—which meant he was probably working for somebody else besides the U.S. government. How could she have been so naive?

As she lumbered past the meat counter, a large hand wrapped itself around her arm. Turning her head, she saw Martinez.

''Don't make a scene, Mrs. Jefferson,'' he warned in a raspy whisper. ''I have a gun, and I'm prepared to use it.''

Maybe he was lying, but she could feel something hard pressing into her side.

''How did you know it was me?'' she gasped.

''It wasn't difficult.'' He laughed. ''After you called the OAN, we did a profile of you. There was a sixty-eight-percent chance you'd call the INS if you were pushed in the right direction. So we arranged for the birth certificate to arrive from San Marcos. Then I had our calls screened.''

''Oh, God,'' she breathed. She'd done exactly what Jurado had wanted—what he'd expected.

''Come on,'' he growled as he yanked on her arm.

Stiff-legged, she let him lead her out of the store. The woman who had helped her was just pulling up beside a cart full of groceries. She stared at Jessie and Martinez as if she wasn't sure what to do.

Jessie gave her a beseeching look. ''Please!'' she mouthed as her captor hustled her away.

A gray van was waiting at the curb. Martinez pushed her

inside. As soon as the door slammed shut behind them, the vehicle jerked forward, sliding in the snow as it headed for an exit.

"Watch it, you idiot!" Martinez growled in Spanish at the driver.

The man's voice came back hard and cold in the same language. "Do not ever call me that."

"Let me drive. I'm used to the snow."

"No. I am in charge!"

Before Martinez could protest, they sped off—away from the shopping center, and away from any chance of rescue.

Chapter Seventeen

Miguel was sleeping in another of his endless series of basement rooms when rapid knocks on the door brought him to instant alertness. Before he could reach for his gun, he heard a woman call his name. He recognized her at once. It was Meg Faulkner, one of Jessie's Light Street friends. Every time he moved, his current address was delivered by Luis in a sealed envelope and put into the Light Street Foundation safe—to be opened only in case of emergency. That way, none of Jessie's friends could accidentally give away the location of his hideout. In fact, if they were pressed, they could truthfully say that they didn't know where he was.

But now Meg was here—which meant that something was wrong. The baby? Was Jessie in labor? Her due date wasn't for three weeks, but the child could be early. And the arrangements were complicated. She was seeing an OB-GYN under an assumed name. But her physician didn't know he wasn't going to deliver the baby. Miguel was going to do that himself, at the Randolph estate, where Cam and Jo had set up a secure medical facility several years earlier. Jessie would be able to stay there for a while without having to worry about being stalked by Jurado's men.

Springing from the bed, Miguel crossed the room and threw open the door, shivering as a blast of cold air hit him in the face.

"What is it? Is Jessie in labor?" he demanded.

The look on Meg's face stopped him in his tracks. "Miguel, I'm sorry," she began.

He grabbed her by the shoulders, his fingers digging in so hard that she made a small sound. "What? Tell me! Is something wrong with the baby? Her?"

"No. Nothing like that! She was at a shopping center in Pikesville." Meg sucked in a deep breath and let it out, obviously struggling for control. "Miguel, I got a call from woman—a Mrs. Flint. She said Jessie was dragged into a van by a tough-looking man. It appeared that she was...was being kidnapped."

Icy talons dug into his vitals. "No."

"Before the man grabbed her, Jessie told Mrs. Flint she was in trouble and asked her to call the Light Street Foundation. The woman hadn't heard of us, but she got the number from Information."

"You're sure it was Jessie who was shoved into the van?" he demanded. "There is no mistake?"

Meg shook her head. "I called Randolph Security right away. Jason went straight to her house. Her car was missing, she's not home, and several coats were lying on the sofa—as if she was deciding what to wear. Hunter went to the shopping center. Her car was in the parking lot, but she wasn't in any of the stores."

Miguel pounded his fist against the doorframe, cursing loudly. "I knew this would happen if she stayed with me. I always knew."

"Don't!" Meg said sharply. "She loves you. She wanted to be with you. It was her choice."

"The baby took away her choice!"

"Not a chance. She got out of one bad marriage. She wouldn't have married you unless she wanted to—unless she loved you very much."

He heard the words, but it was hard to believe them. Then Meg was speaking again. "The important thing is to get her back."

A surge of despair went through his gut like a hot knife. "How?"

"Come down to the Foundation office with me. By the time we get back, they'll have a high-tech command post set up. Hunter is there. And Cam and Jason. He says that the kidnapper will contact us—and we can trace the call."

"Yes, he'll call you because he wants *me*. That's why they've taken her."

Meg nodded. "They won't hurt her."

He didn't know if that was true. All he could do was cling to that hope, because if he thought they would do something to her or the baby, he would go insane.

THE VAN MOVED SLOWLY through the snow-snarled traffic. In a kind of stupor, Jessie huddled against the back door—as far as she could get from Martinez. At first all she could think about was how stupid she'd been to get herself captured. She'd practically begged him to scoop her up. After a while, she realized that blaming herself wasn't going to do any good. She had to get herself out of this mess.

Another cramp grabbed at her middle, and she closed her eyes until it passed. The tension was taking a toll on her stomach. When the pain eased, she looked up and tried to figure out where they were. All she could tell was that they were still in the city. The heavy snow made it difficult to see details—or maybe she simply didn't know this part of town well enough to identify any landmarks.

At least Martinez hadn't pushed her onto the floor. Probably he assumed that in her present condition she was no match for two armed men.

The other guy was named Sombra. Mr. Shade.

The two of them talked rapidly in Spanish as the van crawled through traffic. From the conversation, she gathered Sombra had been in San Marcos until a few weeks ago. Had he been in direct contact with Jurado?

Jessie could tell that Martinez and Sombra didn't like

working with each other. Maybe she could use it to her advantage.

Finally she recognized where they were—on Interstate 95, heading south, along with a steady stream of slow-moving traffic.

When Martinez directed the other man to turn onto Highway 175 toward Jessup, he looked around, his expression suspicious. "That's not what you told me before. The Watson farm is to the west."

"We're going the other way first," Martinez snapped. "To throw them off. If they trace the call, they'll look in the wrong place."

Sombra nodded tightly and followed directions.

Jessie felt a surge of panic. These men weren't being careful about what they said in front of her. That might mean they didn't intend to let her go.

"Right here!" Martinez directed, pointing toward a gas station with a phone near the roadside.

Sombra pulled off the highway and into the space between the phone and the pumps. Cutting the engine, he turned to her, his face set in harsh lines. "Do not try to get away, because we both have guns trained on you. You're going to call your husband," he ordered. "You're going to tell him that you've been taken hostage. You're going to follow directions exactly—" he paused, and his gaze bored into her "—if you don't want the baby to get hurt."

She swallowed, trying not to let her fear get the best of her. "I don't know where to reach my husband."

"I do not believe you," he answered coldly.

"Why not? It makes sense. If I can't reach him, then I can't give away his location to someone like you." She lifted her chin and gestured toward Martinez. "That's what I told you when you were keeping me on the phone so you could track me down. I thought at the time that it was important not to lie."

Sombra considered her claim. "But you must have some way to get a message to him. Or let's hope that you do...."

He let the sentence trail off, and the implications were all too clear.

"He checks in at the Light Street Foundation," she said, holding her voice steady to hide the lie.

"Where you work?"

"Yes."

"Then you'll call your office. You'll say you've been kidnapped."

"They may not believe me," she tried.

"Convince them," Martinez told her, punching out the words for emphasis. "And say we're willing to exchange you for your husband."

"Where?"

"We'll tell you when you need to know," Sombra answered.

Jessie nodded.

"We're going to get out of the van now," Martinez said. "I'll be right next to you—with a gun pointed at your belly."

She made a strangled sound. God, she didn't know what she was going to do about Miguel. But she couldn't let this man hurt her child. "Not the baby. Please, not the baby," she begged.

"It's up to you. So don't try anything stupid. And don't call any attention to us. We're just making a friendly phone call. Do you understand?"

"Yes," she managed.

"Okay. I'll be listening to the call." He picked up an electronic device that looked like a microphone. "With this. And one more important thing. Do not mention our names. Is that clear?"

She nodded tightly.

"All right. Then we'll make the phone call. It won't matter if they trace it. We won't stick around for very long."

But they'll come here, she told herself with all the conviction she could muster. *If I can leave them a message, they'll find it.*

Martinez clamped one hand on her arm and reached for the door handle with the other. As the door opened, another cramp hit her, and she sucked in a pained breath.

"Are you sick?" he asked.

"Wouldn't you be, under the circumstances?"

"You have a point."

Quickly she snatched up her purse as he helped her from the van. Pretending to slip as they rounded the back of the vehicle, she took a long look at the license plate, memorizing the number. With a rough gesture, Martinez helped her up. Jessie could see the gas-station attendant peering at them through the window. Lord, what if the man came over to them? He could get her and the baby killed. She said a silent prayer that he'd turn away.

When he did, she almost cried out with relief. Standing in a daze in front of the phone, she picked up the receiver and started to dial. When nothing happened, she stared stupidly at the instrument.

"You have to put in money," Martinez observed dryly, reaching past her to push the correct change into the slots. When she heard the dial tone, she tried again.

Martinez attached one end of the listening jack to the receiver. Then he pressed an earpiece into his right ear. Hidden from view, the barrel of the gun pressed into her, forcing her to stand there when all she wanted to do was run away.

Erin, who rarely answered the phones, picked up on the first ring. "Light Street Foundation," she said, her voice a little higher than usual.

"This is Jessie."

There was a short pause. "Oh. Hi. How's our mother-to-be?" Her friend sounded casual and chipper, and Jessie's hopes fell. Erin must not know anything was wrong.

Her boss continued to speak in a normal voice. "Did you need Hunter to send over any more of those personnel applications you were checking for Jenny?"

Personnel forms? Hunter? He didn't work for the foundation and she hadn't been checking personnel forms for

Jenny. She had been writing a long-shot grant application. Her heart leaped inside her chest. Erin must be trying to let her know that she'd gotten the message from the woman at the shopping center.

Martinez squeezed her arm painfully and she cleared her throat. "I didn't call about the personnel forms," she said. "Erin, I know this is going to sound…weird, but you've got to believe me. I've been kidnapped."

"Kidnapped?" her friend squeaked as if in genuine astonishment.

"Yes. They—they want Miguel. They said they're willing to exchange me for him."

"Oh, Lord," Erin breathed. "You're not playing some joke on me, are you? Or that husband of yours with his crazy sense of humor?"

Another clue, she thought. Miguel had been much too uptight lately to make many jokes, and he would never kid about something like this. "I wouldn't do that," she said quickly. "Neither would he!" Jessie cast Martinez a quick glance. "One of the men who abducted me is listening to this conversation. He'll hurt me if I don't cooperate. I'm so scared. All I want is for them to leave me and the baby alone," she lied. She wanted a great deal more than that.

Erin sucked in a sharp breath. "I'm sorry. It's just so hard to wrap my head around this."

"I know. But you have to help me. Please."

"We will," Erin promised.

As she clutched the receiver, Jessie clung to the tone of conviction in her friend's voice.

"What do you want me to do? You know I can't get in touch with Miguel directly," Erin said.

"Has he checked in with you today?" Jessie asked.

"Not yet."

"Then he should do it soon," she said, adding another whopper to the string of lies they were spinning. They both knew that Miguel never called in.

"Ask them to try and find him," Martinez hissed in Jessie's ear. "Make sure they understand he has to come in person. Alone. Or we'll kill you. Tell them you'll give him directions the next time you call."

She repeated the message in a trembling voice. When she had finished, Martinez slammed down the receiver. "Come on, let's get out of here," he growled.

"Wait!" She turned and stared at the van. "I have to use the bathroom."

"Later."

"I can't wait until later," she insisted. "Don't you know anything about pregnant women? The baby is pressing right on my bladder. I'll have an accident in your van if you don't let me go now."

He made an angry sound but finally gave in. "Okay."

Luckily the door to the ladies' room was unlocked. Stepping into the small space, she looked around. There was a washbasin in the main room and a toilet partitioned off behind it. Martinez held the outer door open while she shut herself in the stall. She hadn't thought he'd be so close. Trying to stay cool, she sat on the toilet. Holding her purse on her knees, she felt inside for a pen and the notebook she always carried.

"Hurry up!" Martinez called.

"I can't do anything with you standing there like that," she called back.

He gave a low curse, but he closed the door. Quickly she tore off a piece of paper. She had intended to leave a message for Miguel and Randolph Security. But what if someone else found the note?

Making her plea more general, she wrote, "Help! I've been abducted by two men. Martinez and Sombra. Gray van, Maryland license WAX3822." She took her lip between her teeth, praying that Sombra had given away their destination when they'd turned east instead of west. "Destination: Watson farm. Big reward—call the Light Street Foundation. Please help!" After writing the foundation number, she scribbled a second copy of the note, leaving out the part about the farm.

The outer door burst open and Martinez stamped inside. "I said hurry up!" he snapped.

"I'm doing the best I can." Jessie pulled out several sheets of toilet paper then stuffed the first piece of notebook paper into the metal holder, leaving only a small corner showing.

Next she slipped her wallet out of her purse, pushed the second note inside, and set the wallet on the floor on the far side of the toilet, covering it with some sheets of toilet paper.

As she washed her hands, Martinez poked his head into the stall, and she froze. With a growl, he stepped inside, scanned the floor, and snatched up the wallet. When he found the note inside, his face darkened.

"You wrote down our license number!" He looked as if he wanted to slap her. "You are taking a big chance!"

"So are you," she retorted, and began to talk rapidly. "You may have been promised a lot of money for turning in Miguel, but before you can spend it, Jurado will kill you."

"Jurado?"

"Don't you know the name of the man you're working for? Carlos Jurado. Miguel is a plastic surgeon. He operated on Jurado last year in San Marcos and changed his face—so that he could come back as a war hero who was missing in action. And now he's got big political plans. Miguel is the only one who knows who he really is. Jurado's killed everybody else who could give him away. After he kills Miguel, he'll kill me—and you."

"I don't believe you," the INS agent growled.

"What did Sombra tell you? That he's working for the San Marcos government? That Miguel is a criminal? That he's going to let me go when he apprehends my husband?"

His expression told her she'd guessed right.

"Then it will come as a big surprise when Sombra puts a bullet in your back. Then *he's* next. Jurado doesn't leave any witnesses."

"You're lying!"

"If I'm not, you're a dead man."

Instead of answering, he grabbed her arm roughly, and she let him hustle her out of the bathroom. Now her only hope was that someone would find the first note she'd written—and find it soon.

MIGUEL WAITED, FEELING as if he would burst with impatience.

"Got it!" Hunter shouted. "They're at a pay phone in Jessup."

"How soon can we get there?" Miguel asked.

Jason looked outside. "I don't like to fly in weather like this."

"We have to!"

"Yeah." Jason grabbed his coat. "I know."

They tramped downstairs to the four-wheel-drive vehicle that would take them the few blocks to Rash Field, where a helicopter was waiting.

Half an hour later, they were setting down on a patch of open ground near the gas station. While Jason stayed at the controls, Miguel dashed into the office, followed by Hunter and Cam Randolph. "Did you see a blond, pregnant woman and two men?" Miguel demanded of the attendant. "They used the phone here."

The man nodded, looking from the trio to the helicopter as if they were a combat team from Mars.

"She's a kidnap victim," Miguel snapped. "Tell us everything you know."

"Yeah, they didn't look too kosher," the attendant agreed. "They had a gray van. Didn't buy any gas. One guy got out and went to the phone with her. Mebbe the other was driving the van."

"What else?"

"After she talked on the phone, he let her go to the bathroom—and stood outside looking impatient. Then he followed her in there and hustled her off."

"Was she all right?" Miguel asked urgently.

"She looked sick."

"God!" He closed his eyes for a moment, fighting not to scream his anguish. Then he turned to Hunter. "I know her. She would try to leave a message—if she could."

They headed for the ladies' room. Cam scanned the ground outside, while Hunter searched through the trash can beside the sink. Miguel charged into the stall. When he found nothing, he slammed his fist against the metal partition. "I thought there would be something!"

"Look carefully," Hunter told him as he unfolded damp paper towels. "She couldn't just write a letter to us on the wall. She'd have to hide it."

Miguel took off the toilet tank. Nothing. He lifted the seat, then tried the back of the lid. On his knees, he felt along the wall beside the tank, Then followed the stall wall along to the toilet-paper holder. A tiny piece of paper fluttered to the floor. With trembling fingers, he carefully picked it up, read it, then waved it in the air.

"Here! Here it is!"

"Let's see." Hunter scanned the text. "The license number is good. I don't know if the Watson farm is specific enough."

IT HAD STOPPED SNOWING, Jessie noted as the van crept through snarled traffic. Occasionally Sombra cursed. Sometimes he and Martinez engaged in a brief, tense exchange.

Jessie figured that under normal conditions the ride to the farm from Jessup wouldn't take more than forty minutes, but they'd already been on the road for over two hours, and they were still far from their destination.

As the car inched along, the pains in her belly had gotten stronger and closer together, and she knew she wasn't having indigestion; she was in labor. And she didn't know what to do about it. When she'd first figured it out, she'd told herself that she had hours before the baby was born—and Miguel would surely find her before then. Now she wasn't so sure.

It was all happening much faster than she'd expected, judging from the childbirth books she'd read.

Trying to look casual, she snuck another glance at her watch. The contractions were coming every five minutes now. A lot closer than she'd anticipated.

Lord, now what? Fighting terror, she tried to do the breathing exercises she'd learned. But every time a contraction hit her, she clenched her teeth, struggling to conceal her condition from her captors.

At least Martinez wasn't paying a lot of attention to her. Sitting next to her, he looked preoccupied. She hoped he was worried that he'd gotten in over his head. She hoped he was thinking about Jurado and what she'd told him.

Above her, she could hear a traffic helicopter again. It had passed over the highway several times. Fat lot of good it was going to do to report the obvious—that the roads were completely snarled.

The ride was endless, and as the miles inched by, the contractions grew closer together—and more painful.

She closed her eyes, praying that the baby would wait. When she made a small sound of mingled pain and terror, Martinez turned to her, studying her critically. "Are you sick?" he demanded again.

"I'm frightened. You should be, too," she added in a low voice, her gaze holding his until he looked away.

"What?" Sombra asked from the front seat.

Neither she nor Martinez answered. But she was sure that the INS agent was thinking about what she'd said back at the gas station.

"We should call her office again," Sombra said. "See if they've located her husband. The sooner we get this over with, the better."

They were on Highway 108 now, on the outskirts of Clarksville. Martinez pointed to a small strip shopping center. "Over there."

The van pulled into the parking lot near an outdoor phone.

As Martinez turned toward her, another contraction hit;

this time it was a vise-like claw grabbing her middle, and she couldn't hold back a groan of pain as she doubled over.

In the front seat, Sombra cursed. "I've been watching her. I think the bitch is in labor."

"What?"

"Didn't you see it?"

Martinez's face reddened. "How was I supposed to know?"

"You've been sitting next to her for hours."

"It doesn't matter," Martinez snapped. "As long as she can talk to Valero." He tugged on her arm, pulling her out of the van. Then he steadied her on her feet, as he helped her toward the metal phone booth.

"Is it true," he hissed, "about this man named Jurado? Valero operated on him, and he's killed everyone who knows?"

"Oh, it's true, all right," she managed.

Martinez made a strangled sound. "I didn't know. I thought Valero was the criminal."

"You know the truth now."

"Prove it."

She gave him a helpless look. "I can't—until Sombra shoots me. And you."

Martinez looked pale. "Okay. I can show you where to find faxed messages between Sombra and his boss. If I help you, you'll help me? You'll tell them I didn't know what he had planned?"

"Yes," she answered. Then another pain took her, and she gasped.

Martinez's gaze darted around the shopping center. "How—how long do you have?"

"I don't know," she managed.

"Hurry up!" Sombra shouted from the van.

The agent shoved change into the slot, and she dialed the Light Street Foundation. He was holding the listening device he'd used before, apparently too distracted to attach it to the phone.

Again, Erin picked up on the first ring. "Are you all right?" she asked anxiously.

"Yes." The assurance ended in a little cry as a gush of wetness rushed out of her, and she knew her water had broken.

Erin's voice came to her dimly through the phone. "Jessie, please listen to me. Get down on the ground. Get down now."

"What?"

"Get down," Erin ordered. "Roll behind the car to your right."

"I don't understand." She could hardly hear because a whirring noise was filling the air around her.

"The men are coming for you!" Erin shouted. "Get down!"

Martinez must have heard the warning—even without his receiver—because he grabbed her and threw her to the snowy pavement just as she saw a helicopter swoop down from the sky. As she watched in stunned disbelief, a stream of gunfire erupted from the van, and the helicopter returned the fire.

Martinez was pulling her behind the van when she saw one of the copter's landing skids smash into it, breaking the windshield and lifting the vehicle off the ground before setting it back with a bone-shattering thunk. Hunter leaped out of the copter, landing on the roof of the van. Miguel and Cam came right after him, jumping to the ground and heading toward her. Miguel's gun was pointed at Martinez.

"Don't shoot!" the INS agent pleaded. "I can help you prove what really happened in San Marcos."

"I'll take him," Cam said, grabbing Martinez by the arm and pulling him away.

Another contraction seized Jessie, and she groaned. Instantly, Miguel knelt beside her in the snow.

"Jessie, are you hurt? Did they hurt you?"

"I'm in labor!" she managed, her fingers clenching his jacket. All this time, she had been alone and frightened, coping on her own. Now he was here, and she could hardly believe it.

"Here? Now?" he gasped, his face a study in panic as he looked around the snowy parking lot.

Before she could answer, another pain captured her, and she cried out as she grabbed his hand and squeezed it in a death grip, her own fear rising as she realized that everything was happening much too fast. "Miguel, I feel like I have to push."

He made a strangled exclamation, then his expression changed to a kind of calm resolve. "Not yet. Not out here in the snow." Gathering her into his arms, he looked toward the strip of stores, then back into her eyes, his steady expression soothing her. Miguel was here. She wasn't alone anymore. "Jessie, can you pant?" he asked. "Can you do that for me?"

She nodded, trying her best to comply as he bore her across the parking lot.

"Is she okay?" Hunter called urgently.

"The baby is coming! Get my medical bag!" he shouted as he reached the front of a real-estate office. Yanking the door open, he carried Jessie past a startled receptionist.

"Is there a private office in the back?"

"Yes, but you can't go there!"

"The hell I can't!" he retorted, striding past her, kicking open the door to a plush private enclave.

The receptionist dashed after them. "I'll call the police if you—"

"She's about to have a baby," Miguel interrupted as he laid Jessie on a leather couch.

"Oh, my God!" the woman squeaked, her tone changing from outraged to unnerved.

"Where can I wash my hands?" he snapped.

"There." She pointed toward a men's room.

"Get me blankets, if you have them. And something clean to wrap the baby in," Miguel ordered in clipped tones. But his voice became gentle as he bent over Jessie. "I will be right back."

She lay panting, her head turned toward the door where he'd disappeared. Then he was back, kneeling beside her, telling her how much he loved her, telling her everything was going to be all right.

He sounded calm and in control as he stripped off her sodden underwear and pushed her dress out of the way—exactly how she needed him to be at this moment.

Still, she couldn't hold back a cry as the next contraction grabbed her.

"Just a little while longer," he crooned to her. His hand was on her abdomen as she felt another contraction building. "Push!"

She was beyond answering, beyond anything but following the dictates of her body.

"Good. Perfect," he praised her. "I can see his head! Everything is fine. It is only going to be a little bit longer."

Everything is fine. She clung to that through the next contraction and the next, bearing down again and again, groaning with the effort.

All at once the pain was less. "That's the head," Miguel told her. Then she heard him suck in a sharp breath.

"What? What's wrong?" she managed.

"The cord is looped around his neck." He moved quickly, and she couldn't see what he was doing.

"Miguel?" she cried.

"It's okay. Everything is okay. I've got it off him," he said, but his voice was strained as he helped her deliver the baby's shoulders, then the rest of the tiny body.

"Is he all right?" She sobbed when she saw that the baby's skin was tinged with blue. Miguel was working over him, suctioning his mouth with a syringe from the medical bag that somebody must have brought into the room.

For what seemed an endless time, she waited for an answer, her breath frozen in her chest. Then she heard a tiny cough and a high-pitched wail.

"Oh, God," She sighed through the tears that ran down her face now. "Thank God."

"His breathing is strong," Miguel said after a moment. "And his heart rate is a hundred and ten."

"Is that all right?" she asked anxiously.

"It's good. Over a hundred is what we want. And his muscle tone is good." Miguel's answer was thick with emotion as he laid the infant on Jessie's chest.

Her arms came up to cradle their child. "Is he really all right?"

"Yes."

She gazed into her husband's eyes, saw the look of relief, and knew that he wasn't just saying what she wanted to hear. "Oh, Miguel, what if you hadn't been here to help us?"

"But I was, Jessie. I was." One of his hands clasped her shoulder, the other curved around the baby's head. "Both of you are safe now."

He stroked his lips against her cheek, and she closed her eyes, trying to come to grips with everything that had happened. This wasn't a dream. She was safe. The baby was safe. And her husband had made it possible.

When he pulled away, her eyes opened. "Don't leave us!"

"Never again. But I must do a few more things for the two of you," he whispered. In a low, reassuring voice he kept talking to her, telling her what he was doing. He cut the cord, delivered the placenta, then bundled Jessie in blankets and cleaned off the baby before wrapping him in a towel. Finally, he handed the infant into her arms.

She looked down in wonder and gratitude at her son, whose skin was pink now. "His hair is dark, like yours," she whispered, stroking the tiny head.

Miguel nodded, and she gave him a little smile, sensing that this was a time when she could ask for—and get—anything she wanted. But she wouldn't be *too* greedy. "I'd like to call him Michael," she said. "After you."

"Yes," Miguel answered in a choked voice as his lips moved against her face.

She rested again for a moment, then murmured, "I was so frightened when they had me. How did you find me so quickly?"

He stroked her possessively as he replied, "We found your note. With the license number, it was easy to spot the van from the air."

She nodded.

"My wife. So brave. So clever," he told her, his voice breaking.

"Like my husband," she said, burrowing closer to him. He held her as if he would never let her go, and she felt herself drawing strength from his embrace.

A little while later, Cam came in to deliver a terse news bulletin. "Sombra is dead. Martinez is going to cooperate with the police. It looks like he can provide information that will link Sombra to Jurado. And Jed was able to dig up some of Jurado's old dental records. Unless the bastard had all his teeth pulled, we've got him."

"Thank God," Jessie breathed, then turned to Miguel. He looked stunned, as if he didn't believe it could finally be over.

"Think of it as an early Christmas present," Cam said. "But you should keep out of sight for a few more days, until we get things nailed down. Let's go with the original plan. You, Jessie, and the baby can stay at the estate. Do you want me to have Jessie's doctor meet you there?"

"Yes. And a pediatrician. I want her checked—and the baby, too."

"I'll arrange that. When you're ready, we'll leave in the chopper."

"In about a half hour," Miguel said. Standing, he shook Cam's hand. "Thank you. There is no way I can repay you for all of this...."

Cam looked embarrassed. "I've been in some tight spots

myself. I know that friends can make a difference.'' He took a small step back. "I'll go make the arrangements.''

When they were alone once more, Miguel came down beside Jessie, his face still full of wonder. "I can hardly believe it. It is almost over. We can live like a family—like everybody else.''

She laid her hand over his.

"I am so lucky,'' he said, looking from her to the infant in her arms.

"We both are.''

At that moment, little Michael began making tiny noises and waving his arms.

"Do you think he's hungry?'' Jessie asked.

"Probably. And it would be good for you to nurse him.''

"Is that a medical opinion, or do you want to see your son have his first meal?''

"Both,'' he answered softly.

He arranged the pillows so she could prop herself up and watched while she undid the front of her dress. As soon as she brought Michael to her breast, he started searching for her nipple. When he found it and began to suck, she caught her breath. The sensation was sharp at first, then settled down to a sweet tugging.

Miguel cupped his palm around the back of his son's dark head, then laid his own head on Jessie's shoulder as he slipped his arm around her protectively. She closed her eyes, feeling tired but so very happy.

"A lot of men would take this for granted,'' he said in a thick voice as he touched the baby's cheek. "But I know what it means to be with the woman I love. And the child we made together.''

"Yes,'' she replied. "With the man I love.''

"You went through too much for me,'' he said.

"That's all in the past, and I've got exactly what I want.'' Her heart overflowed with love for this man as she thought of the years ahead. The future would make up for the nightmare he had survived, if she had anything to say about it.

"Now that you're a free man, you can open that clinic you've been dreaming of," she said.

She felt a tremor go through him. Then he moved so that his liquid gaze could meet hers. "That was just a dream—to keep me going when I needed hope."

"Is it what you want?"

He swallowed hard, and replied evasively, "I wouldn't be a rich plastic surgeon if I opened a clinic for the people in the barrio."

"I didn't marry a rich plastic surgeon," she countered. "I married a man who wants the same things I do—to help people, to make a difference. And if we can do it together, that's even better."

"Truly?"

"Oh, yes."

"Jessie, you understand me better than anyone else," he said, his voice thick, as he settled her and the baby more solidly into his embrace.

"I hope so." She felt tears blur her eyes as she savored this moment together.

"You have already given me so much." He gently stroked the baby's hair and hers.

She looked from her child to her husband, knowing they possessed riches that money could never buy. They had almost lost each other, more than once. Yet now they were safe—the three of them.

"The luckiest day of my life was the day I saw you across that room at the rec center," he whispered. "I thought I couldn't have you. And now…" Overcome with emotion, he choked up before he could finish.

"Now we're at the beginning of a long and wonderful life together." She completed the thought for him and snuggled into the certainty of his love.

And there's more 43 LIGHT STREET!

Turn the page for a bonus look at what's in store for you in the next "43 Light Street" book by Ruth Glick writing as Rebecca York, coming to you in October 1999.

MIDNIGHT CALLER

Only from Harlequin Intrigue!

Chapter One

Meg Faulkner felt it like a dull ache—disaster looming around the next hairpin turn of the road. Night had fallen hours ago, bringing with it a chill haze that billowed across the narrow ribbon of macadam winding through the thick pine forest. The mist fogged the headlight beams and turned the landscape into a scene from the *X-Files*.

In the TV show, Meg would be playing the unsuspecting first victim of some unseen menace. In real life, there were plenty of reasons why the analogy didn't quite work. She wasn't an innocent victim. She knew what she was getting into. And now that she was having second thoughts, it was too late to back out.

"Damn Glenn Bridgman's hide!" she muttered under her breath as she hunched over the wheel, straining her eyes to see the road ahead. Maybe he hadn't arranged the nightmare driving conditions, but he'd chosen to live in the back of beyond, fifty miles from the nearest town and a couple of well-placed steps from hell. Which was where she hoped to send him, if she ever made it to the front gate of his estate— and managed to talk her way inside.

The car rounded a rock outcropping, dipped into a small valley where the pavement was covered with water, and went into a skid. Meg fought to keep the car from sliding into the wall of rock hemming the right-hand shoulder of the road.

From the trunk of the car she heard a muffled sound like a couple of sacks of oranges rolling around. But she wasn't carrying a shipment of citrus fruit to Mr. Bridgman.

The tires spun on gravel as she surged back onto the road. Breathing a little sigh of relief, she deliberately slowed the heavy car, then glanced at the glowing green numbers of the dashboard clock. Ten after eleven. Probably she should have taken a motel room when she'd had the chance and started fresh in the morning.

She'd voiced that observation to Mr. Johnson, after he'd blinked his lights and led her onto the old logging road where they'd agreed to exchange cars. But he'd told her in his gravelly voice that they'd lose the element of surprise if she stopped overnight. So she slid behind the wheel of her borrowed vehicle with its special cargo hidden in the trunk. Then Johnson had driven off in her car, leaving her on her own.

Nervous energy and fear had kept her going for the past fifty miles. Not fear for herself—but for Tommy.

Thinking about her brother made her eyes mist. She managed to fight back the tears, but she couldn't wipe away the mental image of his haunted face, sunken cheeks, and trembling hands. He was going downhill fast—thanks to Glenn Bridgman.

She'd made the mistake of delivering that opinion to Tommy, and the old spark had ignited in his hazel eyes. For a moment she'd been glad that he was still capable of showing some spirit. Then he'd started defending Bridgman, warning her that he didn't want to hear a negative word about the man, since every member of the team had known what they were getting into.

Seeing that the heated defense was draining Tommy's strength, she'd clamped her mouth shut and gone into the kitchen to fix sloppy-joe sandwiches—one of Tommy's all-time-favorite meals. But even her home cooking hadn't tempted him to eat more than a few bites.

She'd left his small apartment a half hour later, choked

with despair and simmering with anger. Over the next few days, the anger had grown into a roiling cauldron of emotions that had left her vulnerable to a devil's proposition. A man named ''Mr. Johnson'' had been playing the devil. He'd shown up at her Light Street office a week after her visit to Tommy, taken her out to dinner, and made her an offer so tempting, that her mouth had gone dry.

Still, she'd politely refused. No way was she getting into anything illegal, immoral, and insane.

He'd kept talking—knocking down her objections one by one, making it sound like it was her patriotic duty to give Glenn Bridgman what he deserved. Even then, she might have gotten up from the table, until he'd pointed out how far a million dollars could go toward defraying Tommy's medical costs. A million dollars. That was a lot of money—enough to start Meg's brain spinning.

Johnson must have sensed the moment when she'd gone from confirmed skeptic to would-be convert, and he'd started talking faster. Before she'd quite known what was happening, she'd agreed to sign on to his Mission Impossible team.

According to instructions, she'd told her friends she was just going off on a much-needed vacation. Which meant nobody knew where she was or what she was doing, she reminded herself with a sudden chill as a gust of wind whipped clouds of mist into her path like a fog machine on a Hollywood set. Still, she caught a glimpse of a diamond-shaped yellow sign that read Falling Rock Area.

Great!

For the hundredth time since the nightmare ride had begun, she glanced at the odometer. Only five more miles. Then came the real fun. First she'd have to confront the armed guards. Then, if she were lucky, she'd get an audience with the Big B., as she'd started calling Bridgman in her mind. Some luck!

She'd seen a couple of pictures of him. He was tall and dark-haired, with icy, shuttered eyes—the kind of man you'd hate to face in a high-stakes poker game. Unfortunately, that was pretty close to what she was going to be doing.

Mentally she reviewed her prep sessions with Johnson and his staff—all the things she was supposed to say in answer to Bridgman's inevitable questions.

Her mind was focused on the confrontations, so that it was several seconds before she realized she was hearing a rumbling noise above her. In the next moment, a trash-can-size boulder came hurtling down the cliff to her left, crashing through the underbrush and landing with a thud several yards in front of the car. Jamming her foot on the brake, she managed to avoid the obstruction. Unfortunately, it was only the first of several falling rocks that came hurtling down, slamming like cannonballs into the side and back of the car and straight toward the window beside her head.

A scream tore from her throat. The last conscious thought she had was that she'd bartered her soul to the devil—and he was going to collect on the deal a lot sooner than she'd anticipated.

*   *   *   *   *

Don't miss this next 43 Light Street tale— #534 MIDNIGHT CALLER— coming to you in October 1999. Only from Ruth Glick writing as Rebecca York and Harlequin Intrigue!

Looking For More Romance?

Visit Romance.net

Check in daily for these and other exciting features:

Hot off the press

View all current titles, and purchase them on-line.

What do the stars have in store for you?

Horoscope

Hot deals

Exclusive offers available only at Romance.net

Plus, don't miss our interactive quizzes, contests and bonus gifts.

PWEB

They're brothers by blood, lawmen by choice, cowboys by nature.

THE COWBOY CODE

The McQuaid brothers learned justice and honor from their father, the meaning of family from their mother. The West was always in their souls, but now it's the past they have to reckon with. And three women hold the keys to their future.

Don't miss this exciting new series from three of your favorite Intrigue authors!

McQUAID'S JUSTICE
Carly Bishop
January 1999

A COWBOY'S HONOR
Laura Gordon
February 1999

LONE STAR LAWMAN
Joanna Wayne
March 1999

Available at your favorite retail outlet.

HARLEQUIN®
Makes any time special ™

COMING NEXT MONTH

#501 A COWBOY'S HONOR by Laura Gordon
The Cowboy Code
Cameron McQuaid was both a cowboy and a lawman, and lived his life by a code of honor. Yet, when Frani Landon comes to town to catch a killer, Cameron finds his honor—and his heart—on the line.

#502 FAMILIAR VALENTINE by Caroline Burnes
Fear Familiar
A velvet Valentine's night, a threatening attacker—and suddenly, Celeste Levert found herself swept to safety in Dan Morgan's strong arms. He promised to keep her safe and secure, but couldn't offer his heart—until a black cat played Cupid....

#503 LAWMAN LOVER by Saranne Dawson
Michael Quinn's tenacity made him an extraordinary cop. It also made him an exceptional lover. And Amanda Sturdevant remembered everything, every caress and kiss, of her one night with him, but nothing of a long-ago night of terror that had left a woman dead and Amanda barely with her life—and amnesia....

#504 JACKSON'S WOMAN by Judi Lind
Her Protector
Everyone called her Verity McBride, but only Vera knew no one would believe the truth about her identity. But now with a murder charge hanging over her head, she turned to Jericho Jackson for help and found a love for all time—even though he thought she was someone else....

Look us up on-line at: http://www.romance.net